SATCHEL

A CHEROKEE GIRL TELLS ALL

*The hunt always glorifies the hunter
until the lioness tells her tale.*

~ An African Proverb

SATCHEL

A CHEROKEE GIRL TELLS ALL

A Historical Novel by

Martha Gunsalus Chamberlain

Published by CaryPress Publishing

Cover photo copyrighted to Sabrina Photography

ISBN-13: 978-1631030208
ISBN-10: 1631030205

DEDICATION

This book is dedicated with respect and gratitude to these courageous Americans in the United States:

Native Americans who peopled our land and cared for it thousands of years before the white man arrived; and to Enslaved Africans whose contributions to our country can neither be over-estimated nor adequately acclaimed.

And, to those whose stories are interrupted, even lost as the result of untimely deaths, or diseased bodies, or incarceration, or failing memories—unless someone forges the links on their behalf.

Joseph Campbell suggested that we would do well to study the mythology of the land where we live instead of limiting ourselves to Greek and Hebrew mythology. Drawing from her own land, Martha Chamberlain immerses and enlightens us with skillfully interwoven stories of Cherokee history and culture in an impressively imaginative tale. Her compelling narrative includes rich and tragic elements related to histories of both Cherokee and enslaved Africans who lived among the Moravians who settled Salem, North Carolina, in the nineteenth century.

Prepare to be touched and inspired by the courage of central characters faced with extreme oppression by not only white settlers and government officials, but also traitors among their own people, at times blinded by their own concepts of truth, justice and mercy. Her story conveys cherished values and traditions that bear witness to living what the Cherokee call Duyukta—the path of being in balance and harmony.

~ Larry Ousley, Director of the Intentional Growth Center, Lake Junaluska, N.C.

ACKNOWLEDGMENTS

It takes a village . . .

Five extraordinary persons read an early draft, each knowledgeable in more than one area, but chosen specifically for the depth of understanding about some of the major actors in this tale: John Hauser, Moravian resident of Old Salem; Margaret McClesky, United Methodist, Lake Junaluska resident; Darlene Ousley, Cherokee/scholar; Mark Seavet, interpreter for the deaf; Mel White, Afro-American perspective. Without their generous gift of time, expertise and constructive criticism, I could not have completed this story, and without whom this book would be less than it is.

More than a publisher, Durdana Yousuf went beyond the second mile in accommodating requests and delays, offering guidance and finally producing this book. After all that, we completed the work as friends.

The Foreword, written by Reginald F. Hildebrand, generously affirmed what I had hoped: This story needed to be told. Martita Marcaño, Charles Maynard, Larry Ousley and Jim Winkler graciously agreed not only to read the manuscript, but also to write an endorsement.

Thanks to my dear family. They stand with me, no matter what, including our foster daughter Pam and my youngest granddaughter Carrie Reagler who early on said she "loves" the story I told her, especially the part about the horse Thistle and the dog Moonlight. More than anyone, she keeps asking, "Is the book ready yet?" Finally, most importantly, my husband for more than fifty-five years continues to support and love me unconditionally, and that's no small feat. He's the glue, the catalyst, inspiration, listener, mentor, advisor, best friend, extraordinary provider (insisting on a "room with a view" whenever, wherever I need it). He is the key to any success I achieve. (My worst fear about handing him the first copy of this book is that I shall have to start cooking again—after we celebrate.)

Russell and Marcia and Sharon Chamberlain—yes, you guessed it. They are more than son and daughters. They all write compelling prose in their professions, and even when one of them suggested I start over (which I did!), I knew that they know far more than I about these things. So, without their critique, I cannot believe this book would ever have been completed. Also, please do not "blame" them.

The first publisher to whom I submitted it said, "It's not ready." Right-on! Indeed, "it takes a village," to be published. Many individuals encouraged and supported my efforts. To name them all is an impossibility, but some invaluable resources and persons include public libraries in Winston-Salem, Winchester and Waynesville; Salem College library, including Kay McKnight and students who assisted me there; university libraries: the UNC/Duke Special Collections Library Request System, Shenandoah University, McClung Library at UT, Knoxville; lectures/events at Winston Salem University and Wake Forest University; archives at Lake Junaluska, especially Ashley Calhoun and Nancy Watkins; archives in Winston-Salem with its rich collection of Moravian history, including impressive volumes about the Moravians in addition to the Cherokee in the 19th century: special thanks due to Richard Starbuck, historian and Director, Moravian Archives; Museum of St. Philips Moravian Church: Cheryl Harry, Director of African American Programming and Leo Rucker, Interpreter, who have been most responsive to requests and questions. Residents and officials in Old Salem whom I cannot name, warned me: Careful, now! They, too, were right, and I have tried. Other encouragers include: John Larson, Vice-President, Old Salem; Tyler Cox; neighbors and friends like Ann Johnson and Catherine Hendren, Ginny Tobiassen and John Hauser (who, in addition to other help, brought videos, books and ideas to expand my knowledge); John Pierce, responsible for book purchases; Lou Ann Wilson in the Salem Book Store: neighbors in the Old Salem Book Club (mourning the recent loss of two members); authors Nancy Peacock and Charlie Lovett, two authors/resource persons at NCWN conferences, who taught me things I needed to learn. Maurice P. Johnson who introduced me to Happy Hill; Esther Snyman, Bartlesville, Oklahoma, in whose home I stayed (and ate) while researching; the Weymouth Center for the Arts (Southern Pines, N.C.) where Hope Price and Alex Klalo always welcome writers with open arms, providing for hours/days of productive research/writing; the writers and encouragers there, like Erin Chandler and Pat Thompson (who connected me with Theda Perdue's work in Cherokee history). Appreciation for Kelly Carpenter, my pastor at Green Street United Methodist Church in Winston-Salem;

for Sr. Brigid and Sr. Donna Marie and staff at Well of Mercy (Harmony, N.C.), in addition to pastors Ginny Tobiassen and Richard Sides at Home Moravian Church, all of whom continually replenish and challenge me. Barbara Duncan, Director, Museum of the Cherokee, N.C.; Unto These Hills, drama; Oconaluftee Village, Sequoyah Museum in Vonore, Tennessee; Smithsonian Museum of Native Americans in Washington, D.C.; Museum of the Western Band of Cherokee in Tahlequah, Oklahoma; Peggy Parks and Camille Abbott at Museum of Southern Decorative Arts (MESDA), and the Old Salem "living museum" that immerses me every day into Salem history; New Winston Museum; North Carolina Writers Network (NCWN); Winston Salem Writers Network (WSWN); Bookmarks events. The U.S. Bureau of American Ethnology: "The Swimmer Manuscript: Cherokee Sacred Formulas."

At Triad Mac, Macaulay Rivas and Josh Spencer saved the day (and this book) when my computer crashed two weeks before the final edit was due, and rescued me too often to describe here.

I recognize the impossibility of naming all those who have shaped and supported me, from my parents and other family, teachers (like Mrs. Wisely who was my first grade teacher the year my mother died), pastors and mentors and professors (like Harold Crosser at UWC and Alan Cheuse at GMU, who died this year), to my friends across the years, many of whom continue to inspire and encourage me (and stand in line to buy this book), to you all I owe unending gratitude.

Peace . . .

FOREWORD

Many years ago I did some research for my doctoral dissertation at the Lake Junaluska Archives in western North Carolina. At that time, the significance of the name Junaluska was unknown to me, and I must confess that I only began to comprehend the meaning of the great chief's life journey after reading *Satchel: A Cherokee Girl Tells All* by Martha Gunsalus Chamberlain.

Like any good storyteller, the author is no respecter of boundaries that divide people and cultures into neat and clearly defined categories. This is the story of Cherokees and Africans and Moravians, but it is also a narrative of how those cultures interacted, overlapped and created some common ground. Madaya, the Cherokee Indian, and the enslaved African Squire, are not merely markers for their cultures and conditions. They are deftly and skillfully portrayed as complex human beings, navigating their way through an oppressive society, while affirming each other's humanity. Their lives do not follow straight lines, nor are they lived in entirely separate cultural categories.

As a writer of historical fiction, Chamberlain understands that important truths lie beyond facts and footnotes, and that often meaning is most effectively conveyed in stories well told. The very compelling story told here is grounded in solid historical research and folklore, but the author's imagination, empathy and good writing carry it forward.

Perhaps most importantly, *Satchel* helps us appreciate the value of our own story-satchel, as well as those of the people around us. It is by preserving and honoring those stories that we convey the meaning of our own lives. It is through appreciating the stories of others that we have some hope of finding our way to common ground. Readers will embark on a journey well worth taking through the pages of this book.

~ Reginald F. Hildebrand, author, Associate Professor of African American Studies and History, UNC Chapel Hill

PROLOGUE: SACRED STORY

The story of the hunt will always glorify the hunter until the lion tells his tale. ~ An African Proverb

We all know that a story can take on a life of its own. Facts seem irrelevant when witnesses describe what they *saw* or *heard* with their own eyes and ears, or to siblings relating their memories of childhood, or to political candidates. We can imagine the fisherman's tale about the one that got away, or the hunter who took out the fierce lion. Then one day we recognize that the lion and lioness also have a tale to tell.

Of consequence is my obsession with the Cherokee Chief Junaluska as it relates to what we've learned about early U.S. history. I wanted to pay attention to and consider the rest of the story. Learning that Junaluska was a beloved "chief," but not because of election, led me to discover his brilliant military leadership at Horseshoe Bend and other battles. More importantly, walking with his people 1200 miles to Indian Territory on the Trail of Tears before walking back to North Carolina to continue his diplomatic efforts on behalf of the Cherokee Nation, further encapsulated his people's reverence for him.

Ironically, the state of North Carolina bestowed the belated gift of "citizenship" on Junaluska, as well as the "legal right" of Cherokee citizens to live in the state following their military service during the Civil War, long after the Removal. Junaluska was also given one hundred dollars and a tract of land in Graham County to "hold and enjoy, without the power to sell or convey the same." Voting privileges for the Cherokee would be re-instated (after having been granted and rescinded earlier), following their military service during WWII, about seventy years after Junaluska's death.

Standing, although I wanted to kneel at Junaluska's gravesite in Robbinsville, North Carolina, I read this inscription on the bronze plaque:

Here lie the bodies of the Cherokee Chief Junaluska, and Nicie his wife. Together with his warriors, he saved the life of General Jackson at the Battle of Horseshoe Bend, and for his bravery and faithfulness, North

Carolina made him a citizen and gave him land in Graham County. He died November 20, 1858, aged more than one hundred years. This monument was erected to his memory by the Joseph Winston Chapter DAR 1910.

Intending to write the story of the historic Chief Junaluska, I found that research revealed too little, with none of it autobiographical. What was documented was a lifetime of angst as a result of having saved the life of General Andrew Jackson who would later be elected President of the young nation. When Jackson subsequently ordered the Removal in 1838, implemented by General Winfield Scott, Junaluska's failed efforts to save his people from that tragic walk tormented the rest of his days.

Unfortunately, Junaluska buried his own stories deep within his psyche, layered with the dust of silence through nearly a century of his life. Etched only in his memory, the stories of his battles and lessons learned, his association with radically influential persons from President Andrew Jackson to Tecumseh, his contributions to United States history, his personal losses on the Trail of Tears and his return walk to North Carolina, all these stories were lost, unless . . .

Unless my path intersected with the indigenous American girl Ma-da-ya, without whom I could not have told this story. This fictitious Cherokee child became the "lioness" that led me into unfathomable story, sometimes reflecting history, at other crossroads plunging into unexplored territory. It was she who wove together the story of the renowned chief and an enslaved African from Salem, North Carolina, in the nineteenth century.

And I—with no idea of the complexity of my undertaking—followed her from Squire's grave that lies just up the stone steps in the strangers' graveyard at St. Philip's in Old Salem, all the way into Cherokee, and Robbinsville, and Lake Junaluska in North Carolina in the twenty-first century. Yet, little did I realize that was only the beginning. Recognizing holes in the fabric of available history, I embraced this comment by historian Martha Jones: *in the face of silence, a historian might draw upon the speculative imagination of fiction.* These valuable stories could not possibly survive without *speculative imagination* to fill in the gaps. If a historian can employ such methodology, surely a writer of historical fiction can do likewise. That I have done, delving into that rich mulch of *speculative imagination* from which a new story germinated and grew, creating this story that yearned to be told.

Disparate sources both contributed to—and complicated—the telling. History and fiction, old journals and newspapers, genealogies and internet connections, libraries and museums, archives and lectures, interaction with historians and both Cherokees and Afro-Americans, and their association with the Moravian community now known as Old Salem, they *all* interconnect. While that was only the beginning of complex issues surrounding the telling of a story from both a historically separate and culturally different vantage point, I was hooked.

As protagonist in a coming-of–age tale, Madaya, this indigenous American girl, had walked the Trail of Tears with both Squire and Junaluska, becoming orphaned when one by one, her whole family died, among four thousand other Cherokee on the *nuna da ul tsu n yi,* the "trail that made us cry." Suffering tragedy upon tragedy, Madaya—a composite of the Cherokee story—survived into old age to tell her story by delving into her story-satchel with its relics to aid the telling. In so doing, she revealed the stories of Junaluska and the enslaved African Squire.

After five years in Indian Territory, now known as Oklahoma, Madaya walked back to North Carolina with both Junaluska and Squire, with whom ten year-old Madaya chose to live in Salem. Having promised her dying mother on the Trail that he would care for Madaya, the enslaved African also determined to protect the child from slavery, a life he knew well. After all, she was neither his daughter, nor a slave. She was Cherokee.

When the well Squire was digging caved in on him, depriving the child of the beloved one she had been instructed to call *Papa,* Madaya found she could no longer hear. This phenomenon, both physiological and psychological, can occur following the trauma of deep loss, referred to by some experts as hysterical deafness. Alone once again, the girl decided to return to Cherokee. Running away—in the wrong direction—she ended up at a slave auction in Charlotte, North Carolina.

Unknown to Junaluska or Madaya, she was not the only one who grieved the loss of Squire, leading to years of anguish for an African-American child. The eight year-old boy had been told by his dying mother that Squire was his father, but as the boy attempted to overcome his timidity when Squire returned to Salem, the accident left him orphaned and remorseful for his failure to approach Squire with that wonderful news.

Returning to the Cherokee village once again, Madaya as a young woman embraced her heritage while learning even more about love and loss, about friendship and betrayal. The gift of forgiveness eventually assuaged the plague of guilt for the death of her lover John Astooga Stoga, Junaluska's grandson. Living with Junaluska and his wife Nicie, the two women learned the Cherokee syllabary, the newly invented alphabet by the genius Sequoyah, who himself had been illiterate. Together they taught their Cherokee villagers to read and write, even as they continually practiced finger-talking and lip-reading for other hearing-impaired persons like Madaya.

Meanwhile, Madaya's *story-satchel* grew heavy with both artifacts and meaning. In the evenings by the fire, or gathered with other women by the river, Madaya gradually opened her satchel of secrets, those relics collected from childhood, each of which symbolized an episode in her journey. Most of these Cherokee women had escaped into the forest, or chosen to become citizens of North Carolina rather than move from their ancestral homes during the great Removal. These lionesses, too, had tales to tell.

One evening, fingering a lock of black hair that she pulled from her satchel, Madaya locked eyes with the mother of her deceased friend Ilya. "I need to tell you what happened on that night Ilya and I ran away from the boarding school," she began. The women well remembered the day their children had been forced into wagons by U.S. soldiers to be taken to the government's B.I.A. [Bureau of Indian Affairs] Boarding School. But until Madaya emptied her story-satchel, they had lived too long in silent speculation about some of their children's experiences.

Indeed, the world is full of stories, and sometimes they permit themselves to be told, Madaya thought.

The bits and pieces buried in Madaya's story-satchel were meaningless until she linked them to *story.* Opening old wounds of loss and guilt—once lanced with the telling—she began to sense healing, new life bursting with discovery, with miracle and renewal. So it was that Madaya cracked open the door for a glimpse into their history by remembering her own. She related tales about the forced Removal, about the BIA boarding school, about life in Salem among the Moravians, and about her beloved mentor and caretaker, the enslaved African Squire.

Through ensuing years Madaya showed the women how they, too, could do this, how to tell their own stories. Listening to one another with their guilt and shame, their regrets and questions, enabled even the most reticent or the most damaged one to pour out her own tales, passing them on for survival of self, as well as others. That's the way it works, this sharing of stories.

After her lover, as well as both Junaluska and his wife died, Madaya returned to Salem to visit the grave of her "Papa Squire," never imagining whom she would meet, once again changing her life forever. Returning to Cherokee, she again experienced far beyond anything she had even dreamed as a possibility. At last, having learned to "hear" by watching the lips and expressions of those around her, Madaya awakened miraculously to an old, barely remembered way of being.

Like the flash of a distant meteor in the night sky, more than twenty years passed. Madaya returned to Salem this time with her adult son who worked at the pottery for a year. Heavy with artifacts as well as meaning, her story-satchel represented her life. Sleeping with it tucked into her bosom, guarding it, she embraced the story-satchel as an endeared companion in her dotage. She also began to describe the artifacts and their meaning in a journal.

One day Madaya lost her journal that had become as constant a companion as her worn, rabbit-skin story-satchel. After desperately searching for it, one night her *aduli* [mother] appeared in a dream to tell her that not only would the satchel not survive, but also that someone else would find her lost journal. *Remember,* Aduli said: *It is your story that is* sacred*, not the satchel, not the journal. It's not the stuff, but the* story *that must survive.*

And it did, from the perspective of Madaya the lioness.

All eighteen chapters are a work of fiction, drawing on historical background during the nineteenth century and a few facts from the twenty-first century in Old Salem where I now reside. It is neither my intention to misrepresent historical facts nor to represent a chronological reconstruction of the era. Yes, I had to employ *speculative imagination* to birth this story.

My purpose in writing this narrative is two-fold: to remind readers yet again of the courageous—and often tragic—histories of both enslaved Africans and the Cherokee Nation in nineteenth century North Carolina. Some of these persons lived among Moravians with whom I now walk on common ground, both literally and figuratively. They, too, remind us of "the rest of the story."

A second goal is to encourage the reader to tell his or her own *story*—in whatever way is practical, with or without a story-satchel. To forge these links reflects the sacred nature of the story. Ancient peoples, every culture and Judeo-Christian scriptures as well as the holy books of other faiths commend storytelling: *watch yourselves closely so you do not forget the things your eyes have seen, or let them slip from your heart as long as you live,* spoke Moses to the Hebrew people. We know that children participate in the Seder by asking questions and hearing stories in response. Christians partake of the sacrament of Holy Communion "in remembrance" of the Passion story. Such rituals link past to present. And sometimes, these stories reflect personal experiences.

The Rev. Ms. Ginny Tobiassen, associate pastor of Home Moravian Church in Winston-Salem, recently spoke these words: "Every member of the [physical] body can *see* what the foot can do. From seeing it in action, we infer that the foot has received gifts for walking, standing, dancing. But without a story, inferring is all we can do," she said.

So, I ask, how would the foot of a toddler tell its story? How might the foot of a ballet dancer tell her story? How might the soldier whose foot is blown off when he stepped on a landmine tell that story?

Can we allow the lioness within to tell our story? In other words, if you don't tell it, who will? "How much do people closest to you have to infer, and how much do they really *know* the story?" Tobiassen asked.

The end result for my intentions is to link the past, through the present, to the future, lest we forget, lest we die like the endangered species we are.

As Henry Taylor wrote in "Understanding Fiction," I, too, with faulty human understanding,

> tell it again, and see how
> to help you believe it . . .
> I make some adjustment of voice or detail,
> [as] the story strides into the future.

CONTENTS

Chapter One: Abduction

*The world is full of stories, and sometimes they
permit themselves to be told.*

Ma-da-ya knew. Her story was far too big to live and forget. But with whom could she share it now? Alone again, the eighty year-old woman she had become emptied her satchel of artifacts onto the dirt floor of Chief Junaluska's house. *Maybe some things are best left buried,* she thought, *safely hidden, forever forgotten, like my old journal.*

Then she remembered Junaluska's stories, Papa Squire's stories. She believed in the linked stories that survive when all else disappears, *like Salem,* she whispered. Her husband was gone, having passed into the Darkening Land where she hoped to join him soon. Even so, she still had their stories, her story.

Fondling the physical mementoes of her life, her mind wandered randomly like the lazy Oconaluftee River. Madaya picked up a braid of horsehair from her treasures and stared at it, hearing again what sounded like whinnying from somewhere down below the path where she and her *edoda* [father] had walked. The dusty relics from her satchel did that for her, re-created the past that had become her daily companion, whether waking or sleeping.

Pressing the coarse black horsehair braid against her cheek, Madaya leaned forward as though to look into the ravine she remembered. "There she is, in that patch of briars," she'd shouted to Edoda. A Cherokee horse had slipped off the trail in a rockslide, and lay moaning at least thirty feet below the path where they walked to the trading post for supplies. Edoda reached for his gun, newly acquired from the trading post.

"We can't have her suffer, Madaya!"

"Nooooo!" Her scream echoed louder than the horse's cry of pain.

Breaking away, Madaya slid and tumbled down the mountain to reach her. Even these many years later, she rubbed her palms against her arms and muttered, "I don't care about scratches and bumps on my arms and legs. Poor Thistle. She's terrified."

Lying there with her arms hugging the horse's neck, she whispered to her and stroked her tangled mane. Her legs were not broken, or Edoda would have shot her. But Madaya knew Edoda wouldn't shoot while she was holding her, clinging to her neck.

Pity overflowed from Edoda's heart, so he ran to get help. Fortunately, a Cherokee horse is small, like a pony. Men from their village pulled up the animal to the path, blood oozing and thistles sticking out of her hindquarters. That's how she got her name: *Thistle*. Her glistening brown eyes reflected her terror and pain. "She'll be all right, poor thing. I just know it," pronounced Madaya to the rescuers. And she was.

Edoda told people they never knew where she came from. But Madaya knew. Thistle was a gift from the *Galonlati*. She had prayed and prayed for a horse. And there she was. The Great Spirit saw to that.

"Great sorrows and pain can lead us to a path of great joy," *Aduli* [mother] told Madaya. Thistle had suffered to get what she needed, but they had found each other.

"We had only one horse, poor thing. Thistle was old, but served us well. Edoda loved her, too. I knew he would," Madaya said to the empty room.

All that had happened a few weeks before the soldiers came. The adults had been told, had been warned repeatedly that the United States government was sending them to Indian Territory. And—they'd been further informed—they could leave their ancestral home any time to head west. Peacefully. Quietly. Orderly. In whatever way and time that seemed best for them.

A few men like Chief Junaluska, had intervened, pled, even visited President Jackson to request permission for his people to remain on the land, but the only recourse offered was to become citizens of the new country. Decisions split families, sending some into the forest to hide, others choosing to become citizens of North Carolina, and yet others believing they needed to head west where land and opportunity awaited them, "a gift to the Cherokee," they were told. But the right time never seemed *right*, so many others waited, hoping that choice would save them.

The previous night they'd been warned again, that time by an extraordinary, heavenly meteor show. A few misty clouds drifted low over the Smoky Mountains. No moon that night. As darkness crept into every crevice of their village, the storytellers pointed heavenward. Stories coalesced into a vivid night sky where one after another, blazes of light streaked toward the gathered Cherokee people who at first shrank from the dazzling display.

Their outdoor fires shot cinders and sparks to meet the few clouds hovering just above their heads. Parents gestured toward the heavens. Madaya, only five years old then, watched the heavens from the comforting lap of her aduli, whose growing fetus left little space for a daughter on her lap, but Madaya felt her arms pull her closer.

Older children gazed with interest as the stars danced, darting, falling, chasing one another through the night. "Look!" the children murmured in awe. The little ones fell asleep on their mother's breasts. The men, whether *edoda* or *tsodusti* or *edudi* told the awestruck boys and young men stories of hope and despair, victories and defeats, life and death, all the while wondering, watching the heavens into the night.

Even the medicine man considered the meaning of this particular heavenly display. *What portent? What does the Galonlati know about this strange phenomenon tonight? These meteor showers always* mean *something . . . something . . ."*

Anxiety pushed them headlong into the next morning, forcing men to rise even earlier than customary, still pondering the meaning of the meteor-show. Mothers prepared for their walk to the river for water. But the silent forest did not stir as usual, as though afraid that waking up might disturb—or escalate—or fracture the expected normalcy that generally awaited creation. From ants to eagles, from creeping things to hungry night creatures who usually roamed about seeking what they needed to survive, on that morning they instinctively peered cautiously from their protective covers into the hazy dawn, waiting.

Before Madaya heard the shouts of the soldiers, her little dog Moonlight bounded on top of her. He was all white except for a tiny black diamond between his eyes and black socks on his two front feet. He belonged to all the villagers, a gift from one of the traders to Will at the Trading Post; but Will couldn't keep him because he often traveled to Washington. So he asked Madaya to take care of him. Everyone loved Moonlight, but he always came to her at night.

Moonlight leaped onto Madaya's pallet and belly-flopped on top of her. She welcomed his wet kisses washing her face, telling her it was time for them to join her aduli to go for water. She giggled and wiggled, but Moonlight seemed serious. Something was astir.

Walking toward the river with Moonlight, Aduli and Madaya heard the soldiers. Like thunder they rumbled through the valley and into the village, shouting in English. Of course, Madaya didn't know English then, but several spoke Cherokee. Aduli ordered her about, "Back to the house! Come quickly! Madaya, carry this! Put that under the walnut tree! No! Hurry! "

Everyone scurried about, frantically snatching a few pots, clothes, blankets, some dried corn and venison. Madaya grabbed her little

24

satchel of treasures, but when young, everything is special; it held pebbles, a tiny baby doll she had made from cornhusks, her tooth that had fallen out, a milkweed pod . . .

Most soldiers were nice enough. One took Madaya's hand and led her to neighbors standing under the trees, waiting for something—she didn't know what. Other soldiers began shouting "Hurry up!" in Cherokee.

Edoda told Madaya to put Moonlight in the house with some food and water. This was strange, because Moonlight stayed outdoors until bedtime, but she did as he said. One of the enslaved Africans who called himself Squire helped load their belongings. Edoda took his place behind the wagon where he would walk with other men and stronger people, while Aduli and *Enisi* (grandmother) were assisted into a wagon with Madaya and other young children.

That's when Madaya saw Thistle watching her, her brown eyes big with fright. She shivered in terror, looking like Madaya remembered her after falling off the trail. During early morning hours when it rained, she had asked to bring her horse into the house, but Edoda shook his head. "But Thistle is old," Madaya begged, "and she's cold, poor thing." Thistle stood dripping, watching, waiting for someone to untie her. Poor thing.

Madaya shouted to her father, "Edoda! I need Thistle!" She started to jump from the wagon, but a soldier pushed her back. Some of the soldiers laughed even as they struggled to push the horse-pulled wagon forward, but the wheels sank more deeply into the mud.

"Now, now, that old mare will just slow us down,'" a soldier with red hair told her. Madaya heard them arguing and laughing at old Thistle. An officer rode up on horseback and shouted, "Take her!" Not knowing whether he meant Thistle or her, Madaya watched someone loosen the frayed rope that tethered Thistle to the chestnut tree, pile sacks of grain and bundles of pots on her sagging back, and pull her forward. Poor thing. But at least she was going with them.

The children watched the drama, trying to obey, quivering with excitement, boiling with compressed energy. Remembering suddenly that Moonlight was in the house, Madaya jumped from the wagon to get her, and raced toward the house. When Edoda saw her, he shouted, "Madaya! Get back in the wagon!"

"I have to get Moonlight!" she called to him. Without warning the wagon jolted ahead. A scowling soldier grabbed Madaya and pushed her back inside. She tried to explain about Moonlight, but he didn't understand. She heard a loud sucking sound and felt the wagon jerk forward.

"Will we come back home soon?" Madaya asked Aduli who patted her without answering. Before long, they smelled it. Gazing behind them, they peered through smoky haze from fires set by the soldiers as they left their beautiful village, their home. Madaya shuddered and crinkled her nose.

Some villagers had small Cherokee horses; some had chickens; all had gardens. The soldiers burned everything in sight, even the cornfield that was big enough to feed the entire village through the winter.

That's when Madaya saw a soldier hurl a burning stick into the thatched roof of their house. Sobbing aloud, she screamed and jumped from the wagon again. Like an arrow Edoda darted after her and grasped his target firmly, preventing her desperate dash to rescue Moonlight.

With few memories of her edoda, even into old age she clung to that image of the face that looked rugged as a river rock, wet and cracked and rough. That clear memory of him was all wrapped up into feeling his arms tighten around her, even in old age.

Madaya kicked sideways against the soldier leading them back to the wagon, so Edoda held her legs against his strong body as he walked while whispering into her ear. After carrying her a few miles, he told Madaya to check on her aduli.

Back inside the wagon, women were crying and wailing, everyone talking at once, some ready to fight. Those who rode in the wagon were young children or pregnant, old or sick. Besides, the soldiers outnumbered the Cherokee and carried guns. Their strong, massive horses were not like the little Cherokee horse named Thistle.

What could they do?

Dragon flies plagued the horses and mosquitoes sucked blood from the sweating, hungry travelers. They weren't dressed for travel—by foot or by wagon. They never imagined that they would be forced to walk through the harsh winter that lay ahead, never imagined that. Some had been taken from the fields or while feeding their chickens, all wearing summer clothes, not dressed for a winter's march of twelve hundred miles.

Looking behind them, they rubbed their eyes, unbelieving. Smoke and falling ash mixed with tears as they watched the flames eat their homes, their crops, their animals, their village, including Madaya's precious Moonlight. Burying her head in the lap of Enisi, Madaya sobbed. Enisi murmured quietly, stroking her granddaughter's hair. Through the years she had experienced all manner of sadness and tragedy, but never anything like this.

For months to come Madaya would dream of Moonlight's waking her with his wet kisses, looking at her with those big brown eyes, tilting his little white head, lifting one paw toward her like she had taught him to do, begging her to take him with them on their journey, as they always did. Then Madaya would wake up, sitting up straight, wiping her face, wet with Moonlight's kisses—or her tears.

Chapter Two: Stockade

You will use all means to persuade any tribe to come in for the purpose of making peace, and when you get them all together, kill all the grown Indians and take the children. Sell them as slaves to defray the cost.

~ Confederate Governor John R. Baylor

Their respected leader and chief, Junaluska, was in charge of herding his own people, including his wife and child, from Cherokee to the stockades where they waited for the next order from government officials. The harrowing walk through rivers and dangerously wild terrain had just begun, unaware to them. With Junaluska, they felt safe.

After one particularly long day of riding that Madaya preferred, so she could be with her *aduli*, they saw a stockade in the evening mist. Sturdy, strong, protective, the sight of it gave them hope. Aduli would soon deliver her baby; even Madaya had hoped they could stop when the time came, little caregiver that she was. The soldiers prodded them toward the fort, and with the help of a few enslaved Africans, unloaded their meager belongings. Not having eaten that whole day, they were happy enough to feel full again after a bowl of rice and chunks of venison, one of the last times they would eat protein.

Divided into groups of men on one side with women and children on the other, they devoured what was set before them. At last they could lie down under the stars and wrap up in their blankets after the long journey. Madaya fell asleep thinking about Moonlight, holding her aduli close, rubbing her pregnant belly and talking to their baby inside. Aduli had explained that soon they would all have a new home. Surely they must be close to the place they were going.

Kindness came from unexpected sources, like the enslaved African Squire who walked with them, along with other Africans the government had acquired. Officials assured the owners that their slaves would be returned once the "cargo" had been delivered to Indian Territory. After all, it had been explained to some Moravians, as you build your village in Salem, you and your land will be safer with the Indians moved elsewhere. *Agreed*, some thought silently, if somewhat guiltily. They had suffered through some harrowing skirmishes with the Indians.

Of course, Squire was not consulted about leaving. He had been happier than he'd been in a long while, working diligently for his Moravian master. Squire was aware that the man for whom he worked had lost his wife to a fever recently, leaving him alone with his four year-old daughter in this strange new land. In one way, both Squire and Brother Freihofer had similar stories—each had lost his spouse. But the similarities ended there. At times Brother Freihofer fought twinges of guilt—not because of Squire's enslaved status, for that was no fault of his—but more for his lack of knowledge about how to befriend the man. To sit at the Tavern with the slave over a mug of spirits simply was not done. So of course, they had not shared their losses.

What brought Squire pleasure in Salem was his acquaintance with an African free woman named Precious who worked for the village doctor. Having been purchased with some others by a Moravian who would not, could not accept slavery in any form, Precious served the doctor well.

Not until Precious broke the bars that steeled Squire from any conversation, any accommodation other than what was required of him as an enslaved man, he had not realized the depths of his loneliness and withdrawal. He and Precious had met at St. Philips Church, and before long they had told each other everything in those sweet, stolen trysts on Sunday mornings before separating until the next service at the church brought them running. *How devout these persons seemed to be, rushing to St. Philips whenever its doors opened for services*, commented some observers. Somehow in those brief encounters, the couple managed to share everything that mattered to either of them, including the dream that one day they would marry, one day when Squire completed his servitude, another eight years.

So, that day in the spring of 1839 when Brother Freihofer announced to Squire that he would join a contingent of soldiers, likely the next day, for a journey of undetermined length, Squire was stunned. The orders were to help the soldiers collect the Cherokee, a hard day's travel from Salem, and travel from there to Indian Territory. They needed extra manpower to help with the gargantuan move, thus the decision was made to acquire some enslaved men.

"And Sir, uh, how long will I, uh, be away?" Squire ventured to ask.

"Well, it is not known how long that journey will take," Brother Freihofer said. "I am sorry, Brother Squire," he continued sympathetically. Surely this man was not unlike himself in many ways. Brother Freihofer knew him as a faithful, honorable man and a hard worker.

That night after the announcement, whether with Brother Freihofer's sympathy or not, Squire scrubbed himself clean after a hard day's work

30

tilling soil for planting behind his master's house. Strong and muscular from his hard labor in the past several years, was obvious. Of course, neither was his master less fit, for all, whether bond or free, worked to create this new compound, this village called Salem.

Squire was aware that the Moravians did not condone the owning of slaves, yet—and this puzzled him—more than one of their persuasion had leased an enslaved African from the church. After all, the considerable work to carve a sizeable community demanded the efforts of every able-bodied person; they needed these Africans. Yet, neither did Squire understand the unnerving rumor that the first legal slave-owner in the young country was a black man like himself.

Nearly frantic with the news of his imminent and sudden departure, Squire debated how he might contact Precious about this interruption to their greatly anticipated weekly meetings. He knew that she lived behind the doctor's residence that also housed the pharmacy, but did know how to alert her to the message he needed to give. Indeed, more than a message...he needed to touch her, hold her in his arms, caress those rounded breasts that intruded on his dreams at night. Of course, he had never followed through on any imaginative speculations or unbidden dreams. Their public Sunday rendezvous hardly allowed such liberties. Perhaps she would not even—no, he was positive that she wanted him as deeply as he needed her.

Tears of anger and frustration flowed as he scrubbed himself. But such deep feelings primed the well of courage to leave the Negro quarter compound that night before he would leave, to wander cautiously but intently toward the church, up the hill toward the doctor's residence. Finally within sight of the little cottage hidden among some cypress trees, he paused, still pondering how to alert her to his presence. If frightened, she might cry out for help. The good doctor, even with his house full of children, might hear her and run to her aid.

Leaning against the rough bark of a walnut tree, he remembered how, as children back in his African village, he and his brothers could mimic every sound of the night, from the hyena to the monkey. But here, there were neither hyenas nor monkeys.

I can do this, he thought, his flesh tingling with the thought of his beloved. *I must do this for her, for us.* Squire cleared his throat quietly, tentatively, and thought about the owl that frequented the compound where he lived in the Negro Quarter across the fields from St. Philips. *Yes! That's it!* He puckered his lips and out came, "Whooooooo."

Courage flowed from his hooting into the darkness into call after call. He waited expectantly. Creeping stealthily closer to her back stoop, Squire squatted by the back door, and called again. "Whooooo," he sounded desperately.

Perhaps he could write her a note, but he had no access to paper without taking a piece—that he did on occasion—from Brother Freihofer. He hooted again, more weakly than he intended, and there, to his surprise, as he had not really expected her to appear, her form darkened the open door. Her shapely acorn-colored arm held a lantern high, lifted above her head to search the trees.

Now that she had appeared, Squire did not know what to do next. She looked like an angel to him. "Precious!" he whispered loudly. "Precious," he called again. "It's Squire."

"Squire! Come!" she whispered. It was as though she had expected him. Many were the nights she had wished, had dreamed that he came to her. But he was an honorable man; they had never before met secretly, except in their fantasies.

By the time they collapsed into each other's arms, so much closer than they had ever dared in public on Sundays, the miracle of it washed their faces in tears. Closing the door behind her, she could not speak, nor could Squire. One day, they would live together this way! They knew it. The gods knew it. All nature knew it had to be.

Through the hours that followed until nearly dawn, they clung to every word, every embrace, every promising feeling that portended only good for these lovers who sealed their determination that night to make their dream come true.

But, they both knew as he crept away through the brush back to the Negro Quarter, that a long stretch of time would elapse before they met again in this way, maybe even a year or two. They considered that possibility.

Thus Squire re-lived that last tryst with Precious, even as he helped care for the animals on the Trail—mainly the soldiers' horses—and supplies. Some of the Cherokee were boarded at Stecoah, but most of the villagers were herded into a larger stockade, Fort Montgomery in Tennessee. Even while moving farther and farther away from his lover, Squire had looked at the journey west as one step closer to his return to Salem and his beloved one.

Never having been in Georgia or Tennessee, most of those journeying were surprised to see other Cherokee join them in the stockade from areas unknown to them. Maybe this will be fun, the children reasoned. They devised games to make them feel better, but that was before cold set in and they ran out of food. Soldiers promised warm clothes would arrive from the government before they set out on the Trail again. President Jackson and Commander Scott had said so.

Weeks swallowed the days and nights. Small pox, dysentery and venereal diseases soon threatened everyone in the stockade. Like wild animals in a cage, the confined travelers could not escape. One morning a family noticed small blisters had appeared on their children during the night. Soon, their bodies were covered, spreading even onto their faces. Alarmed, the enslaved African Squire first noticed them in his rounds. He searched the huddled masses to find Junaluska who notified the officials.

General excitement ensued and shortly an order was given. Soldiers led that scantily clad family outside without their blankets and clothing. Madaya's edoda told his family and others not to worry. Comforting them, he promised that everything would be all right. Some believed him, hanging on to the assurance like a drowning man to a rope, a frayed one at that. They never saw that family again.

After removing the infected family from the stockade, a few soldiers gathered the family's belongings. They knew the power of the small pox that not only could wipe out the whole tribe, but also the white soldiers. Aduli watched them intently as they collected their blankets and then began distributing them to other families who certainly needed their warmth and protection. But those blankets had touched the infected children and their families with small pox. It wasn't long before other families began to show the same symptoms and were led away from the fort.

Madaya's aduli refused the proffered blankets and tried to warn others surreptitiously. Some were only too pleased to have more blankets. But she knew better. She knew that these European diseases could kill. *Can their diseases be any more cruel than their actions?* She considered this. *Were these white soldiers so ignorant, or were they trying to kill all of them?* Small pox had invaded their temporary shelter, if it could be called *shelter*.

By the time darkness sneaked into their circle again, Aduli felt insistent warning signals that her time for delivery was close. Perhaps on this night her baby would come. She explained to four year-old Madaya how the baby would be born, how the life-giving cord would need to be cut, how the placenta would follow. A few other women stooped to assist the little family. Once the newborn infant dropped onto the blanket, Madaya sneaked away to find her edoda in the area where men gathered.

Startled to see Madaya, he stooped to hear her relay the news about his new son, "Our baby is here!" she whispered to him. Together they skirted the edges to reach his wife, hoping the soldiers would not notice; men were not permitted to go near the women. But his wife needed him.

In the Cherokee tradition, no man—not even the husband—would be permitted to help with the delivery. By the time they reached her, Edoda sensed that everything was not all right. When Madaya opened the blanket to show her edoda his new son, he saw the umbilical cord wrapped around his neck, his face blue and unmoving.

"No, no!" the other women pushed Madaya aside. "He is not alive! Go now; we must help your aduli." Edoda stooped to help his wife deliver the placenta. But something was wrong. A soldier appeared and shouted at him to stop. Edoda ignored him, focusing on assisting her.

"What are you doing here? Leave her alone!' two soldiers appeared, shouting to him.

"She is my wife!" Edoda gasped at their insolence and cruelty. Seeing the young soldiers watch the birth incensed Edoda. "How dare you watch my wife deliver her child?" he shouted at them in Cherokee. Of course, they did not understand him, and were furious about his disobeying their order to leave.

Edoda pushed aside the bloody blanket that held the dead infant son. On his knees between Aduli's legs, he saw a second son emerging from Aduli. The second twin appeared, sucking in great gulps of tainted air that filled the stockade. Another boy, he cried like he was angry, too.

A sharp pistol shot warned everyone to mind his own business. The women scampered aside as, without warning, Edoda slumped forward on top of Aduli.

She screamed, but not with birth pangs...

"Shot for non-compliance with the officer's order,' a soldier shouted at the angry Junaluska when he ran to the scene of the murder after hearing the gunshot. Aghast, watching from a safe distance, Squire saw Aduli's dead husband, Madaya's edoda, sprawled across her belly.

Lifting Madaya and pressing her head onto his shoulder, Junaluska tried to shield her from the brutality, then handed her to Squire. The cruelty Squire saw at the fort reminded him of his own kidnapping and experiences as a slave, both sickening and terrifying him.

Afraid to pick up the squalling, red-faced infant whose father had just been shot. Madaya didn't know then that she would soon become the baby's aduli, a four year-old aduli.

Junaluska pulled Edoda off his wife and knelt beside her to cut the umbilical cord. Squire set Madaya aside and scooped up the bloody human birth debris, all this watched by the immobilized women. The soldiers had ordered Squire to collect and discard—but not bury—the bodies of those who had died during each night, victims of hunger, disease, cruelty. And now, those bodies included Madaya's edoda and one twin son. Squire was fully occupied.

Junaluska discreetly pulled a button from Edoda's shirt and handed it to Madaya, not knowing why exactly, except that at times no words, no kindness, no tears can begin to express what is felt. Madaya looked at him, fully aware of the gift, already mindful of its value. Clutching the button with her fist, she reached inside her flimsy dress and dropped it into her story-satchel, tied around her neck for safekeeping.

Aduli begged Junaluska in whispers to bury her husband and dead baby that night. Squire and Junaluska devised a plan; they hid the bodies outside before the soldiers' return. They wanted to ensure that Aduli's dead baby and her husband would be buried properly. Once the full moon set, with the ground still warm enough to dig a shallow grave, Junaluska and Squire accomplished their mission. Had the soldiers noticed, they too, would have been shot.

Later that night Junaluska returned, but Squire was not with him. He hid in the forest through that long night. Madaya feared he had run away. But picking up her new brother, she gazed into his finally placid face, and smiled at her mother as she thanked Junaluska for his help.

Once alone in the forest, Squire struggled. *I could run away. They'd never miss me. I could go back to Salem and to Precious...*but reality shook him with the facts. Runaway slaves "ain't nothin' to nobody," he'd heard someone say. If he ever wanted to return to his love, to begin life again, he would need first of all to complete this assignment. *Then*—he clung to hope—*then, I can return.*

"I cannot go back to the wagons now, but I will return. I need some time alone. I cannot bury another body tonight," he told Junaluska, who nodded. He understood. So Squire cried his own prayers, weeping for the state of things, as terrible as his own experiences on the slave ship. Back in Zambia he recalled having sung words and phrases that encouraged him through many long nights. They chiseled their way through the debris of sadness and anger and confusion. Repeating them like a mantra, he hummed quietly to the still forest:

> When I despair, my God encourages me.
> When I fear, my God holds me.
> When I am empty, my God fills me.
> When I feel alone...my God cares for me.
> When I breathe my last, my God welcomes me.
> My God loves me, just the way I am.

Sneaking back to the stockade before sunrise dissolved the cover of darkness, he believed he was somehow protected, cared for by a power greater than himself. He arrived at the stockade to see bustling everywhere as preparations to pack up and leave the stockade enveloped everyone. Surely, he had chosen the best way: just move on, continue the circuitous journey that would eventually lead back him back to Salem, to his lover.

The next morning, Madaya held her baby brother as her aduli wrapped their meager belongings in a blanket, praying for strength to continue their journey without her husband at her side. Madaya often glanced up, expecting to see her edoda. Her child-mind could not grasp death, that separation common to all of creation. Of course, no more easily could her aduli fathom such a mystery.

Following the soldiers' orders, the already diminished Cherokee stumbled out of the stockade, mostly single file like ants on a trail. Some elderly, pregnant or ill persons jostled in covered wagons, stuffed in among supplies, while most walked. "Are we almost there?" Madaya asked her aduli.

CHAPTER THREE *NU NA DA UL TSU N YI*

Those [Cherokee] people who were removed on the Trail of Tears, [they were] carrying their Bibles, able to read and write in their own language, [having] their own newspaper, whereas many of those who removed them could neither read nor write—an irony.

~ Freeman Owle, Cherokee historian, teacher, artist

By that time Madaya felt like an adult and her aduli confirmed that her actions showed maturity beyond her years. On the other hand, the child was hungry and begged, "Let me have some milk, too," but Aduli said she needed it for the baby, and she could eat what they were given.

Thankful that her little daughter functioned like a miniature aduli, she often allowed Madaya to hold the infant so she could rest. For some reason, the return of occasional post-partum strength was only a teaser, far from reality. Five-years old by that time, Madaya embraced the care of her aduli. *That is easier than caring for our poor baby*, she thought. His skin felt rough and bumpy, like the back of a frog. Then, the sicker he got, the more he wanted only Aduli to hold him as he rooted for milk, and that was scanty enough given their diet and little water to drink.

They had not named the infant, for each fitting name seemed too sad to give the little one. Aduli longed for Edoda who would think of a good name. Full of joy with his baby daughter, he had named their first child Madaya, meaning first girl. And now, Aduli knew she would be the only girl, her only living child.

Through another long night Madaya's baby brother shook with cold and fever. Lying in the wagon in her liquid excrement, Aduli had become too sick with dysentery to nurse the baby. *Just in time,* thought Aduli, welcoming the attention of Watie, wife of Chief John Ross, who had befriended Madaya and her family. As her own baby had died two days earlier, she offered to nurse the boy. Although she shivered with chills herself, Watie wrapped him in her own blanket before pressing him to her breast. The next day, just when Madaya thought their baby might live, the news came: Watie had died.

Aduli must have known she would not live through another night. Dehydrated, sick and fearful for Madaya and her baby boy, she called to Squire as he made his rounds, looking for dead bodies. "Please, sir," Aduli begged him as he passed by, "you buried my husband and baby back at the stockade. You have shown my daughter and me kindness. I fear that I, too, shall soon die. Will you please, Sir, look after these two children."

Squire promised, thinking he would surely find someone to care for the baby, and probably Junaluska would take Madaya back to Cherokee. Squire fully expected he would be sent back to Salem, and what would he do with two children? But promise he did.

As the baby fretted, Madaya tore off a tiny corner of Watie's blanket, rolled it up tightly and dipped it into some water for him to suck when he got fussy. It's not hard to make a sugar-tit, but with neither sugar nor molasses to dip it in, the starving baby—hopeful for a few moments—sucked vigorously on the little rag, then whimpered like an injured rabbit, too weak to cry or suck any longer at that empty fountain.

Keeping the infant and her mother warm was Madaya's next big problem to solve, for cold had seeped across the valleys and winds blew snowflakes from the mountains, threatening the pitiful stream of refugees. Her aduli seemed hot enough, Madaya reasoned, so she hid her brother under her blanket. She sometimes watched him exhale, each time waiting for him to take another breath, then finding herself trying to breathe for him...*breathe baby, breathe,* Madaya whispered, and then he'd exhale with a gasp. Waiting for him to inhale again, she held her own breath. But with Watie gone, and Aduli without milk, their baby survived only one more day.

Madaya waited for Squire to pass her way again, pulling the little corpse close to Aduli's side under their blanket. Aduli in her delirium did not realize what was happening, so Madaya kept the baby hidden close to her. She would not allow the soldiers to take him away.

Aduli's attacks of chills shook the whole wagon. *"Why does Aduli feel cold?* Madaya asked herself. *When I hold her, it feels like a fire burns inside her body, but the heat never reaches her arms. They get colder.* Like icy fingers crawling up from her toes and fingers, her skin felt cold as the ice that the wagon slid on from side to side. Rocking back and forth on the rutted path was enough to make Madaya feel sick.

Lying down on top of Aduli to get some warmth, Madaya felt better inside the blanket. Finally, Aduli stopped shaking. Madaya tried not to touch the cold and stiff gray body of their baby on one side of her aduli. Burying her nose between her aduli's breasts helped Madaya escape the stench of sickness and body excretions in their wagon. Sleep finally draped over Madaya before she awoke, shivering again. Aduli wasn't keeping her warm any more.

The ice was thick that night. The winds were cruel. Nature attacked like a monster in a nightmare. "Aduli!" Madaya whispered to her, because she did not want anyone to find their dead baby. She would wait for Squire to take him away. When Aduli didn't answer her call, Madaya shook her a bit, but still she didn't move. Then she knew.

Feeling like she must be the only living person on earth, she threw her arms around her aduli's neck. Determined not to let them take Aduli and their baby away, she clung to the remnants of life—and death—beneath the blanket, her tears freezing on Aduli's shrunken, icy cheeks. Her enisi by this time seemed unaware of anything happening around her, even to her daughter and two grandchildren in the wagon with her.

At last Squire came. Madaya asked him for a proper burial for her other baby brother and her aduli. For all they knew, the soldiers may think they were a family. What would they care about a black man's dead wife and baby? Other slaves didn't have their families with them—and of course, neither did Squire—but the soldiers didn't know that.

Hearing the soldiers' boisterous talking, getting closer in their rounds, Squire scooped up the baby's tiny body and placed him under the wagon. Fearing the soldiers might take Aduli's body, Madaya lay down on top of her dead mother, her head up cupped in her hands, her elbows jutting into her aduli's chest, talking to her aloud, telling her a story, acting like she was alive.

The soldiers peeked inside the wagon, checking for dead bodies as they did routinely each evening, checking up on Squire's work. He worked harder than those soldiers ever figured out, attempting to bury each dead Cherokee with respect. For all they knew or cared, he just pitched them into the dark forests as they passed through. Sometimes, Squire was taken away from that job to help clear a road for them to travel the next day. Each return bolstered Madaya's courage and strength.

After the soldiers moved ahead, Madaya lay quietly on top of her aduli and waited for Junaluska to help Squire, but worried that the horses might trample their baby under the wagon. But the wagons had already slowed for the night. Finally, Junaluska walked by and stopped to talk to Squire. Looking up into the wagon, they did not go to her as usual, but stood talking quietly. She could not hear what they were they saying and waited for them to approach the wagon.

Squire told Junaluska Madaya's request; the burial part was not in question, but they soon understood that one of them had to take responsibility for the orphaned child. Once in Indian Territory they would find a suitable aduli for Madaya. But Junaluska did not appear to listen well that night. That was strange enough. Madaya watched Squire put his hand on Junaluska's shoulder, even more strange. As Junaluska walked away, Squire told Madaya that somebody else had died that night—Junaluska's wife Tena.

Junaluska had told Squire he was no longer impressed by the white man's way. He wondered why, if the white people had their holy book for so long, like they say, why they had not yet learned to follow it. Junaluska said that when the white man began to live the *Jesus-way* that he would be happy to recommend the Christian religion to his people.

Observing people like President Jackson instead of Watie, such thoughts came unbidden, but not irrationally. Junaluska cried for his own losses, his wife, his child a few days earlier, his Cherokee people. So Madaya did not want to burden him further about her aduli and baby brother. Squire comforted Madaya, telling her that Junaluska planned to return.

That evening just before the soldiers did their checking, Junaluska lifted Madaya from her aduli, whose spirit had left her. Young as she was, and wise beyond her chronological years, Madaya asked Squire and Junaluska a question. "Why can we not see the *spirit*, when that is the part of us that lasts, but we can see the *body* that soon becomes part of the earth?" The men looked at each other, hoping the other would answer, but said nothing. Squire scooped up the baby-corpse and hid him inside his cloak, then worked with Junaluska to remove Aduli's body.

"You must wrap her in this blanket," Madaya instructed the men, for even she knew this was the custom for burial. For this, the men had an answer, both responding together, "No, no! Aduli wants you to have the blanket," they assured her. Perhaps with both Watie's and her aduli's blankets, she might survive the long winter's walk still ahead. Feeling a strong, protective instinct toward the child, Squire thought, *Yes, I could be her parent.* This trail-walk confused all he thought he had learned from his own suffering through the years.

Madaya watched them carry her aduli and baby brother off the trail, into the trees. Soon the dark forest swallowed them. Straining to see, it looked like nothing had happened, like withdrawing one's hand from a bucket of water. After what seemed a long time, Madaya awoke after a horrible nightmare. *Aduli! answer me!* she cried out. But she was alone under the blanket they'd shared; then she remembered everything.

The wagons were still. All was quiet. She crawled to the edge of the wagon and dropped down. No one stopped her, so she ran toward the forest, then saw Squire and Junaluska walking toward her. Junaluska picked up Madaya and carried her to the wagon. He pulled Aduli's beads from his pocket. She had fashioned them from river clay and painted them in a variety of colors with dyes from berries she collected. For as long as Madaya could remember, Aduli had worn those beads.

"These are for you," Junaluska said, draping the beads around her neck. Finally, that long, slow day and night ended.

Junaluska collapsed later that day with dysentery and delirium, at last succumbing to the great grief that sapped his energy and reserve. As his fever climbed, he mumbled about past battles and told Squire he would have killed Jackson in the Battle at Horseshoe Bend, had he known, had he only known. Squire didn't really know what he was talking about, and of course, Madaya was too young to know the story. She begged Squire to take her to see Junaluska, but he told her to stay in the wagon, because many people were getting sick.

Perhaps I do know how to take care of a child. Squire again reflected on this as he worked. Perhaps he and Precious could care for her back in Salem.

Most of their journey was overland through northern Georgia, Tennessee, Kentucky and Ohio, but that meant crossing river after river in those vast states. "Terrifying not only to the children, but also even the old ones, the soldiers, too, feared and dreaded some of the crossings. Forced off the wagons, even Madaya's confused old enisi had to leave the relative protection of the wagon to walk with the others. As she had walked so little, unlike the others at least she still had moccasins on her feet.

They crossed the Hiwassee where it met the Tennessee River. Crossing that north section of the Hiwassee, Madaya watched in horror as her enisi slid on a rock and went under, gasping for breath and crying for help in the icy waters. Although Madaya could not do much, she tried to grasp her hair and hold her head above water so she could breathe. It wasn't deep there, but Enisi had no strength to get up again. Some Cherokee men noticed and tried to assist her, but the soldiers kept shouting at them, "Move on! Move it! Keep going!"

Madaya could see the water foaming as it picked up speed over the rocks. As the water deepened, a man scooped her up onto his shoulders, but she struggled to get down and pled with him to carry Enisi, not her. But it was too late. Madaya watched her tumbling downstream, arms flailing, finally disappearing in the angry waters.

Five year-old Madaya already felt old, felt like the travelers were all the same age, one condition, all of them like the puppet Junaluska had brought her from his travels to Washington. He had taught her how to make her puppet tell a story. How she did love that little doll. She often retrieved the ragged puppet from her story-satchel to press against her cheek or tuck inside her top. It looked as old as Madaya felt, like a dirty, old rag, yet comforting somehow.

"We are puppets, too," Madaya explained to Squire. "Somebody we do not know, do not understand, bigger than we are, controls us, makes us dance, makes us leave our homes, makes us walk through rivers and climb mountains, makes us go hungry and live in pain. Yes, those white men make us go anyplace they want us to go." Squire agreed, puppets all.

The dwindling band kept moving as they were told to do, all the way to Nashville where they stopped one night. In the morning they awoke to snow, more than Madaya had ever seen. They spent the day and night camped there by the Cumberland River, watching the giant white flakes drift silently down, looking as soft as feathers.

The next morning they managed to move the Cherokee to a narrow spot at the mouth of the Cumberland and Ohio Rivers where a ferry crossed, but on that day the river was frozen solid. The soldiers talked among themselves, wondering what to do next. Looked like they weren't having fun, either. Some of the soldiers skated across easily, and decided it was solid enough to hold the wagons. Again, they made everyone get out—most were barefoot by that time, shoes worn to threads—and walk across the great expanse. From there they passed through Illinois until the great Mississippi River stretched out before them. Now that's a river, a *long person,* the Cherokee called it.

Months into their walk, all they had to protect them from freezing were a few worn clothes and threadbare blankets, but when they got damp and froze stiff, wrapping them around their bodies was impossible. Many died there, sleeping on the ground where they remained, as there was no possibility of digging graves and proper burials. Babies were born only to die, old men cried out for Death to rescue them. They thought nothing could be worse than that hell.

That's when Will Thomas arrived on the trail to tell the depleted, freezing Cherokee about those who, months earlier had escaped into the forests, some successfully. That part of his story offered hope, encouraging them. "You, too, will one day make a home again, in a new land," he reminded them. But then he related to Junaluska and the older men the story about ruthless soldiers and a courageous Cherokee father. Oh yes, they remembered Old Tsali and his sons. But their memory of that did nothing to hearten them in their journey.

While they walked the Trail on which the Cherokee cried, the respected old man named Tsali, with his family, had escaped Removal by pushing farther into the mountains rather than be forced to move west. Legends about them grew like canebreaks. Junaluska had heard rumors during his travels.

A general who had once appeared to see both sides of reasoning about the Removal, said that if he could, he would remove every Indian beyond the reach of the white men, "who like vultures, are watching, ready to pounce upon their prey, and strip them of everything they have." Yet, that same general who wanted protection for the Cherokee, proceeded with forced, and often cruel removal of the Luftee Indians in Haywood County. Some were permitted to stay on the land if they renounced all but their new citizenship in North Carolina; still others escaped into the forest, hoping for safety, even some autonomy.

It was there that Tsali and his family had escaped as fugitives, an estimated three hundred men and their families; Cherokee scouts—yes, Cherokee—captured about one hundred forty of them. General Scott wrote that "those wild Indians have refused, again and again, to comply with the urgent entreaties of both Cherokee and U.S. authorities; they have obstinately separated themselves from their nation, and resolved to live in their savage haunt."

When Tsali was finally apprehended with eight of his family members, Wasitani, Tsali's son, related that a soldier struck his mother with a horsewhip because she stopped to care for her baby. So, to increase the speed of the prisoners, two of the soldiers dismounted so Wasitani's mother and some of the children could ride on their horses.

He said that his mother with her infant in arms was boosted onto a white horse. Suddenly, the steed bolted, throwing both his baby brother and mother to the ground. One of her feet caught in the stirrup. There she lay, while her baby, his skull fractured, was flung to the side. They left the dead infant in the road—without proper burial—and proceeded with the heart-broken mother flung over the back of another horse like a sack of grain.

This provocation resulted in an attack on those responsible by the angered Cherokee. Within minutes several soldiers lay dead, stripped of their scalps. Their enraged Cherokee war whoops catapulted the U.S. army into retreat, while Tsali and some others escaped yet again into the forest.

The fugitives travelled to the home of a white farmer who provided food and drink and refuge for two days, but once again the soldiers pursued them. According to Will Thomas, Tsali, also known as Old Charley, later related that Tsali finally offered himself with his sons as a sacrifice for his people. Accepting this offer, the United States government through General Winfield Scott offered to allow the other Luftee Cherokee to remain in North Carolina in peace as long as they could assassinate Tsali and sons.

So, commanded by General Scott, Old Charley, his brother, and the two older sons were shot near the mouth of the Tuckasegee River. To further etch the murder upon their memory, the soldiers corralled a detachment of Cherokee prisoners to participate in the cruel shooting of their own blood brothers. Helpless, they had to obey. Although the stories that circulate differ, to many Cherokee, Tsali, their Old Charley, was a martyr and a hero.

But there was more. Junaluska asked Squire to remain with him. They huddled together into the night to hear further news from Will. His reports about the murders of the Ridges and Boudinot shocked the listeners. Such tales of disaster and death nearly clotted the blood in their veins.

Will blamed Ross who by then was safe in the north, and who, of course, took no blame for the assassinations laid at his feet.

Squire understood none of these tales, but listened carefully. Junaluska understood all too well, adding a few facts for Squire before Will continued. "A young Cherokee named Elias Boudinot had published the *Cherokee Phoenix*—the first national bi-lingual newspaper in both English and Cherokee," he explained. "Not only local, but also reporting national and global news, Bible teaching, feature articles, advertisements, the paper enticed even foreign subscriptions.

Then Boudinot began to write editorials, often criticizing not only the land-hungry white settlers, but also the Cherokee raids in retaliation. He tried. Ah yes, he tried." Junaluska nodded to Will to continue his story.

"Boudinot, John Ridge and his father Major Ridge became the hated ones by the Ross faction, although John Ross insisted to his death that he had neither knowledge of nor participation in the well-planned and executed assassinations of three Cherokee leaders. In fact, Ross reminded everyone that he himself was guarded by five hundred of his friends, as his life was also threatened. All Cherokee, yes, all devoted to their Cherokee families, yes, yet they were enemies who could not agree on a solution to their mutual dilemma. But this is what we understand happened on that fateful day," Will explained.

"One early dawn morning in June, three assassination parties set out to exact blood revenge for perceived—and sometimes factual—injustices of their Cherokee brothers. Twenty-five Cherokee men surrounded the quiet house at Honey Creek where John and Sally Ridge and their children, a sister and brother-in-law still slept. Three of the intruders crept stealthily through the door to John's bedside. One pointed his pistol at John's head, but it did not fire. In spite of Sally's screams for mercy, the three dragged him into the yard. Attempting to follow her husband, Sally fell as two of the men pushed their rifle butts against her. She watched as two grabbed John's arms while the third stabbed him repeatedly. Then they threw him up into the air and when he fell—still alive—twenty-five men stomped on him.

"The men released Sally who ran to her husband and ordered servants to carry John indoors. His brother–in-law Rollin later wrote about the scene of agony, saying, 'it might make one regret that the human race had ever been created.' Crushed with the violence of it, Rollin related that he remembered 'John's voice had been listened to with awe and admiration in the councils of his Nation, whose fame had passed to the remotest of the United States; to think he now lay pale in death.'

49

"We were later told that the assassins moved on to enjoy dinner of a slaughtered steer they ate with relish in celebration of a job well-done: one down, two to go. We were told that one of the soldiers boasted, referring to John Ridge 'Let his silver tongue be cut out, his right hand be cut off; let his children remember this particular sunrise and know their place.'

"Meanwhile, some men approached Boudinot at the site of the house he was building and asked for medicine, as he was also a doctor. Following the doctor into the house for treatment, one of the assassins plunged a knife into the back of Boudinot, that gentle, soft-spoken, kind, forgiving Cherokee.

"But the end was not yet. Knowing that Major Ridge was on his way to visit a sick slave, the assassins accosted him from the underbrush, just inside the Arkansas border. The men shot five bullets into his head and body. His horse bolted and Ridge fell to the ground, dead. His black attendant raced away to relate the tragedy, while the assassins proclaimed their story of success with pride and victorious reports."

Squire shuddered. "How can this be? Your own Cherokee people!"

Wanting to clarify a few details for his friend, Junaluska reviewed some history he knew well. "A small number of living Cherokees signed the Treaty of New Echota, our new capital in Georgia, and ratified by the U.S. Congress. It passed by one vote."

"Ahhh, one vote," Squire echoed. Junaluska had said *living Cherokees*, because driven by desperation, even names of people already dead were added to that treaty, after which more than fifteen thousand Cherokees denounced it as a fraud. Could anyone be trusted? Many national leaders protested the treaty, including Sam Houston and Davy Crocket, John C. Calhoun and Daniel Webster. But the law was set in stone as solid as the rugged mountains.

The soldiers split up the group so they could cross at two points, some at Camp Girardeau and others downstream at Green's Ferry, through Missouri. Terrified of being separated from Squire and Junaluska, relief overwhelmed Madaya when all three stayed with one group.

Once across the river, soldiers ordered the Cherokee to kill game for the soldiers to eat, with promises to share any leftovers, but when they could find very little, the soldiers punished the hunters for not finding enough game. "Find anything. Kill anything," they finally shouted. They, too, hungered and then anger consumed them. "Don't expect us to share with you," they told their prisoners.

Might those Indians who had preceded them have wiped out many of the bison, only to be followed by ferocious winter cold and starvation that felled the rest of the herd? It was like one more betrayal; reason and fact shriveled beneath the bombardment of confusion and desperation, not to mention hunger, that drove angry words and feelings into the open.

"Have you ever been hungry, Squire?" Madaya asked one night. "You know, the kind of hunger that messes with your thinking. The kind of hunger that gnaws like a rat at your insides, biting, scratching, nibbling. it's hard to explain, Squire. Have you ever been hungry?"

Of course, he would not burden the child with the stories of his days on the slave ship that had brought him to this country. Oh yes, he had known hunger in earlier days. And even now, he knew exactly what she experienced. All were hungry, the highest to the lowest in rank, the whitest to the blackest, the youngest to the oldest, they all withered like sprouts in a desert sun.

At last they arrived in Indian Territory in early spring 1839, having traveled through that interminable winter, mostly on foot. The Cherokee people brought with them the treasured concept of *Duyukta,* the moral code that they translated as *the right way* or the *path of*

51

being in balance. And, they had transported with them the fire that must never be extinguished.

Many families brought embers from their home fires, but those fires all came from the Sacred Fire in the council house that burned seven kinds of wood. Junaluska explained to Squire that the Cherokee had carried the eternal flame safely to Indian Territory where they dug a pit, four feet deep. A fire was lit before adding the fire from the capital of the Cherokee Nation in Red Clay. The fires from two separate places converged into one. Men were appointed to keep it going, and they did; even to this day it burns.

"I like the symbol of a fire that we must always attend, never extinguish, never give up what is ours to tend," said Junaluska.

The United States Army records show that under command of General Winfield Scott, six hundred wagons, steamers and boats or rafts moved sixteen thousand Cherokee by land and rivers, twelve hundred miles to Indian Territory. During the journey that lasted between one hundred four and one hundred eighty-nine days [records differ], they suffered in their summer clothing the natural elements of pelting rain, bitter cold, surprise snowstorms and ice thick enough to impede the crossing of rivers. Disease and weather, hunger and despair devoured four thousand refugees.

Young as Madaya was, she grasped little of the goings-on in their new home in Indian Territory. One day, a surprise awaited her when Junaluska invited Madaya out for a walk. They watched rabbits and squirrels and chipmunks, listened to sweet warblers and mocking birds, picked raspberries and pecans. Suddenly he stopped and announced, "Madaya, I am returning to Cherokee. I will take Squire with me, for companionship and assistance. We will go as friends, for he has become that to me."

"What are you saying?" Madaya shouted at him. "How can you do this, take away the two I love the most, the two persons who are left to me?"

"Now, now," he said, patting her on the head. "I am asking you if you want to go with us."

"Oh yes, yes, yes!" Like a squeezed, over-ripe plum, her huge black eyes squirted tears of joy in every direction.

"I am asking you because you have lost so much," he said. "You are ten years old now, and you have friends here. Hiwassee is most fond of you. She will make your life safe and happy with her and her family. She said she wants to be your aduli. You are still Cherokee," he reminded her.

"No! No!" Madaya cried. "I need you and Squire. That's who I need. That's who I want."

"Well then," he said, lifting her up into his arms, "we shall leave in the morning." Then he asked what Madaya thought a strange question: "Do you remember the journey here?"

They had not once talked about it, *too painful, too far past to conjure up any good at all by talking about it, by thinking of details,* Junaluska thought. Madaya considered: *I have even lost my aduli; she never talks to me any longer, not even in my dreams. Perhaps she will find me again back in Cherokee.* Excitement bubbled up, like a river splashing over hard rocks, washing her clean, giving her hope.

She couldn't wait to tell Squire, but was surprised to discover he already knew the plan. She wondered how many things adults talk about without telling her. Madaya frowned. But this one thing she knew: They were walking home!"

Chapter Four: Soulmates

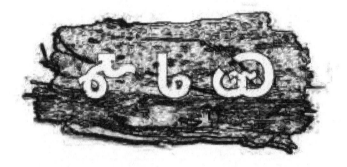

The Indians survived our open intention of wiping them out, and since the tide turned they have even weathered our good intentions toward them, which can be much more deadly.

~John Steinbeck

After five years in "Indian Territory," Junaluska began the trek back home to North Carolina, taking Squire and Madaya with him. Squire was required to settle in Salem again to complete his servitude with the Freihofers. *Maybe they've forgotten all about me.* Squire could hope again. *I could be free!* Squire could dream again. *And soon, my sweet free Precious who works for the doctor will be mine!* He allowed himself to anticipate their reunion, remembering their tender farewell the night before he was sent away—nearing seven years ago.

Junaluska brought him back to reality when he said to Squire: "Having lost both parents on the trail, Madaya needs the love and care of extended Cherokee family again."

"Oh! Yes, yes," agreed Squire. So, he would not have to take care of her, he concluded with genuine relief, but also with sadness. Madaya sometimes begged Squire, surprise overtaking him each time, to allow her to live in Salem with him. She cannot forget his comfort and kindness, and Squire cannot forget his promise to her mother that he would care for her.

"Always remember, you are Cherokee," Squire often reminded Madaya, touched by the girl's tender feelings and dependence on him. He feared that she would be considered his daughter, or worse, treated as a slave who can be owned, managed, and even sold, with no chance to prove who she is. She must *not* be considered his daughter. That he knew.

While little is known about those five years in Indian Territory for Squire, Junaluska and Madaya, Squire's relative freedom during that time only increased the desire to live free again—really free. He and Junaluska became known and accepted as a team. Both worked hard, providing direction and expertise for assimilation into the western Cherokee community that was already well-established before the influx of the newly arrived Cherokee from the east.

In some ways, Squire considered, he felt more freedom than did the others—the newly arrived Cherokee themselves—who often felt snubbed, disregarded as interlopers. And wasn't that the reason the eastern Cherokee felt so strongly about the white European invaders? Yet neither in Indian Territory in Oklahoma nor in Carolina and Georgia in their centuries-occupied homeland did these Cherokee feel invited or accepted, and only sometimes tolerated.

Oh yes, Squire worked hard as he had for Brother Freihofer back in Salem, yet he felt accepted in a different, a more humane way, while working with Junaluska. Yet, considering that he might soon be back with his lover again, Squire knew without a doubt that he would return to servitude, even willingly, to be near Precious.

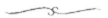

"Strange alliances often begin as a result of tragedy, without which the link of a lifetime would never have been forged," Junaluska reasoned aloud, thinking of his relationship with the enslaved African Squire as they began the long walk home from the Cherokee community that had come to depend on them. "Providential signs," Junaluska rambled on to Squire, "like stars in alignment, or everyday events.

"Yes, they can point to extraordinary links between two individuals that one cannot explain away, or live without," responded Squire, thinking more of Precious and himself than of Junaluska and him.

The growing camaraderie between the Cherokee "Chief" Junaluska and the enslaved African Squire appeared at first to benefit exclusively—or at least primarily—the child Madaya. But this solidarity became only a backdrop for the profound connection between two adult men whose lives were enriched and opened in ways they never dreamed possible in the few years left in their lifetime. To compare their previous walk on *The Trail That Made Us Cry* with the return walk on the trail that made two men friends, that made two men laugh, that made two men live again, is an impossibility. It was that meaningful, and even brought joy to their tiny sidekick Madaya who kept them anchored in reality.

Junaluska was old enough to be Squire's father, or even grandfather, but they needed each other. Both had suffered great loss; each needed the other, but neither one fully recognized it, that is, until the twelve hundred mile walk back to North Carolina. That's when they began to talk to each other, and not just about Madaya. Squire finally told Junaluska about Precious, the love of his life after having lost his wife on the journey from Northern Rhodesia to the United States.

"Let's talk!" Madaya often suggested in the evenings, pulling first one and then the other toward a stump or toward the glowing embers of a cook-fire. So, talk they did, often tiring the girl who would nod off, stretching herself between them, her head on the lap of one and her moccasins tucked under the legs of the other one. Sometimes she surprised them by asking a question, often simple, desiring clarification, and at other times insightful, penetrating, possibly rhetoric only, but certainly engaging them.

On one particular night, she opened the door to a world of revelation for the men who began to own their stories. Knowing that Junaluska had some "talking papers" with him, some of those documents written in the new Cherokee syllabary, Madaya asked Junaluska, "Tell us about Sequoyah. Who is he?" And so the night began with this story.

"Sequoyah was born about 1770 to a white father, a fur trader who deserted his family, and to his mother Wut-the, the daughter of a Cherokee chief. Sequoyah spoke only Cherokee. Observing white traders and settlers and those in the military with whom he served in the United States Army in the War of 1812, convinced him that they had an extraordinary advantage: they could read and write their own language, using their 'talking papers,' also called 'talking leaves' for commerce, reading books, keeping records, recording history, learning about the world, even writing personal letters to send long distances, the way the white people did.

"Artistic, Sequoyah also became a silversmith. But because he was illiterate at that time, he could not even sign his own work; the Cherokee had no written language; he knew no other language. He persuaded Chief Charles Hicks to sign his art for him when selling his work, but Sequoyah could not decide whether to use his Indian name or his European name, George Gist, so Hicks chose for him: *Sequoyah* it would be. For business purposes, Sequoyah often drew a picture of the person for his records; he could draw, but not write.

"After the war for a period of ten years he began to develop a system that translated the sounds—the spoken language of his people—into a uniform *alphabet* of 85 symbols called the *syllabary*. Each character represented a syllable, as well as a sound in Cherokee.

"Sequoyah devised games using the syllabary for his six-year old daughter Ayoka, amazing their friends with his 'trickery.' One day, he sent his daughter Ayoka a distance from their house, accompanied by a skeptical visitor, while inside the house someone told Sequoyah a sentence to inscribe in Cherokee on a slate, using the syllabary. When the child returned, she astonished the adults as she read aloud the magical marks—written Cherokee words.

"Some of the characters in the syllabary appear to be borrowed from the Greek, some from English, but Sequoyah created other characters. He was a genius," Junaluska told Madaya and Squire, "someone who could translate an *idea* into a practical way to preserve history as well as to communicate in a new—and lasting—way. This man, unable to read or write himself, transformed our Cherokee people into a literate nation. Some learned quickly, while some studied and labored for weeks to grasp this new way to communicate."

"When can I learn to read and write the syllabary?" Madaya asked. "Ayoka could do that when she was my age."

"Well, you already speak Cherokee and some English," Squire reminded her. "So, we are a lot alike, aren't we?" he asked her. Madaya grinned. "Yes, we both have ears," she laughed. "But I want to write letters," she insisted.

"Now Madaya, who do you know who writes letters?" asked Squire skeptically.

"Junaluska!" She was right about that. Squire admired the man who not only had gone to Washington to talk to the President but also wrote letters to help settle differences and to procure land—their homeland— for the Cherokee people.

"Write my name here, Junaluska!" Madaya thrust a piece of bark into his hand. He obliged by scratching Madaya's name in Cherokee onto the bark. After examining it carefully, she pushed it into her story-satchel.

"In time," Junaluska went on, "Sequoyah wrote compositions to be read in court, as well as letters sent overland to distant Cherokee to whom he had taught the syllabary. Illiterate observers wondered at this miracle. At last, Indians, too, could 'talk at a distance,'" explained Junaluska, who by this time had only one listener.

The men smiled at Madaya as Squire lifted her away from the fire and into her warm blanket. Curling up into a ball, she clutched her story-satchel that already jingled with its few objects. She had plenty of stories, and even a few memory-jogs to show for it. Junaluska had fashioned her a new bag from rabbit skin, tied together with sinew. Madaya rubbed the white, still-fluffy tail against her cheek, and smiled as she drifted into deep sleep.

It was Squire's turn. Somehow, Junaluska looked to him as the leader, the knowledgeable one, as his story revealed in bits and pieces lifted him high above his own rather confined life as a Cherokee, or so he considered his lot. Junaluska felt he had failed his own people. For one, had he not intervened when the Redstick warrior intended to kill General Jackson would have been simple enough, and then they would not even be here in this wilderness. On the other hand, he knew history to be far more complicated than that.

Perhaps few people, most certainly not those who boast the most about their accomplishments, recognize the value of a life lived well. Not that Squire's life itself revealed significant accomplishments, but the life he lived excelled in one attribute that Junaluska envied and found lacking in himself: forgiveness.

One night after Madaya was asleep, Squire began thinking about his homeland, about the similarities—such as the closeness to and dependence on the natural world, that world just as vital but often unseen and disregarded by those who live in it. He breathed deeply the aroma of the smoky fire and peered into the giant chestnut tree canopy above them, and dreamed of home, "Surely, that is ten thousand miles from here," he said aloud.

"What?" Junaluska asked, not having read the thoughts of his companion.

"Oh!" Squire laughed. "I was thinking of my village in Africa from where I was kidnapped. We often sat beneath our giant baobab tree in the center of our village, with the aroma of our own smoking fire where we cooked...often the same food as you cook. Not deer as you have, but eland, or monkey, or chicken. We, too, pounded corn to make meal for *ensima,* and cooked whatever we had killed for food that day. That was the place we sat to settle any *endaba* [trouble/problem], the same kinds of disagreements that you have here. Amazing, isn't it, in how many ways we are alike?

"Have I told you about my wife?" asked Squire. Aware that Junaluska still mourned the loss of two wives, plus children, he felt sudden embarrassment for having posed the question and asked, "Will my story bring you sadness, Friend?"

"No, no," Junaluska responded, knowing that was not true, but wanting to hear more from Squire.

"We both attended the mission boarding school in Mukoni, far from my village," he said. The girls wore pink dresses, and we boys wore gray shorts and shirts. We had two sets of clothes that we washed weekly. The girls and boys each had a long cinder-block building for their dormitory and a latrine outside each one, and we all ate two meals a day in the big mission house. Before daybreak we all collected firewood for cooking. Then we all marched barefoot—we didn't have moccasins as you do—to the church at the center of the compound. As we marched, we sang in English, *Ahhh-men, ahhh-men, ahhh-men, ahmen, ahmen.* I can hear us now...the deep bass voices of the boys, all of us less than eighteen years-old, along with the girls whose bare feet also scuffed along on the polished concrete floor of the church. I guess there were about a hundred of us, so it took awhile to shuffle in. We sang, read our prayers, received communion from the priest and listened to him read Scripture and preach.

"One day as we marched out in two lines, the boys in one and the girls in another beside them, a girl tripped and nearly fell. Without thinking, I reached out to steady her. This was not acceptable to the teacher who was nearest to me on the sidelines. But, the girl looked at me gratefully and whispered her name: *Monica.* Of course, we all had our African names, but the white missionaries also gave us a familiar name that they could pronounce, usually from the Bible. I was *Sampson*. That's all we whispered, one to the other: *Monica. Sampson.* Again, like you, Junaluska, I have many names. It was not until I worked for the Freihofers in Salem that I was given the name Squire.

"From that day on, I waited for chapel-time with prayers of my own. Would I find her again? Did I dream that she spoke to me? How would we find each other? The rules were strict. The dormitories were locked from the outside at night so that girls and boys could not meet. At night we did not use the latrines, but used pots inside the dorms. During meals we sat separately.

"The only time we might be fortunate enough to meet up was during the dry season when we all helped fight fires in the dry brown tinder-brush that at least once in the dry season would be struck by lightning or the hand of God. The day I found Monica again, surely that was by the hand of God. The fire alarm blasted; we all knew our tasks, having been drilled and instructed, and suddenly, there we were, side-by-side, beating the flames. I felt her nearness, with my eyes, my cheeks, my insides, my outsides, my toes—though I never touched her—and all I whispered was, *Monica!* And she whispered back, *Sampson!*"

He paused, and Junaluska laughed. "I know, yes, I recognize that feeling," he said.

"We did not speak or meet through that whole year, but each time I saw her I knew we would be together one day, forever," Squire said. Then he shook his head hard, as though to shake loose and disperse any memories he could not bear to express. Of course, Junaluska recognized that the couple was no longer together.

"We married as soon as we completed our schooling, six years for us both. That was typical for most students in mission schools, even government schools. Monica was like a goddess, an angel, or, or, she was soft, gentle, kind, with lips as sweet as the fruit of a ripe mango. How we loved each other! In two years we did not have a child, but we were thankful for that gift, because one night a raiding party kidnapped us.

"These were Africans who made their living by capturing people, preferably men, who could be sold to white traders, a lucrative business for all of them. So, the white man was not the only person involved in this transaction. We travelled for days to the coast of Mozambique where they turned us over to white men who paid off the African raiding party, then made their own blood money by selling us to other Europeans who sent some of us to Brazil, some to the Caribbean islands, some to the United States, where we were again sold in the slave markets."

His story resonated with Junaluska who shook his head sorrowfully, speechless. He had once met a white man enroute from North Carolina to New Orleans. He was taking his coffle of enslaved women, called "fancy trade" who would be sold as forcible sex partners. These women, known as "mulatresses" because of their light skin, brought as much as $1200 in a sale. If also literate and beautiful, they brought even larger sums. He learned that half a million persons who walked the Slave Trail—or were shipped on a steamboat on the Mississippi—were sold in New Orleans, the largest slave market in the young country. This went on during those years that the Cherokee walked their own "trail where they cried."

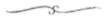

During daylight hours the three-some covered many miles, although they liked to think that Madaya slowed them down. The reason was not, however, because she was slow or had little stamina. Rather, her energy far surpassed their own. But she often detoured, for a view, to climb a tree, to play in a trickling stream. After a particularly strenuous walk one day, Madaya happily wrapped up in her bedroll, and slept within minutes. So Junaluska asked Squire to tell him the rest of that story about him and his wife.

"We did not dare think ahead, or think about being separated," Squire continued. "'Just march,' they demanded, while we clung to each other and prayed all the prayers we had ever learned. *O Monica*, was all I could say. *O Sampson*, was all she whispered in return; we were thankful to be together, but dared not communicate for fear of being separated. Finally, with others we gathered in a large round room where passengers wait for their ship to arrive. Although with neighbors and friends, we spoke little, as the men were watching us. We soon understood what was happening.

"Our group was to be taken to the New World to be sold. Not many women were kidnapped—only enough to satisfy their need for a woman when all were confined to the ship for weeks at a time. The thought of this, of course, terrified Monica. They began calling us, droning on and on, *next, next, next*. Monica gripped my arm as she walked toward the narrow door of no return where the man with the branding iron waited."

"Ohhhhh," Junaluska groaned and turned away. "I can stop now," Squire told him.

"No, you need to tell your story," said Junaluska, marveling that in the six years they had known each other, not once had they confided their deepest hurts and questions.

"A man grabbed Monica and held her arm for the person with the branding iron. I smelled her flesh as the hot iron was pressed into her arm. *Next!* I did not even care what they did to me as I walked forward, boiling with anger. As we walked to the narrow opening onto the ship through the door of no return, I saw a priest standing with holy water on a stand beside him. I heard him say to Monica, "I baptize you in the name of the Father, and of the Son, and of the Holy Ghost. Amen." I was aghast. We had already been baptized, but that was no time for ceremony. We staggered, clinging to each other momentarily, thankful again not to have been separated."

"Strange, isn't it, Friend, how we keep on giving thanks whatever our condition? That must be something of the holy in us, our Creator. I pity those who have no one to thank!" Junaluska struggled to express himself. Madaya stirred, so the men sat in silence for a few minutes.

"After many weeks at sea, on our way to the new world, many friends and neighbors died from terrible illnesses,' Squire continued. "Men were separated from the few women prisoners, and we had no freedom to walk about. But one day I saw Monica, because once sick, they threw us all together, hoping to get rid of as many as possible, as quickly as possible. She had dysentery. Ignoring my own symptoms, I dropped down beside her and tried everything I could think of to help her when the guards weren't looking. I held her one night, even rocked her, and gave her sips of gruel they served once a day. I did not care whether I got worse; I only wanted to comfort her. I thought we would die together.

"When some men came by, looking for dead bodies as they always did, I tried to act disinterested, like I didn't know her or care what they were doing. When they saw Monica with her eyes closed, they grabbed her roughly, thinking she was dead, I suppose. Her eyes opened wide in a panic. Without thinking, I jumped up from my spot and shoved one of the men to one side. Throwing myself over Monica I tried to shield her, but they kicked me aside and dragged her starboard. Stumbling after them, I watched as they picked her up, one holding her feet and another her head. Before I could stop them they heaved her over the edge, into the sea, alive. I ran forward to jump after her, but they shoved me back to my corner and walked on. Grief deeper than the sea threatened to drown me, too, until even in my sobbing, I was thankful. There it is again, Junaluska, I was *thankful.* Monica's suffering was over."

With that, the two friends fell into their bedrolls, exhausted beyond hope of recovery. But when dawn crept softly around them, they awoke with Madaya's laughter as she tickled them under the nose with a feather she had found. In no time, present reality was far better than memory.

Chapter Five: Heroes

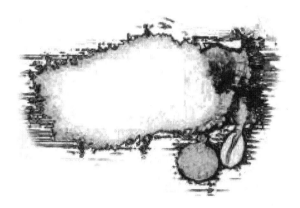

We all have a destiny. Chief Junaluska fulfilled his destiny.

~ Diamond Brown, Jr., Eastern Band of Cherokee

A hard rain kept the travelers in a small cave for shelter for two days, filling Madaya with unadulterated joy. As a child, rather than projecting on their future, she simply cherished these days with her strange *family*. Not realizing how much conversation she had missed the night before, she was happy to settle in for more stories.

She persuaded Junaluska to tell them about Tecumseh. And so he began. "With others, I met with Tecumseh, this Shawnee traditionalist chief whose wife was Cherokee. He represented the northern tribe, along with his brother, a shaman who fueled the fires of angst. Tecumseh despised the white man's incursion into Indian land. He considered them—except for the British—a 'race made of lake scum.'

"Tecumseh urged the Indians to form a Confederacy of Indian Tribes. 'Pulverize those whites!' was his battle cry. Others insisted that recent natural disasters were omens from the *Galonlati* [Great Spirit], urging all Indians to move west of the Mississippi to Indian territories, or at best, to areas allotted to Cherokee who accepted citizenship in the states in which they already lived. Sad days, complex issues with which we all struggled," said Junaluska.

"Forty-six Cherokees including John Ridge were commissioned to attend Tecumseh's gathering, where about five thousand Indians from many tribes appeared, as well as government officials, traders and even spies. Scare tactics, including reported supernatural visions kept the people in an uproar. Meanwhile, we waited, and waited for the great Tecumseh to appear.

"When at last he rode into the encampment in a flurry and dismounted, a collective gasp shot to the heavens from the people who had not realized the colorfully impressive northern chief was lame. But lame or not, through that night Tecumseh hobbled and danced, naked except for breechclout and moccasins, throwing himself about to the beat of the drums. Not enough drama to convince the gathered tribesmen and white visitors, the crowds waited for the great chief to speak. And again we waited. And waited. And waited into a second week. Finally, Tecumseh stood to speak. Interpreters translated his message into many languages and dialects represented.

"'I have foreseen the extinction of the Indian in the East,' he announced. That was enough to cause head-shaking and head-scratching, as well as conversion of many who previously had not trusted him and his prophecies. Then surprising them all, he continued: 'But the time has not come.' Some gasped at this change in his rhetoric, but because it is not customary for the Cherokee to interrupt, they did not respond, nor did other represented tribes. We would hear him out, although anger burned within many who were more than ready to *pulverize the whites*. Although bursting with questions, we reined in their objections and sat or stood, waiting for more.

"'We are outnumbered by those whites made of sand, while we are made of red clay,' Tecumseh explained his tactics. 'We must first form a Confederation. Let the white people alone for now, but when we are a great confederation, then will we confront them.'

"Sometimes passionately and even eloquently, Tecumseh seemed to breathe dragon's fire from his nostrils as he spewed out hatred: 'Brush from your eyelids the sleep of slavery, and strike for vengeance and your country! Red men have fallen as the leaves now fall; their tears drop from the weeping skies; their bones bleach on the hills. Let the white race perish!' he cried. Yet, here he was, insisting on waiting for the right time.

"Ridge surprised us when he stood to make his own announcement: 'If you do visit the Cherokees, I will kill you,' he warned Tecumseh. Big Warrior, head of the Creeks, asked many questions, and finally shouted, 'The *Galonlati* did not send you to us!' Among all the tribes, confusion raged.

"I finally rose to tell Tecumseh this," said Junaluska: "It has been many years since the Cherokee have drawn the tomahawk. Our Braves have forgotten how to use the scalping knife. We have learned with sorrow, it is better not to war against our white brothers. They have come to stay. We believe we can live in peace with them. Junaluska will not raise his arm against them."

Sometimes when watching Junaluska and listening to his stories Squire felt awe rising within him. *No wonder his people respect him,* he mused.

"Not to be outdone," Junaluska continued, "Tecumseh prophesied two natural disasters. As a result, on a given day, thousands of Indians met on the crest of a hill that had been predicted to be spared during a devastating hailstorm. Waiting anxiously through the day, we Cherokee people watched the skies and the valley below. The skies remained clear."

Junaluska sighed with the weight of the memory. "But later, even Ridge was unnerved when Tecumseh's second prophecy did materialize," he said. "'When I leave here,' Tecumseh had told the gathered tribes, 'I will stomp the ground, causing a great earthquake.'

"Weeks passed after he mounted his steed and stormed off. But sure enough, one day a powerful quake shook the earth. Rivers changed courses. Mountains tumbled. Green foam filled great pits in the fractured earth.

"Unnerved, Ridge questioned some Moravians whom he met at the Trading Post: 'What do you know about the disaster and the aftershocks that followed? Is God angry with us? Would the *Galonlati* destroy all of us because of what the white man is doing?' he asked them.

"'Or, were the tremors warnings to the whites to stop their land-hungry encroachment on native lands? Did Tecumseh's brother, the shaman, cause the quakes? What is the meaning of all this?'

He desperately sought answers, but none satisfied him.

"The Creek Red Sticks, so named because of their vermilion war clubs and 'magic' red sticks used by their shamans, attended a meeting with Cherokee leaders to discuss the strange occurrences that troubled all of them. Ridge issued a statement of support for the United States that inflamed the Creek Red Sticks who were already engaged in a civil war in addition to their goal to *pulverize the whites*. Tecumseh and the Shawnee, as well as many Creeks, determined to win dominion over the encroaching enemy."

"You are our hero!" interrupted Madaya. "And here is Tecumseh!" she giggled as she danced in a frenzy around the fire. *So, she did listen*, the men nodded in agreement with the same thought.

During those days and nights in the cave, in the cavernous belly of the earth, the three heard not only one another, but whispers of ages past in the womb of Earth. They gazed at the dark ceilings, watching inky-black bats hanging there, seeing primarily with their ears, hearing their own high-pitched calls bounce back from objects to detect location of enemies, of food, of danger. Then flying with their finger-boned webbed wings, they explored that inner sanctum of Earth that had become the mutual habitat of human and bat.

When the rain finally stopped, the whole world sparkled as they set out again with a promise to Madaya to tell more stories that evening. A pileated woodpecker had awakened them, knocking just outside the cave's opening. "Let's catch her!" And with that, Madaya sneaked slowly toward the unsuspecting bird who realized quickly enough that this intruder meant business.

"Well, it was not only Sequoyah who gave an immeasurable gift to our people," Junaluska continued the next night when Squire begged off, doubtful he could ever continue his stories.

Madaya had been playing, stacking stones around their encampment. The men did not know the extent to which the ten year-old had listened to most of their conversation that evening. "I know some heroes," she said.

"Tell us about them," said Squire.

"Well, Sequoyah was one, and Tsali, and you are both heroes." The men laughed.

"Do not laugh at me," she said. "I know more than you think I do." Of that, they had no doubt.

"Not all heroes are old. We both know a young hero," Junaluska told her, nodding slyly to Squire.

"Who is it?" she asked. "Do I know his story?"

"Oh yes!" responded the men, leading her on.

"Tell me! Tell me about him!" she demanded.

But the men laughed again. 'You will think of the little hero we know, Junaluska told her.

Several moments passed as Madaya continued to stack stones for her fort. Looking up at them she said quietly, "Oh. I mean *real* heroes."

Madaya thought for a few more moments and then said to Junaluska, "Tell us about your big battle on the horseshoe."

On the horseshoe. Junaluska was afraid she knew what she was talking about, even if she did not have the words to describe what she had overheard through the years. Not that he had talked about it, but all Cherokee knew about his bravery in the Battle at Horseshoe Bend. In fact, he and Will had talked about it openly when he met them on the Trail, but that was a long time ago. And she had been a little girl then. What could she know?"

"Well?" she said, after waiting several minutes, still stacking stones. "We are waiting for your story, Hero!" They could not help smiling at her insistence and determination and her very presence that brought joy to them each day of their journey. Surely they would be much too serious for their own good if she were not with them.

"Alright," Junaluska agreed.

"But you can make it short, because I am hungry," she told him, settling in a bit closer.

"A slave-owner himself, General Jackson knew the Creeks had more black slaves than the Cherokee did. Overcoming them in war would increase the numbers of Creek women and children who could be captured and used as Jackson's own slaves, in addition to any Africans they owned. It was then that I determined to defeat the Red Stick faction of the Creek Indians who were aligned with France and planned to go to war against white settlers. I did not want war against the whites. This festering wound was lanced at the decisive Battle of Horseshoe Bend."

"Uh, Creeks had *more* black slaves than the Cherokee did? I didn't know." Squire was puzzled, a bit embarrassed to ask the question. He knew that Africans owned slaves, but not the Cherokee.

"Yes, Squire. The Cherokee owned slaves, too. Have you heard the legend about Good Wolf, Bad Wolf?"

"Yes, I have heard it," Squire answered quietly.

"Well, I want to make clear what I learned from that legend. We all choose which wolf to feed, but of this be certain: The divided heart, rather than belonging to any single tribe or gender or skin color or culture beats in every human breast. Yes, my friend," Junaluska admitted with shame and embarrassment, wishing it were not true, "we Cherokee have slaves, too.

"In addition to the upheaval among the Indians," Junaluska continued, "our young country that was infiltrating the land and culture of the ancient Cherokee Nation was itself in turmoil. By the time General Jackson had been elected as the seventh president of the United States, he sent a message to Congress in which he endorsed the 'voluntary removal' of Indians from eastern United States, 'for it would be unjust,' he said, 'to compel them to abandon the graves of their fathers and seek a home in a distant land,' Junaluska quoted Jackson.

"Sounds good, except that, uh." Squire floundered as he immediately questioned the disparity in the use of these two words: *voluntary removal*. "That is like saying, well, like saying, *forced willingly*." While acknowledging that English was not their mother-tongue, both men saw the discrepancy, and winced.

"Yes, I too had difficulty with those two words used together: *voluntary removal*," Junaluska agreed. "Yet, I also believed this was the only way to preserve my people. And surely, certainly, undoubtedly President Jackson would honor his word to protect us, including the Eastern Cherokee who insisted on remaining in their homes in North Carolina and Georgia if we became citizens of the new country.

"However, neither did the President mention in his reports to Congress during this time that soldiers—more than seven thousand—were ordered to forcibly remove the Cherokee if necessary, nor did Jackson report that more than fifteen thousand Cherokee had signed multiple requests and petitions to continue living on their native land, rather than be moved.

"Some of our Congressmen, men like Henry Clay and Daniel Webster responded to the plan for our re-location with untiring energy, with anger, with eloquence. They worked to prevent the Removal. Congressman Davy Crockett described it as 'unjust, dishonest, cruel, and short sighted.' But their dissent changed nothing."

As wars do, the War of 1812 started earlier, lasted longer, killed more and became increasingly more complex than originally expected. The Northern Red Sticks had allied with the French while the Lower Red Sticks joined the United States to declare war on the British. Following a surprise attack in the Alabama River Valley, the local militia routed the Red Sticks and looted their camp.

"In retaliation," Junaluska went on, "one thousand Red Sticks re-grouped and attacked a small stockade at Fort Mims, brutally killing about fifty of the four hundred whites in the fort, mostly women and children. Then they watched as the fort burned to the ground. Once again, *balance* had to be restored.

"Correctly expecting revenge would again follow that massacre, the Red Sticks waited. They built fortifications to protect about three hundred women and children in the log fort. Thousands of warriors kept watch with cannons ready. Behind them a dozen canoes waited in the event that a quick escape by water was needed.

"That's when I strategized, determined to outdo, outwit, outkill this enemy for all time. With an army of two thousand men, including five hundred Cherokee, we were poised on the land where the Talapoosa River makes a hairpin turn around a hundred-acre peninsula with an island on the lower side." In his mind, Junaluska was there again, thinking, strategizing.

"This was the plan: I stationed men to surround the bend of that horseshoe to prevent any Red Sticks from escaping by that route in their canoes, if the need presented itself. The battle had already raged through the morning with little to show for it, other than the usual carnage.

"Before I could implement the plan, however, I found myself near the general, but thought, *I cannot risk denying the brilliance of my plan by consulting with the general. We can do this. It will work!*

"Looking to one side, I noticed a Red Stick creeping close to General Jackson, arrogantly astride his horse, unaware of what was about to happen to him. Watching closely, I knew it had to be then or never. I thrust out one leg in front of the Red Stick warrior, and I couldn't help smiling as the soldier tripped and fell.

"Sprawled on the ground, he looked up at me, with my spear raised above him." Junaluska laughed. The life of the general—and future president of the young country—had been spared. "Did you, uh, did you . . . Squire could not voice his question, so he got no answer.

Returning to the immediate task, Junaluska swam to the canoes behind the fort and, pulling and pushing, maneuvered them stealthily to the opposite bank where other Cherokee warriors leapt into the canoes, to row back to the opposite bank, all this during General Jackson's frontal assault where person-to-person fighting ensued. Fireballs shot upward from both homes and fort.

"All possibilities of escape dissolved in the aftermath," Junaluska continued. "Of the thirteen hundred Creeks inside the stockade, not more than twenty escaped, mostly women and children. Men like Davy Crockett and Sam Houston were among the recruited frontiersmen that day. The Battle at Horseshoe Bend was a decisive victory in our favor," Junaluska told Squire. Like any good warrior, he felt his breast expand with pride of intended accomplishment, including the unexpected bonus thrown into the mix, like saving General Jackson's life.

"But five months after the victory at Horseshoe Bend," Junaluska withered with this memory of an announcement that stunned him: 'The Creek Confederacy and the United States signed the Treaty of Fort Jackson in which the Creeks ceded 23 million acres in Alabama and Georgia to the young country, opening territory to whites, while pushing Indians farther into the west.'

"It's ironic that now I, with my Cherokee brothers and sisters, have experienced the consequences of President Jackson's order. Announced through his spokesman General Winfield Scott, Jackson's orders resulted in moving sixteen thousand of us westward to 'Indian Territory.' That scandalous betrayal by any other name would still be fraudulent," Junaluska ended the tale, folded up his ego, pulled his knees to his chest, wrapped his arms around them and bowed his head, sighing deeply. He had failed his people.

By this time, Madaya may have been hungry, but she also slept, clutching her rabbit-skin satchel that Junaluska had made for her. But Squire and Junaluska continued talking into the night, each aware that their human condition was one shared by all peoples. At times, they wept to recall the atrocities they had seen, and wept even harder for any they had caused.

When the time came to cross into the Smoky Mountains, all three had to curb their enthusiasm as they neared home. Not sure about all the changes in Cherokee since he had left six years earlier, Junaluska both feared and anticipated the rendezvous. He contemplated what he could do next for his people, wherever they had scattered, whatever had befallen them during that time. Of course, he wondered, too, about Madaya, as he still could not ascertain what her choice would be: to Salem with Squire, or to Cherokee with Junaluska. What would be best for her? Should they let the child decide?

Meanwhile, Squire let his imagination run wildly into his perceived life back in Salem. Whether or not Madaya chose to stay with him, he would be with his lover again. That she waited for his return, he had no doubt. Perhaps Brother Freihofer no longer needed his help, and he might even. And that's where his dreaming got stuck.

What he could not know was that Precious was *not* waiting for him.

Chapter Six: Pathos

*O for the touch of a vanished hand and the
sound of a voice that is still . . .*

~ Alfred Lord Tennyson

As they neared Salem, Squire shook with excitement, his heart palpitating. He wiped sweaty hands on dirty pants and prepared to meet the Freihofers again. Madaya hung back shyly, wondering what sort of people these Moravians were. Squire spoke highly of them to allay her fears, as well as his own. *Will they welcome us?* he wondered. He was only sure about Precious.

Observing Brother Freihofer embrace Squire after his six-year absence comforted Junaluska. He was thankful that Squire had not absconded. Both opportunity and temptation had plagued his old friend. In Squire's absence, Brother Freihofer had hired many helpers, but not one could compare with Squire's attention to detail and expert workmanship. He had the makings of an engineer, a master carpenter, a knowledgeable gardener.

When Brother Freihofer's wife died several years earlier during Squire's absence, he had acquired a new wife, now the stepmother of nine year-old Katarina who remembered Squire. Katarina danced around him, already begging for stories about Squire's travels. Madaya watched her, thinking that perhaps she could have a friend in Salem. The girls smiled at each other, but before they could speak, Sister Freihofer took her daughter's hand and said crisply, "There is a *time* and a *place* for everything," as she pulled Katarina away from Squire.

Still uncertain about Madaya's choice about where to live, Squire picked up a black walnut, telling her they would get to know these people in Salem. "Now, they are inside their shell, just like the walnut inside its hard shell when it falls from the tree," he explained, "but soon we will be able to see inside. You can make friends here, the way you always do, if you choose to stay with me." Madaya took the shell from his hand and dropped it into her satchel without responding.

I need to go with Junaluska. I need to stay here with Squire. I do not know what I want *to do.* Having experienced more trauma in her life than most adults in a long lifetime, Madaya wrestled with confusion. "What shall I do?" she begged for help from her mentors, tears dripping onto her tunic. The men watched, neither remembering having seen the girl shed anguished tears. Not wanting to impose a forced choice, especially when they could not decide themselves what was best for her, they waited. The two men had often discussed as honestly as possible the implications of either choice for all of them.

"I want both of you." She buried her head in Junaluska's soft deerskin pants while Squire looked on helplessly. *Will I know how to take care of this child if she does stay?* he asked himself. *Precious can help me.*

Sensing that Madaya was leaning toward remaining in Salem, Junaluska assured the Freihofers that Madaya is Cherokee, certainly not Squire's daughter. "Squire showed great kindnesses to Madaya's family on the trail that made us cry," he explained quietly. Brother Freihofer nodded that he understood and then surprised them by saying, "I will pay you a stipend, Squire, that you can apply to tuition at the Salem School for Girls. She can study arithmetic and geography, English and German. The child seems bright and clever enough; we Moravians believe that both women and slaves should be educated."

Sister Freihofer listened. *Humph*, she thought. *She can help me with washing, ironing, mending, cleaning, gardening...although obviously she has a lot to learn, this little Cherokee child,* the matron concluded her silent soliloquy.

Suddenly, Madaya turned back to Squire, took his hand, and without another word, she walked from Junaluska. Relieved, the men nodded to each other and Junaluska strode briskly down the path toward Cherokee. He must not allow her to see him vacillating even as he wished she had chosen to go with him. Having lost both his wife and child during their absence, he was unsure about living life without Madaya. Then, he thought about Squire; they needed each other, too.

Turning his head to look back at her, he wished he had not. Junaluska cringed, watching her stare at him for too long. All three hesitated, a still-life of decision. Madaya recalled Junaluska's loss of both wife and daughter on the Trail, and his risking his own life to bury her edoda and the twin brother who was stillborn in the stockade. And later, he and Squire carried the dead bodies of her aduli and her other twin brother into the forest to bury them in the frozen turf.

"Wait!" Madaya cried, breaking the stand-off and running toward Junaluska. "I want to go with you! But please, please take Squire with us. You can take both of us, please!" Always the dreamer, and still too young to realize the implications of either choice, she gripped Junaluska's hands. The men looked at each other, then at the girl. Sometimes love demands more than what seems endurable. Junaluska shook his head and squatted down to speak to Madaya in Cherokee:

"You *are* Cherokee. You *will* return to us when it is the right time. But, Squire has no choice. He must return to his owner. Squire needs you for now, Madaya," suddenly sure that this was right choice. "He has no family but you. You have him. You have me *and* your Cherokee heritage *and* Squire. Stay here for a little while. Next time I come this way, I promise to see you and then we'll talk about this again. You can come to us anytime; remember, you belong to us."

Of course, no one could foresee what would change her relationship with Squire.

Precious had waited patiently, believing her lover would return to Salem to work for the Freihofers and to marry her as soon as the doctor could arrange it. Not long after Squire had left the village to assist the Cherokee with the great Removal, she had wakened one morning long after her monthly menses was due.

Surely not, she thought, although she relished the thought of giving birth to her lover's seed. Squire would be thrilled. That she knew. But it had only been that one night, his last night before leaving her that they had fully expressed their secret love in her little log house.

"I shall approach the doctor," she decided, well into her second month. The kindly old Moravian was fair and beloved by all in the village. So it was, that he did not berate her as he listened to her story. But one caveat she insisted on, was that no one should know that Squire was the father, knowing it could complicate their relationship even more. People could say what they would about her pregnancy as a single woman, but in the end, it had to be this way. Squire did not know, and she did not want Brother Freihofer to learn of their tryst, not yet. The doctor agreed, and treated her as a daughter and friend of the family, taking care of her through pregnancy and delivery. Adding one more child to his household was easy enough; he was renowned for his kindness and generosity.

When a healthy son was born, Precious wept with joy. If only she could let Squire know. Having heard Squire's tales of growing up in Africa, of his wife Monica, of his pleasure in her company, she longed for the day she could introduce the two: father and son. No choice, she thought, but to name their son *Salem,* meaning *Peace.*

But the years rolled on, and though she intended to tell the boy sooner, it was not until Precious was diagnosed first with measles during an epidemic in Salem, and then the pneumonia that would finally take her life, that she determined to tell her son about his beloved father. Only six years old then, he understood that he was loved, and that his father would love him, too, although Squire was unaware of his offspring.

Following her unexpected death, the doctor looked after the boy as one of his own. True to his word, the doctor had not revealed the paternity of the child to anyone. Some wondered if perhaps the child was his. But he knew better. And Precious knew better. The doctor believed that Squire's return would settle everything.

The doctor knew she had told the small boy about Squire, about his father. So on Salem's next birthday, he talked to Salem, man-to-man. The child listened carefully, and expressed clearly that he wanted to be the one to tell his father when he returned.

Following church on that first Sunday after Squire's return, Squire stood with Madaya, and then introduced himself to a young black boy standing nearby. "My name is Squire," he said. Nodding toward Madaya he continued, "Madaya and I arrived back in Salem a few days ago. We'll be living here."

Ignoring Madaya, Salem questioned, "Uh, you are Squire?" Squire nodded, asking the boy for his name. Backing away, mute as the butterfly that flitted about his head, he berated himself for the lost opportunity. What Salem wanted more than a conversation was to climb up on his father's back and hang on for life.

But the time had come. Salem had waited for the right time to tell his father the wonderful news: Squire had a son; Salem had a father. He would tell him this moment!

"Uh, Brother Squire," Salem began, inhaling deeply. But again he lapsed into silence. He assumed the little girl who walked with Squire to be his daughter. Careening like bats in his brain, the boy's thoughts crashed into each other without making sense: *She's his daughter. Squire does not know who I am. Will he like me? I wish my mother were here to help me. Maybe the doctor better tell him. What shall I say first?* His thoughts crashed on and on while Squire patiently waited.

Finally, Squire bent toward the boy and questioned, "Yes, son?" not realizing what that word meant to the boy who still stood speechless before him. "What were you going to say?" he tried again to elicit a response, but Salem turned away and ran to the doctor's family standing just inside the church door. Peering around the doorway, he watched Madaya and Squire walk away.

"Shy little fellow," remarked Squire to Madaya. Squire had recognized the doctor's family and wanted to pursue them, wondering why Precious had not attended with them. She had always accompanied the family to the service at Home Church. Ordinarily he would attend St. Philips, but he had hoped to catch sight of Precious. He had not mustered courage to approach the doctor about her. *He may not even remember me. Surely she has not moved away.* Squire squelched the panic churning inside, telling himself that he would find her no matter where she had gone.

Meanwhile, Salem considered his dilemma. The doctor and he would tell Squire together. That seemed reasonable. So, that was the plan. At the right time they would tell him together. Yet, that "right time" continued to elude his best intentions.

A few days later, desperately longing to break away after his work, Squire decided to walk around the village to re-acquaint himself with the property and the people. But first he planned to visit the doctor's house. Just maybe, maybe Precious would be working in the house or pharmacy on this day. His breath quickened as he ran up the road. Brother Freihofer noticed. *How energetic he is!* thought Brother Freihofer.

On that evening, two steps at a time, Squire brazenly knocked at the doctor's house, hoping to see Precious open the door, as well as her heart to him again. A woman—not Precious—asked him if he needed the doctor.

"Uh, no. I mean, yes!" Squire stammered. She invited him inside.

"Please wait here," she said. He might have asked her. She would know. And he wouldn't need to bother the doctor. Feeling embarrassment, he decided to walk out the door, but at that moment the doctor appeared. Stunned to silence, the doctor wondered if he had seen a ghost. *He looks like Squire!* Salem had not told him of his own encounter, once again waiting for the right time to discuss his plan for them to tell Squire together about his paternity.

"I am Squire, Sir," he began to introduce himself, uncertain whether he was recognized. Staring at Salem the doctor inventoried the young man standing before him. He hadn't changed much. *Why, it must be six, seven, years?* His thoughts chased each other around the most important issue of the moment. *Does Squire know anything about the death of Precious? About his son Salem? About . . .*

The doctor, unlike Brother Freihofer, seemed to wilt and wither in Squire's presence. He reached for the back of a chair to steady himself. "Oh! Yes! Please, sit," he told Squire who was ready to blurt out the most important question of his life. "I didn't know you were coming, " the doctor stammered.

"I have lived every day since I left six years ago, thinking of this moment, Sir," said Squire, smiling broadly. "Can you tell me when I might see . . ." The doctor recognized then that Squire did not know, did not know about the extraordinary, life-altering events for Precious, for Squire, for their son Salem. He wondered if he was up to the task that had befallen him, through no fault of his own, of course.

"Please, please Dorcas!" he called loudly, raising his hand to stop Squire from speaking, interrupting him in desperation. He needed time to compose himself. After all, it would not be the first time that the doctor had to relay bad news to a patient or a family, but this was different. The woman who had opened the door returned. "Bring us tea," he said abruptly. "Please," he then mumbled quietly, attempting to soften his unusually brusque manner.

Anything, he welcomed anything to prolong the time before he must break the news to this fine man, Squire. Just then, two children raced through the room, but the doctor called to one of them, "Salem! Step here, please!" Salem gawked wide-eyed at the man seated before him with the doctor. *Yes, we certainly* will *tell him together,* he thought in a panic. *Finally, we will tell Squire now,* he thought in desperation. *Shall I begin? No, please, you start,* the tongue-tied boy nodded to the doctor.

Dorcas arrived to set a tray on the side table and poured tea, just two cups, with a promise to Salem that he could have some later. *The doctor looks strange, somehow peculiar, unlike his usual jovial self,* Dorcas thought as she left the room with the three seated there.

Salem stared at his father, struck dumb yet again in his presence. Gathering strength, the doctor spoke next. "Salem, you know what we've talked about? About Squire and about, about, uh," the doctor faltered again. "Yes, Sir," the boy said, watching Squire.

"Well Squire, I am happy to see you again," the doctor began in the easiest way to open the door to the big announcement. "This is Salem," he continued. "We have something important to tell you, although we were not prepared to see you today," said the doctor, by now sweating profusely. He took one sip of tea with several sugars, then handed the cup to Salem who promptly drained the cup before setting it aside.

Squire, meanwhile, thought he had heard the doctor say *we* have something to tell you. Strange to involve the boy. He waited respectfully, expectantly, and then the doctor broke the silence as Salem watched his father. "While you were away, Precious became very close to our family, even though she had already worked for us for a long while." Squire smiled broadly, already knowing this had to be true.

"I am so sorry to tell you, Sir, that a measles epidemic hit our community a few years ago, and your dear friend, uh, she got pneumonia. Precious did not survive, Squire, I am so sorry to tell you," he repeated.

There. That was enough for now. Salem opened his mouth to speak, looking at the doctor expectantly, but the doctor shook his head vigorously at Salem. "Take this tray to the kitchen," he demanded, finally in charge again. "We men need to talk." the doctor nodded to Squire who slumped in his chair. Squire groaned. He could not have imagined worse news. The doctor gathered his wits and stood to embrace Squire who stumbled to his feet, then collapsed in his arms, gasping great gulps of air.

"How can this be?" he breathed the unanswerable question. The men sat again, and the doctor thought belatedly what might have relieved the impact. Just knowing he and Precious had a fine son who had been sitting with Squire moments earlier would have been the better way to break the news. He could have told that part, the good part of the story, first. But it was too late. Although he had rehearsed the moment often enough he simply did not know how to introduce the boy and his father who desperately needed that information.

Salem hovered in the hallway, near the door, balancing the tray, trying to hear the men talk, hoping to hear the rest of the story, the good part, the part that would cause Squire to rush to him with open arms, to welcome him as his son. Instead, he heard the front door shut firmly. Placing the tray on a hall table, he ran to the south window and watched them walk down Church Street, the doctor's arm around the shoulders of his father.

Salem leaned against the sill, helpless and alone, wondering what to do next. Why hadn't the doctor told Squire the whole story? The good part, the love part? The doctor who felt he had aged ten years in ten minutes had some explaining to do when he returned home to face Salem again.

Squire questioned why he had survived all those years just to arrive at this dead end, while his son continued to struggle with how to tell his father the rest of the story, as he'd promised both his mother and the doctor that he would do. He had practiced what he would say, and how it would change both his life and Squire's whom he worshiped from afar. Salem would warn the doctor that he, and he alone would approach Squire the next time with the good part of the news, at the right time. At last he was ready.

In the days to follow, Squire threw himself into his work with abandon, and leaned heavily on the doctor who shouldered responsibility for his failure to break the tragic news in a more helpful way. Having agreed that Salem would tell his father the good news as soon as possible, the doctor attempted to comfort Squire, and answered questions about her last days. But days rolled into weeks, while Squire still waited, while Salem and the doctor strategized. They would plan a celebration, a party! On and on they planned, while Squire waited, he knew not for what in his anguished state. He struggled to be present for Madaya who had her own adjustments to make.

"You must tell him today," the doctor insisted one morning to Salem. He knew he could no longer sit on the news that would help poor Squire, of that he was sure. If Salem did not tell him, then he would do so before the day ended. They had been immobilized too long. This was wrong. "Yes, you must do it immediately," the doctor persisted. "If you cannot bring yourself to do it, then I will tell him myself."

"But I want to tell him," Salem imagined repeatedly the aftermath of the good news, and he wanted to do it. He practiced telling Squire the good part, the good news. When each opportunity presented itself, the unsuspecting Squire was amused with the child's reticence in his presence. He could hardly have guessed the reason. But time passed, leaving the three in misery.

Chapter Seven: Collapsed

We need the storm; the whirlwind and the earthquake . . . the hypocrisy of the nation must be exposed; and its crimes against God and man must be denounced.

~ Frederick Douglass (4 July 1863)

Meanwhile, Madaya worked for Sister Freihofer who one day called to her. "Emeline!" she called loudly. Realizing she was the only other person in the house, Madaya ran to see what she wanted. *I didn't know I was about to be named* she later muttered to herself.

"Emeline!" Sister Freihofer announced matter-of-factly, "how would you like to be called *Emeline*?" Madaya looked around the room for Emeline. Nobody else there.

"Yes, Sister Freihofer." What else could she say? Sister Freihofer could do what she wanted to do. Madaya tried, really tried to lay aside petty grievances, but this re-naming of herself pricked her sensitivity like a thorn in her bedroll. Sister Freihofer always chased around words like *Madie* and *Marble* and even *Martin*. *Why, that's a boy's name! She never could pronounce my name properly,* she thought. *So, she may as well call me Emeline.*

"Also," Sister Freihofer continued, "You must not call Squire, uh, uh, by his name. That just doesn't sound right; nor does it look right, uh, to people. An African, and you, living together, for no reason. You say he is not your father. Well, uh, it's better for you to call Squire *Papa*." She looked mighty pleased with her naming spree.

Sister Freihofer might have called him Brother Squire. That was the decent thing to do. But she was young, this new Sister Freihofer, this stepmother of Madaya's new friend Katarina. But Madaya had always called Squire by his name, so thought it strange indeed to call him Papa.

But their re-naming was only the beginning of her troubles. Brother Freihofer's daughter Katarina and Madaya, now eleven-years old, confided in each other their grief about their dead mothers, as well as their antagonism against Katarina's stepmother.

One afternoon, Madaya and Katarina tried to persuade Squire—now called *Papa* by Madaya—to be baptized along with them by the Moravians. But Squire's memories of his branding and baptism by a priest before boarding the ship bound for the new world colored his leanings toward Christianity. Besides, he had earlier been baptized with all the children in boarding school in Africa, again by a Catholic priest, and more recently by the Baptists who invited him into their congregation in Salem. What good was another baptism?

Although he told the girls he would not be baptized, he attended services either at St. Philips or at Home Church—where Madaya could be sure to see her friend Katarina. Following services there, Sister Friehofter chatted with friends, seldom realizing the girls had wandered off, though hardly unintentionally. As often as possible, they studied, played and worshiped together, one a white German Moravian with long blonde curls, and one a nutmeg-brown Cherokee with straight black hair in a long braid down her back. Squire had become adept at braiding her hair each morning. But Katarina had also begged her stepmother to let her attend St. Philips on occasion where Squire and Madaya usually attended. Reluctantly she agreed, as long as they attended with her.

The girls often begged Squire for stories, frowned on by Sister Freihofer, of course. Studying geography one day at school, Madaya asked her teacher to allow Squire to tell his story about the slave ship, and those he left behind in Africa, about which she had heard snatches of conversation between Junaluska and Squire who did not realize she was listening. Spending time with the girls anchored Squire to reality in his insane grief about his loss of Precious, so he welcomed the invitation to talk to the students.

On the appointed day, the schoolgirls gathered to listen, enthralled. Squire looked around at the girls in their simple, long muslin dresses, their bonnets tied snugly beneath their chins. The ribbon tie was a deep burgundy color that indicated their status as young children, while Sister Freihofer's bonnet had blue ribbon-ties, indicating her marital status. Madaya had adopted their style of dress at the urging of Sister Freihofer who sewed the frocks herself for the two girls.

Squire had only twice talked to adults about his private life—to Junaluska and Precious—about his African home and his journey on the slave ship to Charleston, and whenever possible to these schoolgirls who could not get enough of his stories. No others had ever inquired about his wife, thrown overboard with many others while still alive, suffering from rampant diseases on the ship. Other than Precious and Junaluska, no one had ever listened to him talk about the holding room in Maputo in Mozambique, where the kidnapped Africans whose ankles were chained together, waited to be called, to be branded like cattle, to be baptized by the priest who stood at the one-way opening into the ship, that door of no return.

So on that day, Squire stood before the children, telling them about his village in Africa, and about boarding school where he had learned English. As he continued talking, his voice became so quiet that the girls leaned forward, straining to hear him tell about his kidnapping and his experience enroute to the new world. "As we walked through that narrow opening onto the ship, we were first branded, you know," he explained, "like you would brand your cattle. See?" he said, pushing up his shirtsleeve to reveal the mark burned into his upper arm that would forever identify him as a slave. "Next," said Squire, hesitating to speak the unthinkable, "next, a priest baptized us, 'in the name of the Father, and of the Son, and of the Holy Spirit, Amen.'

"Brand, then baptize, repeated until about a hundred of us walked onto the waiting ship at a port on the Indian Ocean. I was fortunate not to have been separated from my wife; not many women were kidnapped, they mostly wanted strong, healthy, young men. A few cried out, but most of us refused to satisfy their hunger for watching us suffer. Brand and baptize, one after another, so for the rest of our lives we could be identified first as slaves—branded, and second as Christians—baptized. Of course, we had not chosen to be either slave or Christian."

Wide-eyed, the stunned students stared before gathering courage to ask questions, encouraged by the teacher, Sister Schmidt. Formerly latent emotion flowed through Squire, as real as the blood in his veins, threatening to drown him. Squire gulped great breaths of air when he finished with head bowed. Finally, he had told his story to receptive listeners, as Junaluska and Precious also had been.

Meanwhile, having heard about this extracurricular activity, Sister Freihofer raced toward the school, her skirts flying. Following Squire's emotionally charged story, he walked from the school with one hand on Madaya's shoulder, and the other resting on Katarina. Meeting them on the path as they left the classroom, and totally misinterpreting what she saw, Sister Freihofer swooned and collapsed. Squire and the girls stooped to call her back to awareness.

Later that day, Madaya cried for mercy when Sister Freihofer demanded that the girls never speak to each other again, and announced that Madaya could no longer be her servant. As a result of a perceived atrocity that had happened at school, their friendship must end. Forever. immediately.

In time, however, Sister Freihofer decided she needed more help in the house and permitted Madaya to come occasionally. The girls guarded against being seen together, but did see each other at school. One day

Madaya heard loud shouting and wondered what was going on. At first, she went on with her work, scrubbing Sister Freihofer's petticoats and underthings. By that time twelve years old, she knew better than to leave without asking permission. But the sound carried from where Squire was digging a well for Brother Fries. Suddenly her feet ran faster than her head could stop them. Squire would know the cause of the commotion. He would explain what the fuss was all about.

Madaya saw what looked like a forest of sturdy brown pant-legs surrounding the well that Squire was digging. Some men threw dirt everywhere with their shovels. Others dug with bare hands like a dog hungrily scratching for a bone. Dropping to her knees, she crawled between the legs toward the hole, but not seeing it, she shouted, "Where's the hole?"

The men pushed her aside. "Collapsed!" someone yelled into the hubbub. "Out of the way, girl!" Falling backwards, she raised herself to her knees and again crawled toward the hole, searching for Papa's legs. Oh yes, she knew those muddy brown pants, stiff with dried dirt. Every Friday evening she washed and scrubbed them so they'd be ready to wear again on Monday. Although, more often than not, Squire insisted on washing his own pants with vigorous scrubbing and splashing that helped to cleanse his embittered psyche. He kept a second pair of pants to wear to church and to work at Fries Cotton Mill at night.

Madaya screamed, "Papa! Papaaaaa!" And that's when it happened. Just like that, no sound, not even the sound of her own voice. "Papaaaaaa!" she called again, by this time sobbing. The silence screamed at her. Madaya looked up at the men and watched their mouths move, but heard nothing. Just before she felt Sister Friehofer dragging her away from the well, Madaya grabbed a brown pebble and clung tightly to it before dropping it into her story-satchel.

"My ears snapped shut, like someone stuffed rags in my ears," she later explained to the Freihofers. " I can't hear the words fall out! Words get stuck there, in the air," she said, pounding on one ear while making a sweeping motion through the air with the other hand.

"Poor Squire," Madaya mumbled over and over again throughout the long days, even as Sister Freihofer hesitated to correct her in her grief. *Well enough; Squire is gone now, so whether she says Papa or Squire, she can call him what she will,* Sister Freihofer reasoned.

Although her deafness plagued her, in the night Madaya could hear in her dreams the voice of her aduli who called to her, dropping bits of wisdom, offering comfort, a safe-haven in the storms that battered the spirit of the broken child.

On the day of Papa Squire's burial, Madaya was led to the front pew of St. Philip's Moravian Church. Sandwiched between Sister Freihofer and her step-daughter Katarina, the orphaned girls held hands during the service, that is, until Katarina's stepmother noticed. She reached across Madaya to firmly grasp her daughter's left hand and push it against her other hand in her lap. Again, nothing Madaya could do about it. But her own empty hand sweated tears for the comforting touch of her friend, for Squire, for her aduli, for Junaluska, for *anyone* to alleviate her abandonment.

She felt her little rabbit-skin story-satchel pressed against her chest with its treasures that now included the tiny brown pebble from the well-site, as close as she could get to Squire and those she loved. Through the years she often let her mind meander there, lifting the stone from her satchel, caressing it, hoping to change the outcome as she re-played the tragedy. At times, the memory brought relief, while on other days nothing but anger burned through her, singeing every cell of her body. On this day of the burial, she clung to the satchel, its contents comforting her.

Across the aisle on the front seat of the men's section of the church, the doctor and his family sat with the young black boy who lived with them. That morning, the doctor cancelled all appointments to concentrate on Salem. The boy wept in anguish on hearing the news. He had tried to approach Squire repeatedly, even a day earlier, but the "good part" of his news now weighed down his grieving heart. Squire never learned about his son, and it was his fault. The doctor, of course, blamed himself.

Standing at the church door with the crowd pushing against Madaya, the mourners waited to exit, watching the heavens burst like a broken dam, pouring its contents over St. Philips. Squirming her way to the front of the group, she could see the empty grave in the churchyard, drinking in the rain while it waited for Squire's body. But the well-hole Squire had been digging was filled to the top. Not with water. With dirt.

Everyone knew Squire. Brother Freihofer even gave his slaves permission to attend the funeral. People from Fries Factory, black and white, stood with them in the mud. Seemed like everyone loved Squire. That's when Madaya noticed the black boy about her age who stood with the doctor. She and Squire had seen him at church, but his shyness circumvented any conversation. Tears washed his cheeks. "He must have known Papa, too," she whispered to Katarina. *But I have no tears today. I am dead, too, on the inside,* Madaya thought.

Madaya could not have imagined the connection between that boy and Squire, beloved by both children. Young as he was, Salem nursed a wound that drained with the pus of self-blame, of knowing he had waited too long for that elusive *right time* to tell his father the good part, the happy part of the tragedy that had befallen them both.

After Squire's accident, Brother Freihofer began calling Madaya *Whisper*, because she talked quietly. The reason for being soft-spoken is that she did not know how she sounded, and she did not usually speak unless spoken to. "It's hard to figure out what people are saying if they don't look at me when they talk," she explained, but no one heard her. Seemed like they were deaf, too. Madaya watched their lips to see what she could not hear.

In time, Sister Freihofer softened a bit and ignored her earlier demands on the children's friendship, and whether out of pity or her need for more help with household tasks, permitted Madaya to work for her more often. Katarina had panicked when she realized that her friend could no longer hear. "It's like someone stuffed rags in my ears," Madaya explained to her.

Sister Freihofer often moved close to Madaya's face when she spoke, as though to aid her hearing: "Speak up, Emeline!" she told her, tilting her chin with one finger, still using her new name. Following the accident, Sr. Friehofer wrote instructions about her day's work, usually in English, but sometimes in German . . . *lucky for her,* Madaya thought. At least she could read, even some German she studied at school. When Madaya struggled with some written words, Sister Freihofer puffed out her cheeks and shook her head, her hands braced against her broad hips. She continued to test Madaya, as though it were her fault that she was deaf.

People at Home Church in Salem often asked Sister Sarah, the deaf woman there, not to talk in church, because she, unlike Madaya, spoke loudly. So she and Madaya learned to hand-talk to each other, neither loudly nor softly. This amused Madaya. Sister Sarah could only speak German, so people looked at them strangely, and sometimes several people gathered around them, as though watching a play. Their lips moved; their hands gestured as they communicated.

Maybe we look odd, or sound peculiar, but we understand each other quite well! Madaya smiled at their game.

Sister Freihoffer had to admit that Squire had impressed her with his hard work and kindness to Madaya, as well as to her own daughter. Both girls excelled in their studies. Junaluska's occasional visits temporarily confused Madaya's resolve to stay with Squire, but stay she did until . . .

Chapter Eight: Rescue

Why do you take by force what you could obtain by love?

~ Powhatan

unctioning as if in a dream, one night after Squire's death while digging the well for Brother Fries, Madaya panicked. Recognizing that not only would her life continue without Squire to lean on, but Sister Freihofer continued to monitor every moment she had with Katarina whose friendship and comfort she needed. Realizing she was still Cherokee and that Junaluska would welcome her "home," Madaya knew what she had to do. Gathering a few belongings and her story-satchel, she waited for darkness.

It had been a long time since she lived in the forest—and even then Junaluska and Squire had been her companions every moment of every day during the walk from Indian Territory to North Carolina. Night swallowed the diminutive figure as she headed west toward Cherokee. Terror stalked her through the long, dark night. Sounds she did not remember, shadows lurking and jerking toward her like monsters as the breeze swayed branches of trees above her, she felt like a child again.

Falling asleep just before dawn, the sound of men talking and dogs barking startled her awake. Peering toward the nearby road, she watched a wagon approach. To her happy surprise, African men and women were packed into a wagon as close as corn kernels on the cob. They clung to the sides and to one another so they would not tumble out of the rough-hewn wagon with few places to hold on.

Without further thought, unafraid of them, of course, Madaya approached from her hiding place. A woman pulled her aboard as they continued to move forward. Someone offered food and a blanket. But when they discovered she could not speak their language, they resorted to clumsily spoken English, finally ignoring her. Was the girl stupid? Perhaps deaf? A runaway slave? Tiring of conjecture, their conversation soon no longer included Madaya.

The sunrise in front of them promised a bright day. That's when Madaya realized her mistake. They were heading east, not west to Cherokee territory. *I'll turn around as soon as they stop,* she conversed only with herself, and tucked away a dry crust handed to her to eat later, but they continued on and on, to finally arrive in Charlotte after dark. A woman offered her a place to sleep under her blanket on the ground. Madaya was not ready to set out for the west in the dark.

Early the next morning she saw a high platform with a large sign in English: SLAVE AUCTION TODAY. Crowds of people milled about, mostly white men. But off to one side, groups of black men stood, as though waiting for their turn at something. Jumping up with her little bundle, Madaya did an about-face toward the direction from which she had come, heading west, but was scooped up by someone who pushed her forward into the crowd. With the others, Madaya was treated roughly. Terrified, she watched, realizing too late that she should have stayed in Salem until Junaluska returned.

Madaya shivered with a sudden flashback of Squire's stories of being kidnapped. All the reminders from both Junaluska and Squire flashed like lightning strikes through her brain. *You are Cherokee. Always remember that. You are not a slave. You are not Squire's daughter. You are Cherokee! How did I get mixed up with these people?* she asked herself.

Probably because she seemed to be alone, a man pushed Madaya forward and lifted her onto the platform. In no time she was considered an imbecile, because she neither spoke the language of the Africans nor heard the commands shouted at them in English. She responded in Cherokee, thinking, hoping: *Maybe they will understand I am not African. I am not a slave,* "I am Cherokee!" she shouted aloud in her mother-tongue.

With no response from anyone in the confusion, Madaya edged close to a black woman with her three children, also on the platform. Hiding as much as possible behind her, she saw a white man wrench a hysterical child from the mother. His little arms flailed in wild desperation as his mother was pulled forward with two other children clinging to her skirts. Although Madaya could not hear, she watched the mother's contorted face mouth a scream.

With the younger two children still clutching her skirt, the mother lunged for the man who held her baby. The two older boys were yanked from their mother's side. Terrified, Madaya could watch no longer. Peering over the edge of the platform, she saw she could escape behind the fray by jumping three feet to the ground. But the assistant to the auctioneer noticed her. Pulling her forward to the auctioneer, he whispered to him. Staring at her, they noted Madaya's strong constitution and beauty.

After all, she had already walked to and from Indian Territory and had worked diligently in Salem. Her physique and beauty and hints of womanhood, now in her twelfth year, appealed to the white, bearded auctioneer. Smirking, he shouted, "A silent worker!" he roared with laughter. "The best kind! What a beauty!" he boomed. "A gift indeed for the buyer!"

Slaves not purchased at the auctions would board a ship for the Carribbean, if not sold at another slave market in Wilmington. Another sign advertized: SALE OF MULES AND SLAVES NEXT WEEKEND. Grinning white bystanders—all men—mostly farmers, needed primarily brawn and muscle on their farms and plantations, as well as adjacent cotton mills. But the bidding on Madaya began with this announcement: "A gift indeed for the buyer . . ." the auctioneer repeated. "She will be good for a lot of things," the auctioneer shouted, "in the field, in the house, in the bed . . ." he grinned as the bids escalated to a frenzy at this valuable find.

Junaluska had visited Madaya and Squire several times since they parted, and he had been on his way to see her after hearing about Squire's death. Crushed in spirit, he clung to the memories of their camaraderie and their deep, though unlikely friendship. *If only, if only I had taken Squire with me to Cherokee, this would all be different. Once again I have failed those I love, but I will bring her home with me.*

On the way to Salem, Junaluska stopped to visit his old friend Will Thomas at the Trading Post, where he would pick out a gift for Madaya. Will, too, had heard about Squire's death, as well as Madaya's disappearance, and told Junaluska that Madaya may have headed for a slave market, because the driver of a wagon-load of enslaved Africans had stopped for supplies earlier, headed to Charlotte. Any not sold there would be sold to another courier for the port in Wilmington.

Vulnerable, Madaya was considered a slave, headed perhaps for the Caribbean for a lifetime of servitude—exactly what Squire and Junaluska had feared. To think Squire's life had been cut short ravaged his senses. But for now, Junaluska's mission loomed before him.

Without a farewell to Will, Junaluska jumped astride his horse and raced toward Charlotte, galloping as desperately as he'd ever done, even into battle. Searching the crowds gathered at the auction block, looking for Madaya, the Cherokee chief pulled up tightly on the reins, halting near the raised auction block. Jumping from his steed into the morass, his appearance aroused quite the commotion among the crowd. Muscular and taller than many, impressive in his typical deerskin pants and moccasins, like a scythe in a wheat field, he easily cut through the mass of men bidding for Madaya. In one giant leap he cleared the distance onto the platform.

Like an apparition, Madaya saw Junaluska approaching her, as if in a dream, a miraculous sight. Junaluska strode toward the auctioneer and swooped Madaya up into his arms. Heaving sobs of relief, she buried her head on his broad shoulder, determined never again to let him go.

Annoyed at the interruption, the auctioneer demanded that Junaluska set her down again on the auction block. "Look at her!" Junaluska retorted. Insisting in English that the child was Cherokee, not a slave, not African, Junaluska proved his point by doing a persuasive demonstration with her hair. He loosened her braid and held up the black straight locks. So different from the gathered Africans, her hair was long and straight as straw.

Not hearing their exchange, of course, Madaya trusted Junaluska to save her, still clinging to his neck. Some of the crowd agreed, perhaps even sympathized, and shouted for her release. Anger boiled in the auctioneer. The child would bring a good price—that he knew. Yanking up both sleeves to her shoulders, he searched for her branding mark. Of course, finding none, he shoved them both away from him in disgust. Red-faced with fury and disdain, he cussed and returned to the dastardly job at hand.

Junaluska took Madaya back to Salem, stopping only to explain her identity yet again to Brother Freihofer. He requested that Madaya be permitted to see his daughter Katarina before they left for Cherokee. Tearfully, the girls promised each other to meet again. Katarina stooped to pick up a hawk's feather and handed it to Madaya. "For your satchel," she whispered, "so you'll always remember me." Sister Freihofer stood awkwardly beside Chief Junaluska, but was helplessly speechless during the girls' whispered promises to each other. He marveled that although Madaya was deaf, they communicated, quietly intent on their conversation.

Finally turning to march back to the house, Sister Freihofer stopped twice to demand Katarina's return with her. Ignoring her mother, Katarina, too, was speechless, tears of affection and loss streaming down her cheeks. She watched Madaya and Junaluska mount his horse tied beneath the crape myrtle tree, its pink blossoms showering over them. As they disappeared down the rutted road, Madaya raised one arm high, waving her feather while clinging to Junaluska with the other arm. They quickly dissolved into a mere speck in the dusty distance dividing them.

Melancholy draped over Junaluska like a heavy cloak as he now concentrated on the painful reality of what had happened to his old friend Squire. He had been a man of character, a man worthy of emulation. And there was no one to whom he could offer sympathy, except Madaya, of course. He considered her loss of Squire who had provided unconditional love and acceptance for the child.

Madaya told Junaluska about their recent half-day trek into the hills with Brother Freihofer on one horse and Madaya riding with Squire on another, joyful beyond words for both of them, just days before the fateful accident. He had loved the child, this Cherokee girl.

While many Cherokee had been forced to Indian Territory in the west, Junaluska had returned to live with those who had chosen citizenship in North Carolina. Now, Junaluska wanted to ease Madaya into her newly acquired Cherokee life, by birthright, to be sure, and also by choice, even if the tragedy in Salem had escalated the immersion once again. What Junaluska did not know, and would never know, was that another person besides Madaya and him deeply mourned the loss of Squire. That boy-child of his in Salem still waited, in limbo, waiting for, he knew not what. He would wait years for that life-changing discovery.

Junaluska and Madaya arrived in Cherokee as a new year dawned at the Spring Corn Dance, perhaps the most valued of all the community rituals. Every spring, even the missionary schools excused the children to participate in the ceremonies and dancing, believing it to be primarily a time of thanksgiving and feasting. Madaya connected tentatively with her culture again, drinking it in to assuage her thirst.

During the Spring Corn Dance, each Cherokee offered forgiveness for old grudges and sins—with the exception of murder—cleansing both mind and spirit to introduce a new beginning for all. Indeed, they were *born again*. Even unhappy marriages were set aside and new life began for many. But discarding what they no longer needed tantalized European observers who thought of them as wasteful, while the Cherokee simply were not intent on accumulating as wealthy consumers and hoarders, storing up treasure for themselves. Instead, they gratefully accepted renewal, believing their needs would be met for another year.

Preparing for this celebration, the women cleaned their houses and the surrounding grounds, sweeping and scrubbing both their homes and the council house. Old, broken pottery was discarded; tattered baskets were thrown away. Even corn that remained from the previous year, with the exception of seven ears that represented the seven clans, was discarded in the ceremony of renewal, of beginning again. After first saving a few embers to light a new fire in the council house from which all other fires were lit, they extinguished the old fire.

The women filled their hand-woven baskets with fresh, young corn and prepared a feast for all to enjoy, embracing their legend of Kanati and Selu. The legendary couple had one son plus their adopted "Wild Boy" who emerged from the river where Selu had washed the game her husband had acquired in a hunt. Although they tried to tame Wild Boy, a mischievous lad, he enticed his brother to join his antics. One day the two youngsters followed their father to better understand his successful hunting ventures. Hidden from sight, the boys watched their father carve arrows from the river reeds.

Before long, he had climbed a mountain, still tracked by the boys. When he lifted a large rock, a buck ran out and was put down by the father's arrows. He quickly replaced the stone. When he left, the boys tried the same procedure. To their amazement when they lifted the same rock although with some difficulty, a deer ran out, and then another, and then another. In their excitement, they forgot to seal the hole, and the animals all escaped.

From that time on, Kanati could no longer find the animals he needed to kill for food without roaming the countryside, ever searching and stalking the animals. And so the male Cherokee is always seeking, roaming, hunting to obtain food.

Returning to the cave, Kanati found not animals, but tiny vermin-like fleas and bedbugs, and decided to release them on the boys as a punishment for their disobedience. Now that the family could not easily find game, they sometimes went hungry. But Selu planted and provided vegetables. One day the mischievous boys also followed her to the storage house for their supplies. Spying, they watched their mother rub her stomach, and suddenly corn appeared in the basket. When she rubbed her armpits, beans filled another basket. Surely, they reasoned, their mother must be a witch, and must be killed.

Knowing their intentions, however, their mother instructed them to clear the land in front of their house, and to be prepared to drag her dead body around the cleared space seven times, and then to remain awake through the night. But, being the lazy boys that they were, they only cleared seven little spots and dragged her body only twice around their cabin, resulting in a few spots of blood-soaked, fertile ground that nonetheless meant corn could grow with a lifetime of cultivation in those few places. Fortunately, the boys properly followed one of her directions, to save seed-kernels from the growth to plant next year's crop.

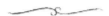

Home at last, Madaya would transform from a young girl into a beautiful Cherokee woman. She would not allow her deafness to isolate her, but instead learned ways to teach others to communicate—not only for her own benefit—but also for others with a hearing disability, so that all might share stories, information, and yes, loving relationships. Living with Junaluska and his new wife Nicie further shaped her understanding of being Cherokee.

It was here that Madaya met Junaluska's grandson, John Astooga Stoga who readily assimilated hand gestures from his playmate and friend. They not only grew increasingly fond of each other, but also of the grand old "Chief" Junaluska and his wife Nicie. Although not an elected chief, Junaluska had endeared himself to his people through his advocacy for Cherokee rights, his success in battle—and not least—his extraordinary comforting presence on the Trail That Made Us Cry, the *nu na da ul tsu n yi.* To them, he was surely and forever *Chief.*

They had been told it was coming, but a few weeks later, the sound outside their houses terrified them. Shouting in English. Horses neighing. Already a speaker of Cherokee, English and some German, Madaya had no idea what lay ahead for her and her new friends in Cherokee.

The United States government officials had met with the parents in the village months earlier in the council house to read the edict and discuss the frightening news. The army captain explained the purpose and expected excellent results when he revealed the government's fine plan: They would take all the children from their ancestral home to immerse them in the white man's ways. The children would be taught to read—English, of course—and to learn the white man's religion. That sounded good to some of them.

"Will you teach about our religion, too?" someone asked. The officer laughed heartily and then spit on the ground without answering. Moments later he said, "Are there any more questions?"

Suddenly, here they were to collect the children. It was a hot day for fall. They had prayed for a breeze and some rain, and rain it did. Rain had soaked the earth all that night before they came. Steam oozed out of the muddy mess like fog over the paths to their houses.

Their shouts were in English. *Who are these people?* she asked. An officer grabbed her by the arm and pulled her through the slushy pools of mud. That's when she saw her friends in a wagon pulled by horses, but no one looked like they were having any fun. It reminded her of the day the soldiers had kidnapped them, burned her village and started the walk on that *trail that made us cry*.

Ilya, Madaya's best friend was sobbing, Aduli! Aduli! Aduuuu-li . . .' She screamed for her aduli and fought to get away from a soldier. But he lifted her up and into the wagon. It had been a long time since Madaya had called for her aduli. She wished for Nicie who was visiting in another village that day. She watched Junaluska's mouth carefully as he explained what was happening.

"Do what they tell you," he encouraged her. "Nicie and I will visit you soon," he promised.

Some parents argued and begged the soldiers for mercy. "We will take our children to school ourselves," they pled. "We will pack their things so you don't need to supply them," one aduli begged.

"Nah! They don't need anything. We supply everything they need." Parents surrounded the wagon, trying to comfort them, but the order was clear from the U.S. government: *Take the children to the boarding school in Oconaluftee.* It was that simple. "We'll take good care of them, we promise," one young soldier said. He spoke Cherokee, but didn't look Cherokee.

While trying to climb into the wagon, Madaya dropped her precious satchel and it fell into the mud. Before she could stoop to pick it up, a soldier pushed her inside the wagon. Ilya's aduli scooped it up, wiping it on her apron before she threw it to Madaya in the wagon. The satchel by then held a collection of things precious to a young girl, and it meant much to her as she walked the trail, lived in Indian Territory and later in Salem.

The wagon jolted forward. The children waved and cried and reached for their families, whose hands touched the wagon as they ran alongside, slipping and sliding in the mud, tears streaming down their cheeks.

"We will visit you! You will be all right! Be brave, little ones!" They watched their parents recede in the distance, still reaching, still calling them by name.

Chapter Nine: Betrayal

We must either butcher them or civilize them.

~ U.S. government official

" "We bumped and sloshed along, whispering and plotting our get-away after arriving at the school. We could not imagine what lay ahead, being treated like babies by the white teachers and caregivers. They even dressed us girls, like playing with big dolls. Some boys were as tall as the soldiers, but to them, we are all children. We are not stupid, but we have to learn a new way to live."

The only generosity shown to the students was the use of notebooks, as many as they needed to do their work. The woman who taught English encouraged the girls to write in a journal, in addition to school work. Nothing could have pleased Madaya more than this assignment. But she learned quickly that writing everything that had meaning to share with Junaluska and Nicie when they visited, was not likely the purpose of their generosity.

As a result of her deafness, Madaya did not have as much opportunity to converse with students, most of whom were impatient with her seemingly slow grasp of stories and jokes they wanted to share, in English, of course. Unlike most of the other students, speaking in English was easy for her, but other than her friend Ilya, not many would talk to her. So, Madaya happily wrote in her brand new notebooks, so she could remember to tell Junaluska and Nicie everything when they visited. She wondered if she should hide her journal. Meanwhile, she wrote, and wrote and wrote:

> When we arrived, the teachers stripped us and confiscated our clothes, followed by scrubbing so hard I thought they were trying to rub off my brown skin. Is this what these white people call school? I know better, because I attended school at Salem Female Academy. We whispered to each other in Cherokee sometimes before realizing the number one rule: Do not talk in your language. No Cherokee! No other languages! Only English! But few of us know English.

> Of course the boys and girls were separated, even brothers and sisters. When clean enough, we lined up for the barber. One terrified girl escaped and hid under her bed. When they found her, they made all of us watch. One held her down while someone cut her hair, very short. We think that was meant as a punishment and a warning, because most of the white women had long hair. The rest of us girls kept our long hair so we could pull it back behind our ears, or make a long braid, or pile it up on top of our heads like the white teachers do. Who wants to look like them? The boys' treatment was even worse. When we all met for supper, they looked like rabbits skinned for roasting.

> An older girl helped the teachers. She even dressed us, first with underwear and then a long dress with buttons all the way down the back that she fastened for us. She was nice enough, playing with her Cherokee dolls, live dolls. We heard rumors about the boys who wore pants with buttons in the front. They didn't know how to unfasten them, so often they just wet all over the front before they learned how to open their pants to pee.

The worst part is learning our new names. Why do these white people want to change us, just like Sister Freihofer did, calling me Emeline! First, they fastened cards with our new names on everybody's back. The teacher had to do this because when she took the attendance roll, none of us recognized the names she called out. So, she walked around with her list, looked at the names on our backs, and made us repeat it until the sound of it was printed on our brains. Of course, I could not hear, but when I had see my name written in English, I answered Present *when Teacher looked at me and said:* MARY! *The first English word that many learned was* Present!

Writing all this—in English, of course—somehow makes me feel better. It is also good practice for writing in English. Do the white teachers not understand that only our bodies are present? The teachers even guess our ages, and give us a birth date to remember. Our clothes, hair, names, language, birth, religion, yes, they strip away all of it, as cleanly and completely as our mothers skin the bear after a hunt.

"They teach us their religion, too. They never asked me what I know, what I learned from the Moravians in Salem. We have to eat their foods or go hungry. At home, we eat when hungry, get up with the sunrise, go to bed at dark. But here, the white people live by watching clocks. They look at their wrists and scowl at the numbers. Some younger children do not know how to eat with a fork and spoon, or how to cut food with a knife. One little girl forgot—but only once, because matron smacked her hands with a ruler.

When the bell wakes us in the morning, we make up our beds quickly and dress for breakfast, they call it, usually a piece of corn bread and prunes, or corn meal boiled in water, but it's not good like ours. I'm hungry for black walnuts from our trees, and freshly picked blackberries, and smoked venison and corn cakes.

When Ilya read some of what Madaya had written, she made a face. "Ugh! That *hash*, that hot tea instead of coffee, ugh!" she said in Cherokee. Madaya placed a finger on her lips and shook her head at Ilya. "No!" she whispered back in English, terrified that someone would hear them, punish them, confiscate her secret journal. "NO!" she repeated and turned away from Ilya, wondering where she might hide her writing.

The next day the English teacher told the students that she would collect their notebooks, both their school work and their journal every Friday so she could read them over the weekend. *Hmmmm, I need to take out some pages before I turn in my notebook!* Madaya thought and tore out each page with meticulous care, folded them carefully, and placed them in the bottom of her story-satchel that she still wore around her neck. Then, she realized that she needed to turn in her journal, too. She had a lot to write in a separate notebook to hand in with her lessons that she kept in yet another notebook, perfectly written in English. *Life is getting complicated, just like the white persons' lives,* she thought. *They want to make us into their likeness, and they are succeeding.* This did not please Madaya. She began to write again:

> *We hear about new diseases that scare some of the children. One is called* homesickness. *The teachers warned us against it. A boy in another school was so homesick he became ill. He tried to run away, but was found and returned to the school. You can't imagine what happened to him. The white people did not know how to treat his disease, and he soon died. What he needed was to be sent home, poor boy. The superintendent wrote to the parents that their son had died like a man. "We have dressed him in his good clothes and tomorrow we will bury him the way the white people do."*

> *Homesickness disease also causes us to catch other white man's diseases. We have our own graveyard, because so many students die, mostly from white man's diseases, like measles, diarrhea, mumps, small pox. In one BIA school, sixty-eight children got sick with scarlet fever; eight died and thirty were*

sent home to die. They told us this, I guess, to warn us not to get sick.

Lessons are difficult. Everything is difficult. The BIA sends us used clothing. Volunteer teachers sometimes come, believing it is a good deed to help poor ignorant Cherokee children learn, so we can become civilized. Junaluska, do you know Harriet Beecher Stowe and Booker T. Washington? They teach English or read to the children in some schools, but they did not come to our school.

Today we learned about Captain Pratt, known as the "Father of Indian Education." He did not graduate from high school, but served in the U.S. Army before he devoted his life to "obliterate the Indian" from people like us all over the United States! Not just Cherokee, but Apache, Cheyenne and Crow, Sioux and even Eskimo, he persuades or kidnaps as many as possible to attend the BIA schools. Pratt opened the first BIA school in Carlisle, Pennsylvania. Most white people think that native children have only enough mental ability to do mundane tasks.

To the officials, we are all "pagans" to be cleansed of our Indian identity. It's true that many of the children cannot read or write when they arrive here, but after only a year, they are studying science and arithmetic, history and art, plus speaking and writing and reading English. The purpose of education is clear to us. One student explained his goal in his journal: "to remake myself into the likeness of the invader." I think the teacher liked this because she wrote his goal on the blackboard for all of us to copy.

Junaluska, I wish you could teach here. They would learn a lot from you. Some teachers base their teaching of English on a book called First Lessons for the Deaf and Dumb. *One student wrote an essay that showed what he was learning. But, it also shows how they shape us, like our mothers taking a piece of clay and shaping it into what they will. Look what he wrote!*

Does he believe this? Teacher was proud of him, and copied it down for all of us to read aloud.

"The white people they are civilized.
They have everything and go to school too.
They learn how to read and write so they can read newspaper.
The yellow people they half-civilized, some of them know how to read and write, and some of them know how to half take care of themself.
The red people they big savages. They don't know nothing."

Madaya added a few notes to the journal for the teacher to read before time to turn it in on that first Friday. She tried to be honest, yet not overtly critical, and hoped she succeeded with entries like this one:

We work long hours, tending gardens and preparing meals, doing laundry and scrubbing floors, making and mending our own clothing, except for underwear and stockings supplied by the BIA. Menial tasks that have to be done are ours to do. The boys learn many skills like carpentry and brick-laying, farming and milking, shoe-making and even brick-making. Before long, word about our skills other than studies and vocational ability will reach our parents. They will hear how much we are learning. The teachers seem surprised to see Indians who learn to read and write English, to look like and live like "civilized" persons, and also to excel in many fields of learning. But we are thankful to be learning so many things.

In her next private journal she quoted another Indian student who wrote in still imperfect English: "Maybe white men better with cannon and guns, but Indian just as good in brains to think with."

Teacher did not seem to mind this observation, but reminded us what one BIA speaker said in a graduation speech: "Let all that is Indian within you die!" And, she reminded us of yet another speaker who said, "You cannot become truly American citizens, industrious, intelligent,

*cultured, civilized, until the Indian within you is dead."
Then she asked us to write in our journal about what this
means to us. She would NOT like to read what I write in
my private journal.*

One girl, friendly enough, asked Madaya in English to teach her some Cherokee, "At night, after Matron checks on us," she whispered. Suspicious, Madaya asked the girl in English what tribe she represented. "Creek," she smiled broadly. Madaya shook her head and responded in English, "I cannot do that. We will get in trouble," feeling rather superior for having sensed a trap. The students always tried to speak in English, except when alone, because twenty lashes for speaking Cherokee, or any other language, wasn't usually worth breaking the rules.

But one night at boarding school, Madaya and her friend Ilya were overheard talking in Cherokee. Like others, Ilya and Madaya briefly and quietly chatted in Cherokee on their way to the latrine with some other girls. Unknown to them, Matron had bribed certain girls to report anyone speaking Cherokee or any language other than English. Officials did not understand the animosity and prejudice that existed among the tribes who were thrown together in close proximity in the dormitories.

The next day Matron called for the two culprits and demanded they take off their tops tucked into their long skirts. Both Madaya and Ilya sobbed while other girls ran to see the commotion. Matron was calm. "This will teach you to speak English," she said to Ilya, and then with each lash she'd repeat: "Speak English. Speak English. Speak English." After giving Ilya ten lashes, she started on Madaya. Both thought that was the end of it, but Matron turned back to Ilya for five more and ended her beating with five additional strokes on Madaya's back. Unaccustomed to corporal punishment, they could not understand what was happening to them.

"Apply this ointment to Ilya's back," Matron instructed as she watched the procedure. Then Ilya did the same to Madaya's wounds. Pulling on their blouses over the clotting blood, she sent them to the dining room that way to eat their dinner, all the time watching them carefully. After dinner she said, "Now, straight to your beds." Still wearing their bloody clothes, they cautiously lay down on their sides, facing each other. All was quiet and dark in the dormitory. Ilya scribbled a note on her hand: "Run away tonight! Come to latrine after me."

Madaya whispered, in Cherokee, "Noooo! Please don't leave me!" That was the second big mistake—talking in Cherokee again that night. Most of the girls did not know how to befriend Madaya with her deafness. Ilya treated her normally, as they were accustomed to using hand-signs and facing each other as they talked. But many questions swirled in their heads that they could neither discuss nor solve. *How can we cross the river at night? Can we find our way in the dark? Shall we wear our lace-up shoes or moccasins?*

Hours later, after everyone appeared to be asleep, they separately stuffed a few clothes inside their long skirts and pockets. Madaya saw Ilya arrange her pillow beneath the blanket to look like she was sleeping there. Ten minutes later, Madaya followed, her heart pounding so loudly she was afraid it would waken the other girls. Slipping on her moccasins, she felt for her satchel around her neck. But the secret journal, where could she hide it? Deciding to take it with her, she pushed it into her roomy pocket where they carried seeds for planting or whatever they needed for work that day. Reasoning that she could run faster in moccasins, she also knew that heavy lace-up shoes would better protect her feet from the rough forest floor and snakes that are difficult to see at night. She chose moccasins.

Madaya caught up with Ilya and struggled with what to do with her journal and satchel on this side of the river. Coyotes and wolves howled in the distance, but they usually did not come close to the school. The river was a twenty-minute walk from their buildings, but no moon or stars shone that night, a gift. Of course like any Cherokee, they could swim, but at river's edge they debated. Swim with our clothes, or strip? They had both gone to bed in their clothes, as the dried blood on their shirts would have pulled off skin had they tried to remove them. The other girls did not think it strange, under the circumstances, to see them in bed with their day-clothes on.

At the last minute, Madaya spotted a hollow opening like a shelf in a tulip tree that seemed made for safe-keeping. Stripping to her undergarment, she added her precious satchel and her private journal crammed inside the pocket, and then wrapped the skirt into a flat parcel. "HURRY!" Ilya whispered, thinking she heard wolves in the distance. Pushing it as far into the opening as possible, they slid down the bank into the Oconaluftee River. Feeling for the satchel around her neck, she nearly panicked until she remembered it was in the secret hiding place. Once the water deepened, the glue of dried blood loosened, and their wet shirts clung to their skin, soothing the lacerations.

"Is that wolves?" Ilya shouted to Madaya when she heard yelping in the distance. Of course, Madaya did not hear her as they both aimed for the opposite shore. "No! It's the dogs! They're coming!" Ilya screamed when she realized someone must have discovered they were missing from their beds. That Creek girl had reported them again, and bloodhounds had picked up their scent. But Madaya never heard them coming.

Desperate now, with dogs and shouting men tracking them, they stumbled and swam on through the murky water, deepening toward the center. Madaya was glad her feet were free of those heavy shoes she had considered bringing. Kicking and gliding through the river, she knew the rapids were farther downstream. *Why did we leave our clothes on the riverbank?* She questioned in a panic. But of course, the dogs already were hot on their trail.

The current quickened. Ilya shouted to Madaya, even knowing she did not hear her, "We're close to the rapids!" They had drifted downstream farther than they realized. "Ilya!" Madaya screamed her Cherokee name, for what did language mean now? "Ilyaaaa!" She felt the rush of tumbling water throw her against giant boulders. Pushing herself, she called Ilya again when she saw the opposite shore not more than ten yards ahead. Had she made it? Swim! Kick! Suddenly Madaya's feet touched bottom near the shore. "Ilyaaaaa!" she shouted again.

Breathless with physical pain plus frantic heart-cries for her friend, Madaya figured Ilya must have made it into the forest. Then the bloodhounds surrounded her; the dogs could be vicious. She wrapped her arms around her head for protection, praying for Ilya's safety. Someone grabbed her arm and shouted, "Madaya, get up!" Shivering with cold and exertion, she stumbled along with the men and dogs through the quiet water below the rapids. Madaya sighed with relief. At least Ilya had made it safely and even her satchel was safely hidden. She would tell Junaluska about her hiding place when he came to the school.

Pushing her back to the school, the men did not know that Madaya pictured Ilya racing to their home where her parents and Junaluska would soon rescue them. Handing her a dry sleeping gown, the helper placed her in a bed in the infirmary for a sleepless, painful night. Early the next morning, Madaya was told to dress. The teachers and matron had gathered together and sent for her. *What else could they do to me?* she thought. *Maybe her parents and Junaluska and Nicie are already here!* That was her happy thought as she followed the messenger.

Matron met her and said, "Follow us!" The women took her to a small room Madaya had never seen. Instead of seeing family, she screamed aloud when she saw Ilya lying on a small table, with a sheet pulled up to her neck. So, she had not escaped to their village.

"Is this what you expected?' they asked Madaya. "This is what happens when you disobey." Madaya fell across Ilya's body, purple and bloated and almost unrecognizable with her face cut and bruised from the rapids. "Ilya! I'm here!" she screamed and sobbed. She wanted her to know she was there with her. But her eyes were closed; she saw no movement beneath the sheet. Then Madaya knew. Yes, she then knew what happens when students disobey.

"We will bury her, now," they said. Cupping Madaya's chin in her hands, she said slowly in her face, "Come with us." Matron reached for a scissors and cut strands from Ilya's long hair and handed them to Madaya, saying, "So you will remember for as long as you live . . ." She gently patted Madaya's shoulder almost kindly, sympathetically.

"I had not the strength to spit in her face," Madaya later told Junaluska and Nicie who had been called to pick her up.

Once again Madaya settled into her Cherokee village life. On the way back from the school when Junaluska came for her, she found the journal where she had left it. Although she insistently pushed receding memories into subterranean mulch that tended to grow and change her recollections over time, at least she always had her story-satchel and journal to remind her of those experiences.

In fact, even as many of her stories dimmed with time, John Astooga Stoga insisted she tell her stories to him. He and Madaya often sat together to tell their tales. A few years older than Madaya, he had not been taken to boarding school, but could already speak and write English. First as playmates who climbed trees and fished, swam and played stickball with other children, before long they recognized a growing fondness and unbreakable bond between them. He knew how to articulate clearly; they communicated well.

The boy-man, already being trained as a warrior like his grandfather, kept his softer side secret, except when with Madaya. He spent hours translating the Book of Matthew into the new Cherokee syllabary, having learned English by reading the Bible with Junaluska's help. With Astooga Stoga's urging, Madaya emptied her story-satchel and secret journal to relate the tales that seemed to her like ancient legends that had happened to somebody else. Had she really experienced all these things? Their trysts included looking into the carefully guarded wealth of stories that each understood and accepted.

By the time Astooga Stoga left for battle, both knew their secrets were safe, as well as the intense love they felt for each other. Several months after he left for home, a knock at Junaluska's door early one morning awakened the three.

Chapter Ten: Hell

I am tired and sick of war. Its glory is all moonshine. It is only those who have neither fired a shot nor heard the shrieks and groans of the wounded who cry aloud for blood, for vengeance, for desolation. War is hell.

~ General William Tecumseh Sherman

There stood John Burnette, stooped and shaking. Madaya remembered him well, first from his kind attention during the longest walk, the "trail where we cried" when she was four and five years of age, and through the years during visits with his old friend Junaluska. Looking at the old ones, Madaya thought, *Each one of us has stories to tell.*

John Burnette often shared adventures and affection with Junaluska, Nicie and Madaya when he passed through Cherokee. An old man now, he rode a horse that looked as old as Burnette himself. As a 22 year-old white man, he had served in the U.S. Army and had accompanied the Cherokee on their walk to Indian Territory.

Burnette limped slowly to Junaluska's pallet and knelt beside him. The two embraced. His unfathomable respect and love for the old warrior added to his discomfort about the news he kept to himself for a bit longer.

Then, standing to one side as though to address them all, Burnette held the reins of his shocking news for several more minutes. He had struggled through the night with his thoughts, but now he stood before them. Into early morning hours he debated with first one approach, and then another, knowing its effect on his old friend and the two women. *I will first, oh no, I cannot break the bad news first. Instead, I will read them the letter I am taking to Sequoyah, and then tell them the news. I cannot offer my condolences about Astooga Stoga until I tell them . . .*

Admiration for these courageous Cherokee people as well as guilt for his participation in their Removal continued to pain him like an ever present, festering blood blister on the sole of his foot. Each step he took still reminded him of the thousands of steps on that journey. He'd grown up hunting and fishing in the Smoky Mountains; he knew these *first people;* he revered the Cherokee and their ways; and, he loved the old chief.

He pulled a letter from his pocket. Burnette had written his grandchildren on his eightieth birthday about walking the "trail where they cried" with the Cherokee for more than a thousand miles. He wanted them to know. He carried a copy to be offered for publication in *The Phoenix,* but first, he wanted to share this confessional moment with Junaluska and Nicie and Madaya. She moved closer to Burnette so she could read his letter rather than try to lip-read. So, they listened:

> *Being acquainted with many of the Indians and able to fluently speak their language, I was sent [as a soldier in the American Army] as interpreter into the Smokey [sic] Mountain Country, and witnessed the execution of the most brutal order in the History of American Warfare. I saw the helpless Cherokees arrested and dragged from their homes, and driven at bayonet point into the stockades. And in the chill of a drizzling rain on an*

October morning I saw them loaded like cattle or sheep into six hundred and forty-five wagons and started toward the west.

One can never forget the sadness and solemnity of that morning. Chief John Ross led in prayer and when the bugle sounded and the wagons started rolling many of the children rose to their feet and waved their little hands goodbye to their mountain homes, knowing they were leaving them forever. Many of these helpless people did not have blankets and many of them had been driven from home barefooted.

The trail of exiles was a trail of death. They had to sleep in the wagons and on the ground without fire. I have known as many as 22 of them to die in one night of pneumonia due to ill treatment, cold and exposure. One noble woman died a martyr to childhood, giving her only blanket for the protection of a sick child. She rode thinly clad through a blinding sleet and snow storm, developed pneumonia and died in the still hours of a bleak winter night.

"I knew her!" Madaya cried out. "She gave her blanket to keep my baby brother warm!" Nicie gazed at Madaya in wonder. So much she still did not know about her life. Reading on, the old man—who had refused to sit down—crumpled his cap, kneading it with one hand like bread dough pressed against his body. With the other quivering hand, he held the letter.

The long painful journey to the west ended . . . with four thousand graves reaching from the foothills of the Smokey [sic] Mountains to what is known as Indian territory in the West [now Oklahoma]. And covetousness on the part of the white race was the cause of all that the Cherokees had to suffer . . .

Now, too late, he accepted that it would have been best to tell them the bad news first, and then give them the letter, because, *what they really need to know is the news, not hear this letter*, he reminded himself again. But he did not know how to reverse his decision, so taking a deep breath, he read on.

Finally, after reading the letter and expounding on the greatness of the old chief, he plunged ahead. What he really was trying to say to Junaluska about his grandson John Astooga Stoga, and to the women as well, was this astounding information:

"I regret, my friends, that I am the one to tell you," Burnette finally began, gazing steadily at Nicie and Madaya who watched his contorted face, his mouth. Madaya backed away from him, unwilling to be a target to the news she felt was coming. She moved toward Nicie, her eyes riveted on the messenger's face, his lips, his movements. They waited.

"Astooga Stoga was, was, was," he finished in a whisper. Catching her breath mid-inhalation, a tightly controlled groan escaped Madaya's lips.

"Noooooo!" Madaya crumpled to the floor with the understanding of what she had feared. Nicie dropped to the cleanly swept, smooth dirt floor of her house, pulling Madaya closer to her. She listened anxiously as the news pulverized the girl into a sobbing, diminutive heap, although she had understood only his first few words. That had been enough. Junaluska stared at Burnette and nodded to him to continue with the rest of his story.

"Well, the white Cherokee Chief Will Thomas, whom you know is the adopted son of Yonaguska and a Confederate Colonel, " Burnette continued, floundering pitifully about irrelevant information. "At one time during the Civil War in our country, Thomas led his company in guarding bridges and railroads. Well enough. Following a period of monotonous reconnoitering, several companies of the Sixty Ninth Regiment were ordered to Powell's Valley between Jacksboro and the Cumberland Gap. One Indian company headed for Baptist Gap, led by Lt. John Astooga Stoga. The unsuspecting Cherokee warriors did not feel like warriors at all, as life had become routine, even boring, without any recent major skirmishes.

"This all changed in an instant about ten miles north of Rogersville, Tennessee, near the Virginia border. Union soldiers appeared, and the unsuspecting Cherokees fell like autumn leaves in a windstorm," he said.

It was as though the earth had stopped in its track. Time stood still. Nicie lifted Madaya's head to rest on her lap and stroked her hair. She no longer watched Burnette, and instead gazed upward through the hole in the roof through which both smoke and prayers found their way into the heavens. Nicie heard a soft groan with each exhalation from Madaya who clutched her satchel with its relics of her still young life. Moving her fingers to feel the objects, she found the treasured heart-shaped stone and pressed it against her breast. Astooga Stoga had given it to her before leaving for battle, assuring her of his love.

"Yes, the valiant Astooga Stoga lay dead," Burnette finished his news report with a shudder. There. He had said it. *Please no more details*, the old soldier pled silently. But not having heard his last words, Madaya lifted her head and stared at him, watching his lips, waiting for more. All she had understood was the name of her lover, but watching Burnette struggle with his news confirmed the worst. Then, unwilling to learn the details, she buried her head in Nicie's lap.

"The decisive battle at Cumberland Gap resulted in tragedy when a regiment from Indiana ambushed the Cherokee company," Burnette droned on, for the sake of Junaluska. After they shot a Cherokee soldier, the Cherokee, rather than the expected retreat, turned to battle hand to hand with the Union troops, energized by fury and revenge. No time to load guns! No time to strategize! Their anger unrestrained, the Cherokee scalped several of the Federal wounded before Colonel Thomas could command his soldiers, not only to cease their vengeful acts, but also never to mention the scalping.

But he knew. Thomas knew better. Word did spread. The Cherokee would pay for their "vicious, heathen retaliation," referring to the scalping as news of their actions spread.

Finally retreating, leaving behind their own dead as well as the fatally wounded and beloved grandson of Chief Junaluska, John Astooga Stoga, they disappeared into the forest. Junaluska had neither the strength nor the words to respond to the news of his beloved grandson's death to whom he had given the respected peace pipe.

The gentle old soldier nodded to Junaluska as he limped out the door on his way to see Sequoyah.

Junaluska considered this: Both white soldiers and Cherokee warriors forget that war is war. Acts of violence cannot be divided into who did what to whom and who started the fracas. Violence begets violence. Restoring *balance?* Questioning this foundational tenet of his people, he posed some questions to himself: *What if forgiveness were heaped upon forgiveness? Or restoration? Or reconciliation? Or, it didn't matter now. John Astooga Stoga was dead.*

Suffering yet another heartbreak, Madaya wept in exhausted pathos through the day and into the night, sometimes gasping for breath as her sinuses and nose clogged with mucus and tears. Through the night she clutched the heart-shaped stone that Astooga-Stoga had given her just before he left to participate in the preparation rituals before battle. In early dawn of the next day, her soul and body spent, she whispered to Nicie, "I need Nanyehi."

Nicie ran to Nanyehi's door, tripping over her own feet in haste to bring any relief possible to the young woman. On their way back to Nicie's house, she relayed the latest news to Nanyehi about Astooga Stoga's death in battle, but she could not have realized the import of their meeting. The time had come for Madaya to share her secret, for she had learned from Nicie that the revered Nanyehi had once confessed a grave failing on her part. She would understand fully what Madaya was ready to confess.

Arriving at Junaluska's house, Nicie's faithful friend Nanyehi wrapped Madaya in a loving embrace before leading her to the fire. Words less important than presence, she sat in the shadows with Madaya at her side, adding kindling to the smoking embers. Picking up a large wooden spoon, she squatted, briefly stirring a pot brewing a stew of squirrel and chunks of pumpkin, then placed the handle of the spoon in Madaya's hand, with purpose. Nanyehi knew the healing power of working with her hands could begin at once. Women know this.

Known by all as Beloved Woman, Nanyehi and Nicie had bonded following the disastrous battle in which Nanyehi's husband had been killed. Young as she was at the time, Madaya remembered that Nanyehi left behind her baby daughter with her enisi to follow the departing warriors that included her husband Kingfisher who would meet the northern Creeks head on.

"My husband will forgive me," Nanyehi had reasoned to herself that long-ago day. "This will be a decisive battle. I must go with the other War Women to help prepare food, carry water and care for any wounded, as is our custom." Had she asked, she knew Kingfisher would not have granted permission. His love for her was too intense. She belonged in Cherokee, nursing their baby, not in the battlefield. But, surely she belonged at the battlefront where she could help win the fight as well as caring for the warriors, especially her beloved husband. *Which is the right choice? How does one decide between two perceived "right" choices? Or, even two perceived "bad" choices?* Nanyehi struggled, then chose.

Accepting the bundle of food from Nanyehi as she bade farewell to her husband, Kingfisher began the march with Chief Oconostota leading with the war song. As usual, the young warriors whooped and forged ahead, while the more seasoned ones followed, their steps measured, intent on their mission, sensing the meaning of all such encounters.

Nanyehi had surreptitiously watched the three days of preparation for that important confrontation with their enemies who had deceived them repeatedly, killing with impunity. The women chatted quietly as they stirred huge pots with the black liquid imbibed by the warriors as part of their cleansing ritual before going into battle. Kingfisher with the other men separated themselves from their families following this pronouncement in the council house four days earlier: *Prepare for war.*

The men had fasted for three days, as well as partaking of purging rituals, drinking the emetic black drink prepared by the women. Three times a day the warriors participated in going to the river, known as the *Long Person*, to wash away the blood following the scratch ceremony in which the medicine man followed ceremonial rites for the warriors.

As a young girl Nanyehi had once watched these preparations from her secret perch in a black walnut tree. That was enough to impress the child with the warriors' courage and strength. Yet, learning about their commitment to bring victory with a show of human scalps hanging from their lances, twisted like a rope around her neck, making her gasp for her next breath.

How can this be? she questioned. This she could not accept. *Surely there must be a way of peace among us, all of us children of Kanati and Selu.*

Nanyehi embraced the unique place of Cherokee women. Women's role is matrilineal; she lives with her clan where her husband joins her and her extended family—not his. Gender-specific work defines them, keeping their world "in balance." While the men hunt to supply not only food but also furs and skins and sinew for trade and home use, it is the women who prepare the game their men bring back to the village. They raise and harvest the crops, prepare meals, make the clothes, create and fire clay utensils, and take care of the children. Also, it is the women who are "communitarians," caring for the poor and any guests who arrive.

Puzzled, however, the white man watched these women attend meetings, participate in discussions and vote in the council house. They worked from sunup to sundown, while Cherokee men appeared to the white observer to be lazy and controlling of their women.

Yet the antithesis that most shocked European observers, caused whispers and a shaking-of-heads as they saw these same strong women in charge of torturing any prisoners of war, sometimes lasting a whole day. During these vengeful acts, the women wasted no pity on their prisoners, torturing them, encouraged by cheers and laughter resounding from the other women who watched in the crowded theater. That is, women other than Nanyehi.

Following any battle, it was the women who chose to adopt any desirable prisoner into their family to help restore "balance," thereby replacing those male family members they had lost in battle. But Nanyehi often plotted escape for her prisoners of war; she found that pardoning them—not torturing them—was written into both her heart and brain. She could not, would not participate in the torture rituals.

Most customs and gender-division of labor Nanyehi accepted. But as Beloved Mother, even though she had become known as one of the War Women, Nanyehi's white cloak of peace made of swan's feathers draped around her, vital as her skin. She had seen too much, experienced horrors that would threaten to sink her beneath despair and damnation if she responded otherwise. Peace was her mantra. Peace, peace, peace was her mantra.

Chief Junaluska understood Nanyehi's divided heart as one akin to his own. He understood well the Cherokee legend of the two wolves at war within the human breast, one evil, one good. The outcome of that ongoing battle hinged on choice: *Which wolf do I choose to feed?* Junaluska and Nanyehi had talked about this. They both knew that the divided heart, rather than belonging to any single tribe or gender or skin color or culture beat in every human breast . . . thus the ongoing struggle.

During one long night some weeks before Junaluska could persuade Nicie to walk with him to the healing springs in Sitico, Nanyehi reflected on the depth of love she harbored for the old chief and his wife Nicie. Although she absorbed their forgiveness and acceptance following her failure, her part in Kingfisher's death continued to haunt her. She continued to re-live her decision to follow her husband Kingfisher into battle years earlier. Perhaps he would still be alive, but that's when she got stuck in the mire of memory, sucking her down into despair, rescued repeatedly by Nicie and Junaluska.

Accepting their gentle nudges to move on, to immerse herself in forgiveness, she learned to offer to herself thoughts of peace, peace, peace. to loosen the grip of regret and failure. And now, it was her turn to hear Madaya's cry for help, her search for inner peace.

"Only you can help me," she whispered to Nanyehi, "because you, too, failed the one you most loved."

Nanyehi was not sure she had heard correctly, but this was no time to ask Madaya to repeat her anguished cry. What could she possibly mean?

Chapter Eleven: *Confessions*

[You are] *making the word of God of no effect through
your tradition.*

~ Jesus (St. Mark 7:13)

itting with Madaya who stirred the stew, the women tasted the
broth, rich with wild mushrooms and crushed rosemary, inhaling
the tempting aroma. Nicie took a bowl of the stew to Junaluska and
sat with him as he ate. Nanyehi allowed her mind to wander, recalling
vividly that long-ago day when she followed her husband and the other
warriors as they left for battle.

Careful to avoid detection even by the war women who followed close
behind the warriors, they cut their way through the copses, sloshed
through swamps and forded streams, pushing ever more deeply
through the mountainous thickets toward the Creeks' hideout.

Nanyehi shivered even by the fire where she and Madaya sat on this
night, remembering her trepidation at the close of the first day's
journey through the forests. As night draped over their encampment,

Nanyehi surreptitiously approached her brave young warrior-husband, cautiously weaving her way closer to the firelight that would reveal her presence, moving ever closer to Kingfisher. When finally he noticed her like an apparition through the smoky haze, first in alarm, then in tenderness Kingfisher reached for his Nanyehi.

"What has happened?" he gasped. Kingfisher barely touched her, aware of the taboos that protect the warrior, assuring victory in battle. Jumping to his feet, he led her gently into a thicket for secretive talking-time, *but only for a few moments*.

"Is our baby well?"

"Oh yes!" Nanyehi replied.

"Why would you leave her?" he demanded. Tenderly placing a finger on his lips, Nanyehi traced his smooth-shaven, painted face with both hands, fingertips crawling upward to his ears, leaning into him, *but only for a few moments* she thought, nearly bursting with love for her brave husband.

"No! Nanyehi!" Kingfisher pushed her away. She recoiled even with the memory of his anger. Their forbidden embrace could negate days of rituals to protect him in battle, the fasting, the emetics, the scratching, the bathing, and refraining from sexual contact. "Why didn't you tell me what you planned to do?" he demanded in desperation.

"You would have refused, but I need to be one of the War Women. I am strong. I am young. I can help bring victory over the Creeks. Yes, I will work with the war women to bring peace for the sake of our little one," she finished lamely, thinking that was a reasonable tactic.

Of course, she did not realize the impact of what would happen next. Stooping, she reached up from the ground on which her husband stood towering over her at his feet, and grasped his ankles while speaking. Her fingers crept upward along the strong outline of his muscular calves, moving slowly, intentionally closer, inside his thighs now. Moonlight on her upturned face tricked Kingfisher into believing that his love for her trumped all else, and he yielded, *but only for a few moments.*

"Nooooo!" Kingfisher groaned while pulling her to her feet, feeling her warmth, her breath, her rounded breasts dripping with milk for their baby, her open lips, her tears streaming in rivulets down her cheeks, her black hair soft and silky against his war-painted torso. Overcome with his love for Nanyehi, he welcomed her embrace, and they became one, *but only for a few moments*, before she disappeared in the thicket.

Nanyehi slipped back into the darkness to work with the war women, to prepare powder and bullets for guns procured from white traders. To make them more lethal, women chewed the edges like a teething baby, roughing the edges of each bullet, also making the missiles more painful when they struck their targets.

As dawn approached, the warriors hid in a swamp to await the approach of the Creeks.

Nanyehi crept closer to Kingfisher who squatted like a coyote with an eye on the silent forest, listening for the approaching enemy. He felt Nanyehi's presence—or spirit—for she lingered in the shadows, more than fifty feet away. He neither turned nor spoke.

A breathless runner arrived and whispered the Creeks' proximity. By the time the sun climbed overhead, they would be victorious, the treasured scalps of the Creeks swinging from their lances. At last the *ada-we-hi* announces, "Ha-yi!" The Cherokee warriors believed the declaration: "The enemy is doomed!" Oconostota cried out to his hungry warriors: "Let your arrows pierce the hearts of our enemies! Let your guns make the earth tremble! Let your lances stab the mighty beasts who bear each warrior! Our enemy is at hand!"

War whoops cut through the early dawn. Nanyehi heard the mighty roar of shouting, plundering, shooting, neighing of the Creek's horses, but her distraught brain distinguished nothing but chaos. In spite of her good intentions, her inexperienced hands fumbled with the precious bullets, some falling to the ground. Too late, she wondered why she had come. Oconostota shouted to retreat, for some reason. Instead, Nanyehi watched her husband jump up from his hidden position, disregarding the command.

"Why retreat now?" he shouted. It is not for the warrior to assess his leader's reasoning, but Kingfisher stood, courageously vulnerable, ready to strike.

Did he not hear? What is he doing? Frantically, Nanyehi leapt toward him, reaching for her husband. Nanyehi's cousin Dragging Canoe—a warrior if ever there was one—shouted to her and to Kingfisher to lie flat. Dropping to the ground, she heard bullets sing overhead and then noticed Kingfisher again.

I thought he was standing, she thought. She slithered toward him, her belly flat against the earth. "Kingfisher!" she shouted into the mayhem. Seeing her husband prostrate, unmoving, she pounced on him, then clawed at the gaping hole spurting blood as she screamed, loud and long.

"Noooooo!" She cradled his head in her arms. His eyes stared straight into the black night sky. The Creeks would *not* have his scalp, she determined. A strange power consumed her, but Nanyehi remembered nothing more.

Other survivors later told Nanyehi that she rose like Phoenix from the smoldering ashes of battle, shouting commands to the warriors. Gripping Kingfisher's rifle, she fired accurately, felling a Creek warrior, possibly the one who shot her husband. Other Cherokee warriors rushed to her aid with a renewed sense of mission, but Kingfisher was dead.

Later that night, Dragging Canoe found her sitting alone by the river where she was hiding in shame and grief. "Cousin! We warriors grieve with you, but it was you who inspired us to fight on. As we pursued the Creeks into the forest, they retreated. We have wrapped Kingfisher and laid him across his horse. The news will spread quickly. You will be remembered always as a great warrior, honored as a Beloved Mother."

"Please leave me alone, Dragging Canoe," Nanyehi cried out in anguish. "I want no more talk of war. It sickens me. Allow me to immerse myself in sorrow and silence. That is my only request." Dragging Canoe bowed to his cousin. "That I will do, Brave Beloved Mother," he said. A bright orb of light pushed aside the smoky clouds overhead, shining down on the bereft mortal whose guilt wrapped like a noose around her neck, strangling, tightening, suffocating her.

Attempting to release the grip of her memories yet again, Nanyehi pulled at the imagined rope around her neck with one hand, while the other rested on Madaya who continued to stir the stew, weeping silently. Nanyehi turned from the fire and gathered the grieving, distraught, twenty year-old Madaya in her embrace. Nicie prepared sassafras tea and listened.

"I know your story, Nanyehi, about how you followed Kingfisher, and what you did just before battle," Madaya began. Nanyehi nodded. How she knew was not important, but Nicie did recall their conversation within earshot of the younger woman. *But she can't hear! Yet, of course she knows*, Nicie reasoned quietly.

Whatever relevance could that have to Astooga Stoga's death? Nicie's mind raced ahead, although her body seemed to move more and more slowly with the burden of recent events weighing her down like a rock hanging from a chain around her neck.

The only words Nicie had later spoken to Madaya were these: "Our friend Nanyehi failed Kingfisher, and now agonizes. We must show her forgiveness." That was all, but Madaya correctly assumed the meaning in those words, even without details. And besides, she had watched Nanyehi closely as she told her story to Junaluska and Nicie. She had *listened*. Now, it was her turn to confess.

"First, Astooga Stoga and I love each other," Madaya began talking in present tense, her voice hoarse and spent with grief. Both Nicie and Nanyehi understood perfectly. Surely her lover could not *really* be dead.

It defied reason. Madaya knelt by her bedroll and retrieved her *story-satchel*. Reaching inside she withdrew the heart-shaped stone, the last gift from Astooga Stoga. Holding it up, she continued speaking.

"We know we cannot marry because he is of the same clan, but we will find a way. We . . . will. . . marry." The older women nodded, glancing at each other. Marry? The word slithered between them like a rattlesnake with a life of its own. Madaya at last sipped her tea and scooted closer to the fire, wrapping up in a cocoon of woven tapestry created by Nicie for Junaluska.

The three women were well aware of the rules created to help prevent birth defects that can result in children born with close biological connections. A woman traditionally married a man from another clan, and he moved into her family, her clan. "So, we *will* marry when he returns to me," Madaya repeated, still unable, unwilling to believe he would not return, just as she refused to accept that she could not marry anyone within her own clan.

"Astooga Stoga had performed all the required rituals before leaving with the other warriors," she said, knowing that her mentors already understood all this. "The night before he left," Madaya began, then hesitated, asking herself this question: *After offering my dearest friends a story, a confession, a spoken acknowledgement of my sin, will my lover still be alive?*

The silence blackened like a storm cloud brewing.

"Well, on that night before he left, I crept toward the gathering of the warriors as they continued to prepare themselves for survival for their long journey and warfare ahead. I watched the camp from my hideout, high above them in my secret retreat in a chestnut tree. Agile as a squirrel, I climbed its branches causing a shower of nuts to fall onto the forest floor."

Actually, this place was no secret to Nicie in whom she'd confided for years. But what Nicie did not know were the secret signals that passed between the two friends, first as children, and after they had become lovers. For several years since Junaluska had brought Madaya back to their village, the two children had played together in the forest and in the Oconaluftee River with other Cherokee children, but their growing fondness for each other changed everything as they passed through puberty to the ripe, sensual beings they had become as young adults.

Both Junaluska and Nicie knew more than Madaya imagined they knew. But they did not know the communication skills the young ones had created to replicate birdcalls. True mocking birds they were. No human and likely no birds could distinguish their sounds from those familiar calls and trills, songs and warnings from the throats of mourning doves, whip-poor-wills, gray catbirds and dark-eyed juncos. In an emergency, they signaled with the cry of a crow. Not only had she taught Astooga Stoga sign language, but together they devised ways to hide from other children.

"Well, on that night," Madaya took a deep breath and shook the blanket from her shoulders, suddenly burning from the fever within her breast. Guilt, heavy as the buckets of water she had hauled when she worked like a slave girl in Salem, weighed her shoulders downward, her heart sinking ever lower in her breast.

A guttural "caw . . . caw" startled the women. Madaya was calling Astooga Stoga with her head lifted, her eyes seeing beyond the door in the early dawn. Like a ventriloquist's echo, the sound bounced back through the door and around the three women and Junaluska. No one dared speak. Madaya waited, reimagining sliding down a chestnut tree, grabbing footholds and jumping the last few feet to the earth beneath the tree.

"He has heard. He comes to me," she explained to her listeners, re-living each moment as though happening in the present.

"'Madaya! What is wrong?'" Astooga Stoga mouthed the words while looking into her face.

"Nothing!" Madaya answered him. "He takes my hand, but *only for a few moments.*"

Nanyehi winced, remembering how often she had repeated those words. Had Madaya *heard* her as she told her story to Nicie?

"My heart pounds. I whisper to him that I am going to the river," Madaya continued.

"'No! Not alone. Not tonight. Not safe,'" Astooga Stoga gasped, although Madaya could not watch his lips in the darkness as he warned her. She did not hear him, but felt his presence as she turned to race through the ferns, quick and quiet as a fox.

"I cannot stop to look behind me, but I believe he is following." Madaya glanced behind her. "I drop my shawl and slide beneath the waters."

"Keeping his distance, Astooga Stoga begs me from the shore, 'Please, please, Madaya! No!' I see his arms outstretched, pleading, motioning me to get out of the river. I plunge in again, and surface to watch him, still standing on the slippery bank. I reach my arms toward him. He throws his breechclout to the ground and kicks off his moccasins. I dive beneath the water again and then feel his arms lifting me up against his taut, war-painted body."

Madaya paused and glared at Nanyehi before saying directly to her: "*only for a few moments,* I think. I do not know whether they are my words or yours, Nanyehi. In spite of all we have been taught and the purification rituals he completed in preparation for battle, his lean, hard body is all I crave, the only right thing to do. *Only for a few moments* whirls in my head, bombarding my reasoning with false promises.

"So, I open myself to receive my lover, lifting me body and spirit, soaring beyond all we have learned and believed, canceling all reason. We were made for each other, that I know." The women stared, speechless. Madaya shrugged, suddenly exhausted and more vulnerable than the night she ran away from Salem as a child struggling alone through that night in the forest.

Returning to the present moment she added, "I also knew that was not the right time, not the right place, but it was, it was *only for a few moments . . ."* she finished helplessly, sobbing again. Beaten like kernels in the pestle, Madaya curled into a tight ball, wrapped her hands around her head and wished she were dead with her lover. Nicie held her close, whispering comfort into the spirit of the distraught girl.

Nanyehi slipped out the door, weeping for herself, for Madaya.

Several weeks passed. Little more than a child herself, Madaya had hoped she was pregnant with Astooga Stoga's child, but when she awoke one morning with the sticky, red sign that proved she was not, she mourned her imagined loss and further confided her secret hope to Nicie.

Although Astooga Stoga negated by his behavior the power of the ritual that could have protected him in battle, Madaya did not blame him. She blamed only herself. She caused his death. She murdered him. Nicie reasoned with her. The medicine man offered forgiveness.

Arriving at her door once again, Nanyehi attempted to comfort her.

"Madaya," Nanyehi said, holding a white swan's feather that she had plucked from her cape of swans' wings. Madaya did not reach for it. "Why do you give this to me?" she asked Nanyehi.

"I want you to remember always what we both learned in great sorrow," she said. "Peace, not war, must be our mantra, no matter what happens. War robbed us of the ones we most loved."

Madaya knew the story well. Following the battle in which Kingfisher had been killed, the red war chief Oconostota and the white peace chief Attakullakulla presented the most revered warriors with the honors they deserved. Dragging Canoe received the coveted eagle feather for the most scalps presented after the last battle. Following all the other accolades, Attakullkulla announced one more award, equal in rank to the Greatly Honored Man titles bestowed. Calling Nanyehi forward, Attakullakulla draped a cape of swan wings around her shoulders. She would forever more be known as *Ghigau,* Beloved Woman, emissary of peace.

Nanyehi's new position included being a member of the War Council and leader of the Women's Council. During the first meeting during which they would decide the fate of the captive Creek warriors who had escaped scalping, Nanyehi as head of the Women's Council listened to the varied suggestions from those gathered: *Kill them all! We can burn them at the stake! But first, we torture them!*

But Nanyehi stood before them, her white cape on her shoulders, and told them of a dream she had. She and her enisi had walked into the river to bathe when they saw the great white wolf on the opposite shore, just standing there, just looking at them. Several women attempted to explain this vision. Nanyehi as leader spoke her own understanding. "I am the voice of peace for our people, and I will lead in this way: We shall release one prisoner who will return to his tribe with this message: 'We have not, and we will not torture or kill any of our captives. Instead, we will adopt the prisoners into our tribe.'"

Several women nodded their approval. Others scowled, some with good reason, some simply speechless with departure from protocol, from tradition. But this was the beginning of Nanyehi's influence as Beloved Mother, woman of peace.

The massacre at Cumberland Gap had murdered more than Astooga Stoga. Little wonder that Junaluska is dying. No doubt about that. Deaths of warriors hardly surprised him, but this loss was his beloved grandson, John Astooga Stoga. While the debilitating weakness of old age wrapped like a python around him, threatening to overtake the giant of a man, still rugged features dominated his physique. Hard, sinewy muscles shaped the contours of his broad shoulders. The fingers of his right hand drummed incessantly at his side, as though attempting to tell yet untold stories. Whether describing a battle or luring the love of his life, his whole body gestured. His physical beauty, hardly waning at nearly a century of years, beckoned Nicie to kneel beside him.

"Call the children," Junaluska said suddenly.

"The children?" Nicie realized he, like her, was struggling to hold on to reality, whatever that meant, for neither could she grasp the reality of the day's events.

"The grandchildren, and all the little ones in the village," he clarified. "I must tell them more stories."

"Now, now, you must rest," Nicie told him.

"No, no, you must call them now," he argued.

Perhaps he is fully in control of his senses, thought Nicie, *but clearly he is confused. Clearly, we cannot call them on this night. Perhaps they can come in the morning . . .*

Nicie slipped out the door to find some of the children to invite them to come in the morning to hear Junaluska tell stories.

Madaya forced her body to kneel beside Junaluska's pallet. Laying her head on his chest, they both felt comforted. Junaluska unexpectedly pierced the quiet with a loud call for his grandson, John Astooga Stoga, possibly a cry of mourning. Half expecting Astooga Stoga to appear at his grandfather's beckoning, yet knowing he would never enter that place again, Madaya comforted the old man, stifling a sob as she gagged on the lump rising in her throat.

Chapter Twelve: *Ani Yun Wiya*

The earth does not belong to people. People belong to the earth . . . All things are connected. Whatever befalls the earth befalls the people of the earth. We did not weave the web of life. We are but a mere strand in it. Whatever we do to the web, we do to ourselves.

~ Chief Seattle

After a restless night Junaluska announced, "I want to sit with you by the fire." Delighted, Madaya and Nicie prepared a doeskin pallet where he could recline or sit as his strength dictated. They tended the fire night and day to ward off the chill that seemed to send him into delirium, just as the fever perpetrated the chill that began the cycle. But on that morning, Junaluska was with them as truly as he'd ever been.

"Where are the children?" he asked. "I'm ready." Nicie smiled at him, relieved with his display of energy and his memory of last night's request.

The news had spread quickly. Junaluska is talking! Junaluska is telling his stories again! Junaluska is calling us! And come they did, from every direction to hear his tales. The children clustered around him, touching him, rubbing his hands. They compared their own smooth hands with Junaluska's furrowed hands with pulsing veins like a map of the river of blood that flowed beneath his parchment-like skin. In a rare mood he talked expansively about his early life and the legends of his people.

Once again Madaya and Nicie listened. They were good at that. Even in her deafness, Madaya listened. *They think I cannot hear those stories,* Madaya shook her head with the knowledge that deaf people are often misunderstood and underestimated. *They hear with their ears, but I listen with my whole body,* she mused.

Young and old treasured the musical intonations of Junaluska's voice. They loved him ever more deeply as he taught them. His knowledge of the world and his people created a classroom to be envied, although few heard his discourses. The women heard the stories, as if for the first time, engaged in the joy of the moment, and the children regarded the old chief with awe. Raindrops, sizzling with tiny explosive pops and snaps like exclamation points to his discourse, occasionally dripped onto the fire through the hole in the roof.

"In the beginning, thousands of years ago in the land of our Cherokee ancestors, lived the *first people,*" he began. These *Ani Yun Wiya,* our beautiful, earthy, brown-skinned Principal People—like you," he gestured toward the women and children, "roamed the forests, built their villages near rivers, lived in harmony and peace with flora and fauna—and sometimes their neighbors. This has changed," he shook his head, "but what has not changed is respect and devotion to the land—not *our* land—remember: we do not own land as the white man does; rather, the land owns us."

The women nodded. Nicie was unsure about how much Madaya understood, yet she was shaking her head vigorously in affirmation. *Does she hear with her eyes, with her whole body?* Nicie continually wondered about that.

"Who dares to claim as one's own, we ask the interlopers, these Europeans, who dares to claim ownership for the mysterious heavens, the living rivers, the expansive land, these gifts of the Creator to all those who live on earth?" Junaluska's usual shaky, waning voice of old age grew loud as thunder and strong with passion.

"Oh yes, we Cherokee treasure the myths of our origin, in spite of Europeans who want us to believe their stories, but will not listen to ours. We tell our children that Earth was once a floating island suspended by four cords hanging from the sky vault, made of solid rock. Long ago, the animals and people lived above the sky, but in time they became crowded, so Water-Beetle explored beneath the waters for new space. Diving to the bottom, he returned with mud that he deposited to mark the beginning of a small island; this he repeated until eventually it became Earth, the earth-island. The sun moved across the arch above it, drying the mud. Another world lies beneath the Earth, the *Below,* the same except for different seasons," he explained.

"We Cherokee do not claim to know *when* the animals and plants were first created, but our ancestors describe instructions given by the Creator to the animals: 'Stay awake' through the long nights. But only a few managed to do so, so today it is those creatures who have the gift of night-vision . . ."

"Like the owl!" "Like the panther!" the children shouted answers.

"Yes, and likewise, of the trees that were able to stay awake, only a few evergreens could do so, while all other trees were condemned to 'shed their hair every winter,'" Junaluska continued. "And you know that at first there was only a brother and sister to live on Earth, until he struck her with a fish; she was told to multiply, until this proliferation of human life—every seven days—became greater than intended." Junaluska grinned. "So, even to this day, a woman bears only one child in a year."

"Tell us about when you were born and how you grew up," a child suggested.

"And about Arrow Woman and Yona and the Great Uktena," said an older girl.

"No! I want to hear about your great battles," added a diminutive boy.

Junaluska groaned. "I don't like to talk about fighting," he looked pensively toward the child. "Perhaps you will find better ways to maintain balance, to solve problems among our people. You can begin now, while you are young."

"Ohhh," groaned the disappointed boy, turning his attention to marking a trail with his finger in the dirt floor.

"My aduli was Immookalee and my edodah's name was Kauna. I can tell you more about them later, but first, you know we are preparing for the Bread Dance. I was born at the time of the Bread Dance in 1775. You know how important that is to us Cherokee. We celebrate because we have lived through another winter, and have just enough food in storage. Just enough! Our cribs do not burst with extra food, but just enough to sustain us until our new crops produce. That's why we dance and eat, celebrate and thank the Great Spirit, *Galonlati*, for our food, just enough.

"Who is responsible for our food? Yes, it's the women. They plant, cultivate, and call on the shaman to pray for rain during dry seasons. Even our enisi sit on high platforms in the fields—you have watched the old ones—flapping their arms and screeching to scare away birds and small animals that would eat their crops. Their work never ends, even in old age."

The younger children giggled as imagination sparked flapping arms and squeals of delight. "When you help them gather and store berries and nuts, seeds and roots and leaves, you help prepare for the times that come; we never know when we may not have enough food for the winter, so we dry and store the crops. We do not eat roots or grains without drying or at least roasting or cooking them in soups and stews, or in making drinks. What does your aduli put into her bread?" he asked the children.

"Pumpkin . . . beans . . . chestnuts . . . corn . . . squash . . ." the children called out answers. "All are familiar with both sources of and ingredients for their foods.

"Yes, but they first soak the dried beans before using in cooking and baking. But what's the most important thing that they pound in the mortar?"

"Corn!" whispered a shy little one.

"Yes, they soak dried corn in lye made from wood ashes to remove the husks. Tell us how they make the large mortar that many Cherokee use to make meal. "

"I helped my edoda haul a large log from the forest. He carved a basin at one end." one boy answered. "He built a fire in that end that burned for many days, and then he carved a smooth bowl into the charcoal-burned space where my aduli pounds the corn into meal."

"That's how they make a canoe, too, but it takes much longer to burn out a whole log," one said.

"My aduli uses a stone for a pestle; it is wide and flat at one end and narrow at the other end."

"Finally," Nicie added, "we build a fire on a stone or clay hearth and shape our loaves for baking. When it is hot enough, we heap hot coals over the loaves, and then cover them with leaves, or a pot or basket. Some women shape small loaves, wrap each one in corn leaves, and boil them in water."

"Then we tear off pieces to dip into bear fat or oil made from hickory nuts, or acorns, or black walnuts," one child offered. "My aduli collects honey before the bears get it, said another. "And my aduli taps maple trees for sap to make sugar."

"And what are the three sisters?" asked Junaluska, attempting to get the children to settle down. Once opened up, they could not easily close the lid on their eager participation. But, Junaluska felt a chill coming on. Nicie noticed his shivering and wrapped his blanket snugly around his neck and started to speak, but the children out-spoke her.

"Corn and beans and squash, " the children shouted in unison. "First, the corn takes nitrogen from the soil, and when it sprouts, the beans planted around the base restore the nitrogen. As the corn grows tall, the bean vines wrap around the stalks," one of the older ones explained.

"Squash is planted last around the edges; it helps hold water for the 'sisters.' The harvest dries on the ground, and we help collect it later to store in cribs through winter months." Madaya smiled, remembering that she had put a tiny bundle holding seeds for the "three sisters" into her satchel back in Indian Territory.

"My aduli makes a drink from the cornmeal and water. After it turns sour, they drink it cold, but not me—ewwww . . ." a girl giggled.

"When a lot of guests come," Nicie interjected, "I make soup with that sour corn broth, or another soup made of honey-locust pods. We sit around the fire, and pass around a big clay bowl with a wooden spoon—carved by Junaluska. We break pieces of bread to dip in the soup while visiting. It's the women who take care of guests and show them hospitality," she nodded toward the young girls listening to her, their dreams swirling as they hope to become a woman like Nicie.

Abruptly Nicie arose and helped Junaluska to his feet. She saw that he had exhausted his reserves. The children each touch the old chief before Madaya ushered them out the door. They made hand-signs—made up or not—to communicate with her. She taught them ways to talk with their hands to make communicating easier, while Nicie taught the children from the new Cherokee syllabary that nearly everyone in their village had learned.

On that night she and Nicie both wondered if they had heard the last from Junaluska. But before he closed his eyes to sleep, he told them, "Before we go to Sitico Healing Springs, I have one more request.

Tomorrow I want to tell the children about my birth, my growing-up years, my naming, my lessons learned. They need to hear it from me," he said, "before it is too late."

"Now, now." Nicie reminded him that his only task was to sleep to renew his strength.

"Then, the Bread Dance begins," he sighed, already dreaming of this festival he associated with his birth, anticipating it with pleasure. "Just enough . . . always just enough," he whispered. But Nicie was thinking of other things. *Perhaps he will still be able to meet with the children tomorrow. Perhaps.* Nicie considered this, then ended her thought with a prayer.

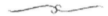

Two days later, the village buzzed with excitement. The women had completed their cooking and baking. "I'm happy we don't dress up for the Bread Dance," Nicie told Madaya. But each woman would wear her best shawl to show respect for the drum in the center.

At last all was ready. Several men assisted Junaluska to an honored seat at the stomp ground. Women and girls entered from the east side, carrying their food offerings to the center. The men arrived to sit on the sides, ready to do the drumming. The drums for the Bread Dance were smaller, with water inside, differing from the larger ones. The drummer listened for a certain tenor, then flipped the drum so the water hit the skin, creating a richer sound.

"Let the drumming and dancing begin!" someone shouted. Eight each of men and women prepared for and led the dances. Anyone was welcome to join in, but they followed the eight chosen ones. Drumming awakened a primal urge, a deep-centered call to solitary response, even while dancing in community. The dance merged the physical and spiritual yearnings into one, creating connections with the Great Spirit and one another in this celebration.

The Bread Dance exhausted everyone, most especially, Junaluska. But as the children begged for another story, he revived. Something about a story provides a life-giving transfusion that energizes both teller and listener.

Even before they had settled around him, one child asked, "Tell us about where the Sacred Pipe came from, the pipe that you gave to your grandson." They all knew about the brave Astooga Stoga. Madaya shivered with the reminder of her lover who had shown her the Sacred Pipe before leaving for battle. But she forced herself to concentrate on Junaluska's story, watching his lips, his expressions, his gestures. That's how she listened.

"When the animals could still talk to men, Waya [uncle] told me, they taught the Principal People lessons about the earth and how to preserve it. Now, Arrow Woman was a brave warrior—even as a woman she could shoot an arrow straighter than any man in her village. She could throw her knife to split a slender branch. She could throw a spear into the eye of a hawk flying above her!"

Both boys and girls all began talking at once, testing their prowess in their imaginations, hurling a spear, throwing a knife, shooting an arrow.

"One day while hunting, Arrow Woman noticed the tracks of a bear who trailed blood as he walked. When she saw the angry red injury on the hindquarters of the Great Yona, she followed the bear to a grassy field, but as she watched, the field turned into a lake—the sacred lake of the animals, *Ata-ga-hi*, that no human had previously seen. She watched him plunge beneath the water; moments later he re-appeared, completely healed of his injury.

"When Yona the bear noticed her watching, he told her that the lake is the home of the Great Uktena, although no person had ever seen the mighty dragon creature. 'You must never reveal this location,' Yona told Arrow Woman. She watched him walk back into the forest.

"As Arrow Woman sat and gazed at the lake, calm because *Unole* the wind was asleep, a surprise intruded on her reverie. She saw the Uktena raise its head above the waters. Arrow Woman readied her spear to fight, but Uktena spoke to her: 'Put down your weapon. You will not be harmed.'

"She relaxed, knowing he spoke truly, and watched in wonder as Great Uktena dove into the lake again and surfaced, holding in his mouth a crooked stick and a leather pouch that he laid at her feet. 'This is the Sacred Pipe of the Creator,' he began to teach Arrow Woman. 'The bowl is made of the same red clay from which you people were formed.' Uktena showed her how to attach the bowl to the stem. Just as a man and woman are separate until married, so the bowl and the stem must not be joined unless ready to use it.'

"Uktena opened a pouch holding the sacred *tsula* and first placed a pinch of the tobacco on the ground, and then another pinch into the bowl before adding a tiny ember, infusing it with glowing life. 'This stem is man: strong, made from a plant, supporting the bowl, just as a man supports his family. This bowl is woman who carries the children and brings forth life, a container for the Creator's work. The smoke is the breath of the Creator, so when you draw it into your body, the smoke will cleanse you. As it leaves through your mouth, it rises to your Creator who will receive your dreams and hopes and desires. But remember this: the Creator knows the truth in you. If you are not true, not worthy, do not smoke the pipe.'

"On and on, Uktena taught Arrow Woman the prayers to be used with the pipe, as well as the appropriate times to smoke it. 'Remember all I have taught you,' said Uktena. 'The one who is worthy to carry this pipe and enact the rituals carries great responsibility as a pipe bearer, to respect and protect Mother Earth, as well as family and tribe. The one who carries the pipe does not own it. He accepts the responsibility until it is time to pass it on to the next bearer.'

"'You will never find this place again . . .' Uktena reminded her, and with that, he disappeared in the Atagahi, with not even a ripple to mark his departure.

"So, my beloved Waya was the respected pipe bearer in the community for his extraordinary contributions to the tribe. During skirmishes between the British and the French who fought side by side with the Indians of many tribes, Waya told his war-stories at the dances and rituals.

"I regarded Waya with admiration and not a little envy. More than once I told my uncle, 'One day, I'll be like you.' Sometimes Waya looked away on hearing this, either from humility or perhaps from fear of what lay ahead for me, the young Cherokee boy whom he loved."

Nicie nodded to Madaya to take the children outside. Junaluska had wearied with the telling and struggled to stand to his feet, with a few of the older boys taking his arms and guiding him toward his pallet. Then he stopped and turned to the boys to ask a question they could not answer:

"Can any people can survive without passing on their lessons learned, before it is too late? Too late, too late," he continued to murmur as they eased him onto his pallet. He drifted into his old-man dreams even before the boys turned to leave.

Chapter Thirteen: Lessons

The present is the tree that springs from the roots of the past.

~ Charles Lovett

Although the whole village collapsed for a few days following the Bread Dance, Junaluska awoke after a deep sleep and said he was again ready to tell his stories. The village children arrived to gather around the old, honored warrior. But on that day he seemed like anything but a warrior as he began to reminisce about tender memories. He wanted to teach them vital lessons, he said, about important things he had learned in his long life, but they begged for his birth-story.

"Among many other names given to my aduli was *Immookalee,* meaning waterfall," Junaluska began. "She told me about the day she ran to her mother with the news: the babe within her had announced his living presence with a swift kick—or punch. Assured that I was on the way, she called together the Cherokee women who gathered around her on the riverbank for prayer, as was their custom.

Her happiness lifted Immookalee in spirit and body as she walked into the swift current, buoyed up with prayers of her own: *Make him strong; make him good; grant him courage; give him long life* . . . believing, but not knowing that her prayers would be answered.

"And just look at me now, an old, old man! At least that part of her prayer was answered," he told the children. "As were the prayers for strength and courage and goodness," breathed Nicie.

"When a baby is expected," Junaluska continued, "not only parents, but also the whole community observes certain taboos. We do not fish in a river where a pregnant woman is wading upstream. We refuse food cooked by a pregnant woman. A warrior does not participate in battle if he knows about his wife's pregnancy. Nor would he wear hats with folds that could cause creases in the infant's head, or dig a grave, or play stickball.

"Also, my aduli took precautions she during pregnancy, like not eating speckled trout that may cause skin blemishes in the forming child. Usually, eating meat is taboo, but if she really wanted meat, it had to be trapped, to avoid contamination from the spilled blood, considered debilitating for both the fetus and a warrior. If she combed her hair backward, the baby's hair might bristle rather than lie flat. Feasting on black walnuts might cause the baby to develop an over-sized nose. Wearing a neckerchief may cause the umbilical cord to wrap itself around the neck of the fetus. She refuses to view a corpse, visit a menstruating friend or relative, attend or even visit the sick.

"Europeans criticize our behavior, thinking that we men keep our women under strict regulations, especially a pregnant woman whom they believe we consider unclean, contaminated."

"But!" exclaimed Nicie, laughing, "they don't understand the power of the female. We believe that menstrual blood flows when a child is not meant to be born," Nicie nodded to the older girls who hung on every word. "So, rather than making us weak, this monthly flow of blood signals our powerful and even dangerous influence—on the warrior, on the husband, on the sick, on the whole village. During menstruation, women often confine themselves to a small dwelling away from the community where they do not need to cook or even care for the children. Other women, or even the husbands, may prepare simple food, such as hominy, and leave it outside the door. "

"This mysterious power of blood connects male and female to the beliefs and legends that accompany our roles," Junaluska continued. "Both the warrior's shedding of blood as part of his function to keep our world in balance, and the monthly flow of blood from the female means that whether warring male or menstruating female, each individual is powerful and respected. The white man is slow about accepting this equality.

"To prepare for an uncomplicated delivery, Immookalee refused to eat squirrel meat, as that could cause the baby to go up, like a squirrel in a tree, rather than down during delivery," said Junaluska. "Loitering in a doorway may cause a slow delivery. She drank a pinecone concoction to guarantee long life for her baby, and see what a long life I have had! To give me a chance to be a quick learner and able to retain in memory anything once heard, she made a drink by pulverizing cockleburs in water taken from a waterfall.

"Like all Cherokee women in the villages, when contractions began, Immookalee entered voluntary isolation. Some women went to the forest for delivery, but she preferred to remain in her house, attended by a midwife. Most other family members left them alone to their task. A clay bowl of water and woven cloths were stacked beside her. Early that morning, wanting to do her part to prepare for the delivery, Immookalee walked to the river to dip clear water into the vessel.

"My aduli told me that, wanting to be helpful, my edoda started out the door with the bowl to fill it at the river, but my aduli laughed at him. Why was that?" Junaluska asked the children.

"Men do not carry water!" the boys laughed boisterously.

"That's our work!" several girls answered.

"My aduli had shaped the clay water-pot with pride, as she did with all the utensils she made. Marking it with stamped cross-hatching, she inserted a corncob into the bowl before placing it into the fire. As it heated, the oils from the cob sealed it, making it waterproof. After the delivery, the midwife would place the placenta into the bowl.

"My *enisi* had woven a blanket with its colorful warp. I can still picture it, as my aduli used it for much of my early life, but she used it to wrap her mother's body for burial when that time came. Before delivery—my delivery—that blanket lay open beneath her, ready to receive me when I dropped onto it.

"The carved instrument for cutting the lifeline from the placenta to the baby, waited, ready for it's only task. Carved for this purpose by my edoda, Immookalee was proud of its curved, polished handle, with its edges sharp as flint. A small, tightly rolled ball of flexible sinew, awaited its unique task: to tie off the umbilical cord, propelling the infant into Life on its own.

"Then, quick as an arrow hitting its target, birth changed everything for me, for my aduli, my edoda, even for our village, as all births do. Your life." Junaluska nodded to each child in turn, "Your life affects others. We are all connected," he said.

"Kauna was my edoda. He liked to tell me about those days, those thoughts he pondered during pregnancy and birth of his first child. He wondered, *What will my life be like with a baby?* He was proud to participate in this mystery and miracle, the birth of this creature, part him, part her, part of the past, part of the future, and the *Now*.

"He wanted to witness the birth, so he stood with a medicine man behind my aduli's head. We know that Cherokee men do not watch childbirth, but he told me about it so often that I can picture him squatting behind her, rubbing her lower back as birth pangs came and went, regular as the white man's clock that ticks, then tocks, then ticks, then tocks, but unlike the clock, these contractions moved ever closer, stronger, harder, as her body did its work.

"The medicine man stood with him behind my mother and chanted, his low undertones punctuating the silence between contractions. Ignorant of the gender of the unborn child, he repeated various formulas to hurry the birth. Louder, still louder, he called forth the child:

Little boy, little boy, hurry, hurry, come out, come out! Little boy, hurry; a bow, a bow; let's see who will get it.

He followed this with an enticement to the possibility of a girl-child to make her appearance to *claim a sifter*, referring to the work of the woman-to-be.

"Some women knelt or even stood, but were never supine during delivery. When the moment arrived, Immookalee squatted and dropped the baby onto the soft landing prepared to receive him. The baby boy dropped on his back and emitted a noisy squall. Stunned with the kicking miracle before them, my edoda and aduli watched and listened in wonder. Immookalee sponged her baby boy in cold water.

"Immookalee told me," Junaluska went on, "that when she was born, the midwife panicked when she saw the baby *age yutsa* [girl] drop face down, a limp figure between my mother's legs. If an infant landed on his or her back during delivery, that was considered a good omen, but if face down, the midwife wrapped the baby loosely in the cloth on which she had been born and raced to the river. The midwife held their breath as she placed the infant into the cold waters. When the loosely wrapped cloth fell from the newborn child and drifted downstream, carrying any 'ill-fortune' away, she exhaled with relief and gratitude.

"So, there she was, her new daughter who would grow up to become my aduli, kicking and breathing and squalling with strong, clear lungs. Some Cherokee mothers, even after a normal delivery, dip their babies into the river daily for two years to assure a strong constitution."

"It was into this paradise, climbing the rolling Smoky Mountains, that my edoda carried the placenta of his newborn son. Kauna told me he considered carefully how many years before he wanted his young wife to bear their second child. Three? Perhaps two? That would be a good interval. The number of ridges Kauna would carry the placenta would predict the number of years before Immookalee would bear another child."

"Of course," Nicie added, "Edodah needed only to refuse her husband when she was not ready for another child." Junaluska ignored her comment. Nicie opened her mouth to speak again, but then likewise ignored her husband's silence.

"By nightfall the next day, Kauna buried the placenta on a rugged ridge jutting into the sky above him. He showed me that spot one day, the place where he had buried what had been my nourishment for nine months, returning it to the Earth that nurtures us." Junaluska paused. "And soon, soon I shall become part of our Earth that feeds us, and that we in turn feed her."

Junaluska was immersed deeply in his story-telling, even gesturing with his hands, fingers fluttering downward to show the path of moonlight filtering through the hickory and oak leaves in the generous, giving forest. "The hypnotic symphony of cicadas beckoned sleep for my edoda.

"But first," he said, "Kauna prepared a fire to keep coyotes and foxes, wolves and bears as spectators from a safe distance.

"Gazing into the darkness from within the circle of light, he listened for movement, waiting for pheasant, or squirrel, or rabbit to roast over his fire. In the fall hunt Kauna had shot a deer with his bow and arrow, followed by the ritual of asking forgiveness for having to kill her. But for small game, like the rabbit he finally killed with his river reed blowgun, he simply offered his thanks to the *Galonlati* who had blessed him not only with a healthy, first-born son, but also food to eat in the wilderness.

"That evening back in the village, my aduli fell asleep and dreamed that she chased a rabbit up the mountain path where she had watched her husband wave to her as he began the climb with the placenta. Her dream of chasing a rabbit is not strange. You know that we Cherokee embrace various legends of the trickster. At that very moment, as can happen when two soulmates are separated, her husband, my edoda, smiled as he thought about the myths while roasting a skinned rabbit pierced with a stick, roasting over the embers for his supper.

"The next day, his task complete, Kauna headed down the mountain, sensing the excitement that emanated from the village as they prepared for the Bread Dance. We know that this ritual offers public acknowledgement of thanks to the Higher Being for *enough* food through the winter, but for Kauna and Immookalee, their gratitude centered on their new-born son—that's me," Junaluska smiled at the children.

"Spring was playful that year of my birth in 1775, teasing even fauna and flora with slippery trails and icy water, while at the same time greenery brazenly burst through frozen soil. But by the time Kauna returned to my aduli, the forest floor could no longer contain itself, pulsating with life, wild grape and rhododendron, coral honeysuckle and mountain laurel. And still further inside Mother Earth, veins of gold hid from roving eyes of invading plunderers, intent on robbing those who belong to this place. I like to think about giant hardwood roots twisting tunnels deep into Earth, and about colonies of ants that make their own little tunnels and food-storage pantries." Nicie smiled at her husband's poetry, even in telling stories.

"Weeks later my Immookalee wrapped her still nameless baby son in soft deerskin from my edoda's hunting expedition," Junaluska told the children. From the little frame onto which I was snuggly wrapped and secured, I watched my aduli hoe corn. They told me that although I was safe and content, I began to wiggle and the frame tipped over from its leaning position against the cottonwood tree, onto the ground. Unhurt but still wiggling, I at last had a name: *Gulkalaski*, meaning *that which falls from a leaning position.*" The children giggled, imagining Junaluska as a surprised baby on the ground.

"Kauna and Immookalee agreed that the Great Spirit, *Galonlati* had named me. Later, I re-named myself after failing to accomplish what I intended in battle, confirming again that Life shapes us with extraordinary power. You can be more than, bigger than your name, or much, much less." Junaluska sighed, weary with both his telling and the memories.

One thing was certain: Junaluska would fulfill his destiny with contrasting peace-loving forays and battle-scarred victories, with kindness and brutality, with mercy and retaliation. Immookalee and Kauna's Cherokee *atsutsa* [son] would live a life of questions and ambiguity. He would live the Cherokee way, attempting to balance the contradictions that necessarily come with life.

The newest member of a Cherokee village became the beloved ward of his mother's clan that included his aduli's eldest brother. It was he who assumed responsibility for teaching his sister's son the ways of the *tsalagi*, the Cherokee. In this sociological understanding of the matrilineal community, the mother's brothers became the mentors who taught by example and by telling and re-telling the myths and legends, and by teaching lessons of trust and integrity, honesty and courage, kindness and loyalty.

"On one particular morning Waya, my *tsodusti* [uncle], called me," Junaluska continued. "Imagine this with me," he told the children, "I am now in my eleventh year; I remember it well.

"When the sun sets today," Waya said to me, 'we will go into the forest. There, I will blindfold you, and you will spend the night listening to the call of the wolf, breathing in the smoky embers, thinking about our world and your place in it. You will hear me walk away, but remember this: This is your home. You are not alone. I will be with you.'"

Junaluska shivered with excitement even after all these years—or was a chill coming on? Nicie draped a blanket around his shoulders. Having heard about the many rituals his friends experienced as they yielded to the shaping of their manhood, Junaluska had known that this time was different. The door to his own manhood opened slowly, gently. And he entered, filled with great admiration, respect and longing, fully trusting his mentor.

Twilight drifted over Waya and Junaluska as they settled into the appointed place. Descending darkness reminded him of water closing around his whole body when he slid beneath its surface to swim. His uncle squatted before him to give further instructions.

"'You will not leave this spot tonight,' Waya told me again. 'You will not remove the blindfold even if you feel afraid. You will honor your *tsodusti* and your *tsunigayvli* [ancestors]—and your word—by refusing to remove it. Then, when fingers of sunlight reach through the leaves above you to touch your forehead, I will come to you and remove your blindfold.

"'Remember this, I will be here with you. You will not be alone. Then we will talk about what you learn this night,' he explained to me. I felt the beaded blindfold tighten around my forehead," Junaluska told the children. "It covered my eyes to block out all light. I reached through the darkness for my *tsodusti*. He touched me gently on the shoulder and I relaxed into the knowledge of his presence. Soon, I no longer felt the gentle pressure of Waya's strong hand. Everything gradually changed: light, sound, breathing, heart rhythm. I waited in silence, at times so loud it astounded me. I felt myself shivering, though not from cold. I leaned into the bark of the towering elm behind me.

"Waya?" I called out. "No answer. Then I just listened, crying out only once more in the long night when I felt a slippery creature gliding across my limbs stretched in front of me. Waya!" I gasped again. My breathing quivered, almost stopped. Hearing no response, I bent my knees against my chest and wrapped my arms around myself, drifting into and out of illusory awareness.

"Long, long before *tsodusti* released my blindfold, I realized I had not heard him leave. You, too, will learn that skill," Junaluska told the boys. "When the blindfold fell suddenly onto my lap, I heard Waya say: 'I told you that you would not be alone. I sat near you through the night. You are never alone, my child. Remember this.'

"I learned that lesson well from Waya: *I am not alone. I am loved. I am cared for, even by the natural world that is a gift to me. I will never be alone.* Waya never misled me. You children, too, will learn these lessons in different ways," Junaluska lifted both hands, slowly moving them above the seated children as a blessing. "You will never be alone!" he told the children. "These lessons will guide you on your journey on earth."

"Later I learned another valuable lesson, this time from my brother's deceit," Junaluska recalled. "When it was discovered that my younger brother had stolen a gold nugget from a visiting white trader, Waya called both of us to his side and described to us the watchful, all-seeing eyes that not only protect us, but also note such acts. Stolen! I glared at my brother, wondering how he could do such a thing.

"'Any of us is capable, even likely to do dishonest things.' Waya looked into my eyes. He could read my thoughts. 'All actions, as well as the model of honesty we are taught from birth to the grave, shape the emerging hunter and warrior,' Waya told us boys. 'Tomorrow you will learn a new lesson,' he said. Neither of us knew his plan, but we did not voice our questions.

"Before sunrise the next day, Waya awakened us brothers. Walking beside the horse that we might have ridden, we groaned inwardly, but did not speak. Our *tsodusti* told us he would accompany us on a hard day's walk to the Trading Post. I moaned aloud, but neither of us said a word. *Walk? Why not ride the horse? And why did I have to make this journey with my brother and tsodusti?* Questions, annoying as wiggly worms, crawled around inside me as we walked on.

"My brother carried the stolen gold nugget in a deerskin pouch that he had been making as a gift for our mother. Admitting his guilt to the white man with the return of the valuable nugget, and also having to give away a treasure of his own in the cleansing process, plus the stress of enduring shame and physical pain during the long walk, cured my younger brother for life from any leaning toward dishonesty. Nor was the lesson wasted on me. I remembered again: *I am never alone. What I do and the way I live affects everyone within my circle of being.*"

"One afternoon we boys in the village were practicing with our blowguns. We not only created targets made with thistle, but also fashioned blowguns from the canebrakes by the river. This indigenous bamboo calls to boys and men alike to be cut and used as weapons to kill small game for eating, such as rabbit and squirrel. You boys know that seeds—even pebbles—can pack a mighty wallop in the hands of an expert hunter with a blowgun."

They nodded their heads, thinking of many stories they could add, but Junaluska continued. "One day, I heard the medicine man calling the boys of the village. We ran to the respected leader to hear whatever he had to tell us. 'Listen closely,' he said.

"'In every living person, a frightening contest takes place. It happens within you. It is like a terrible fight between two wolves. One is evil: he is fear, anger, envy, greed, arrogance, self-pity, resentment, and deceit. The other is good: joy, serenity, humility, honesty, confidence, generosity, truth, gentleness and compassion.'

"I couldn't help calling out my question. *Which wolf will win?* I asked him, thinking myself rather clever to respond so quickly. The elder peered into my eyes, way down into my soul. Everyone listened to the silence, because it was so loud. He did not answer for a long time. I knew he wanted to hear more from me, but my tongue froze in my mouth, cold and immobile as a dead body in a dark tomb. Finally, he answered my question: 'The one you feed,' he said.

"I understood that more fully as I reflected on it for a lifetime, for that's what it takes, a lifetime of practice, a lifetime of choosing every day which wolf to feed.

"By the time I reached puberty, I already could look straight into the eyes of my edodah and my tsodusti, Waya. In a ceremony when I was eighteen years old, Waya bestowed on me the treasured sacred pipe, called the peace pipe by Europeans. It had belonged to my great grandfather. I have already told you how the peace pipe came to be, but I want you to remember that the pipe is not the *symbol* of things that are sacred; it is in itself sacred. You will use it with others when decisions must be made, decisions that will affect our people, decisions about war—and peace," Junaluska continued solemnly.

With Nicie and Madaya assisting him, Junaluska struggled to stand and walk toward his palette, the children watching in silence. Madaya led the children to the door, knowing it would surely be the last time Junaluska would tell his stories to the receptive children. They, too seemed to sense it, and left quietly.

Stroking, soothing, whispering, Nicie wiped Junaluska's brow with a mixture of *agrimonia gryposepala*, brewing in a pot for drinking. But Junaluska could not tolerate the spicy concoction, so Nicie gently massaged the warm liquid onto his forehead while Madaya offered sips of wild senna roots crushed in water for fever.

Sometimes she mixed it with ginseng root, procured by the medicine man who observed numerous regulations during a hunt for the plant. Considered a sentient being, ginseng is believed to be invisible to any unworthy to gather it. The medicine man passes by the first three ginseng plants, honoring its value, and asks permission to cut a small piece of root from the fourth, leaving enough for the future. He buries a red bead in its place to thank the plant known as the *Great Ada wehi.*

Exhausted that night after having talked with the children, Junaluska announced to Nicie: "We shall leave at dawn."

"Now, now, that can wait," encouraged Nicie, knowing well the plan he had espoused for several days as his fever undulated, unrelenting.

"Healing springs in Sitico," Junaluska gasped. "We can walk together," he tells his wife, clutching her hand. The medicine man had already performed his ceremonial scratching with sharpened flint, after which he poured water over the bleeding wounds, in lieu of "going to water" that Junaluska was no longer able to do.

Together Nicie and Madaya wrapped their beloved one in tender ministrations. Watching them walk away together the following morning, Madaya wanted to run after them, wanted to care for the old couple. She owed them her life. Junaluska clung to Nicie's long braid with one arm around her neck, while she steadied him with an arm around his waist. With his other arm he leaned hard on his walking stick. Turning back inside the house, Madaya knelt by Junaluska's bedroll. Smoothing it out, she noticed the tie belt he had stopped wearing recently, and slipped it into her satchel. *I will tell them I need this to feel close to my beloved one*, she thought.

Noticing her need for the healing touch of nature, Madaya began to walk through the village, losing herself in the coolness of early morning mist. Inhaling deeply the restorative morning air, Madaya was aware that such extraordinary circumstances and stories surround every life, even if not recognized, not understood. Young, to be sure, but Madaya was one of those persons known for having been born *old,* mature beyond her chronological age.

On that confessional night long ago, she had accepted Nanyehi's story as a lesson, so she might never repeat that tragic mistake herself. But somehow, tantalizing her tender conscience, Madaya again considered the fact that she, too, had trespassed onto the holy ground of her own lover's preparation for war.

"Ahhhh! Madaya!" She turned quickly to the greeter who leaned against a cottonwood tree at the edge of the compound. She hadn't realized she had walked that far in her reverie. She recognized the strong, muscled body of Degataga, the insistent pursuer of her affections. *He must have been following me*, she thought.

"I want to show you something," he said. Trusting him, thinking little of it, she followed him to the riverbank to see what he had found. Dropping his loincloth and laughing at her surprise to see him naked at the river's edge, he grabbed her arm and pulled her down the slippery embankment.

This in itself is hardly strange. Cherokee children grew up swimming naked, laughing and making jokes as young ones do. But this was different. Resentment and anger bubbled up like lava within her when he tried to persuade her to swim with him.

"Don't you know I am thinking only of my beloved Junaluska who even now is walking to healing springs?" she screamed at him as she clambered up the bank. *And doesn't he know that Astooga Stoga is dead, that the love of my life is gone?* she thought as she raced back toward home.

Fast as the wild horses that roamed the valley below, she arrived breathless at Nicie's door. Drawing a deep breath, she entered the safety of her home, now deserted without Nicie and Junaluska.

But Degataga was not so easily dissuaded. The next morning he knocked at the door. Madaya called out, "Who is there?" He responded quickly, but not hearing his response, she opened the door a crack. "I have important news," he said, facing her. "Junaluska?" she cried. *Why would Nicie send Dagataga with a message? Perhaps they need me!"*

"Nicie needs you," he confirmed her thoughts, stepping inside. "We must go quickly," he said, tilting her face toward him with both hands, he pressed full lips against hers. "Now that Astooga Stoga is dead, you are free to be mine," he whispered passionately.

"Nooo!" she screamed. Its sound rang so loudly in her head that she seemed to *hear* it with her deaf ears. Degataga pressed her close against his broad chest as she collapsed momentarily into his arms. Then Madaya broke from his grasp, still screaming, shoving him out the door. Women pounding dried corn to make bread dropped what they were doing and raced to her door. Leotie arrived just in time to see Degataga fleeing. *Was he laughing as he disappeared? What had he done to her? Was she raped?* The women cradled her in their arms and tried to make sense of her blubbering sobs.

What Madaya most feared had happened. Not only was her lover dead, now Junaluska was gone, too. Crushed in spirit, she thought immediately of Nanyehi who would know what to do. One of the women ran to get her. Nanyehi raced to tell Madaya the good news: "It's not true, Madaya!" she gasped. "Degataga confessed. His story was a trick. He knows nothing about Junaluska and Nicie," Nanyehi comforted her.

Madaya crumpled into her arms. Nanyehi assured her that Degataga's uncles would determine a fitting punishment for his cruel deceit. She insisted on spending each night with Madaya until Junaluska and Nicie returned.

Two days later, Nicie did return . . . alone. They had not made it to the Healing Springs in Sitico.

Chapter Fourteen: Discovery

Historical trauma is: *cumulative emotional and psychological wounding over the life span and across generations emanating from massive group trauma.*

~ Maria Yellow Horse Brave Heart

"Madaya, this quilt is yours," Nicie told her. "I want you to wrap my body in one of the deerskin wraps that Junaluska gave us." Madaya doesn't want to believe the time has come to talk about this, *but death is not to be feared; it is part of life for all creatures,* she reminded herself. Such thoughts flooded her mind, but could not get through to her heart where she harbored intense love for her friend.

Junaluska had brought the coverlet to his wife from the Trading Post. "It's a quilt," he had told the women, "made by a woman in Charleston." She had appliqued birds on eight squares of the exquisite wrap. Every day in their village they watched these same birds: goldfinch and robin, black-capped chickadee and mocking bird, red-winged blackbird and cardinal, ruby-throated hummingbird and Eastern bluebird, with an owl perched on its own over-hanging hickory-nut branch that stretched across the top width of the quilt.

Before long all the village women gathered to marvel at the tiny stitches used to applique the colorful birds onto cotton. It had always reminded Madaya of the birdcalls she and Astooga Stooga had perfected when they were children.

"But before that time comes," Nicie whispered weakly, mouthing the words carefully for Madaya to see, "I ask two things of you, dear child," Nicie said, her eyes bright, her mind clear. Madaya laughed aloud, reminding her dearest friend that she is far more than a child.

"You are my friend, my sister, my daughter—the only daughter I have. I am blessed because the Galonlati has given you to me."

Humbled, Madaya waited, tears dripping onto her hands that caressed Nicie's hands. "First," Nicie said, "promise me again that you will continue telling your stories that we need to hear. I owe you much," she paused, breathless with exertion.

"No, no, Nicie! I owe you and Junaluska more than I can repay."

"Now, now, Madaya . . . one more thing: Bury my sacred satchel with me, for these are the symbols I treasure. You already know their stories, and it is the story that will live on as you tell it. These physical symbols in my satchel will become dust, like me. But I want you to have something to remind you of me through the years." Nicie reached into her own satchel and pulled out a woven bookmark she had made for her. Both Nicie and Madaya believed in the power of the satchel, this link to their stories. She cupped Madaya's hands between her own.

Madaya tells her that she wants to keep Nicie's treasures. "But yes, I honor your request. I can part with them because they are only symbols of your beautiful, well-lived life. It is your story that must last. And I will have this bookmark, woven by your precious hands, to remind me of you always," Madaya said, laying her head against the fluttering heart of her dearest friend, her sister, her other aduli.

Madaya mourned her losses, praying for light to shine on her path forward. That night as she rifled through her satchel, she found the nearly illegible scrap of paper on which she'd copied this hymn from the Moravian hymnal, sung at Squire's funeral in Salem:

> When rising floods my soul o'erflow,
> When sinks my heart in waves of woe,

Jesus, thy timely aid impart,
And raise my head, and cheer my heart.
~ Count Nicholas Ludwig Von Zinzendorf, translated by John Wesley

Once Nicie rested beside her husband in Robbinsville, Madaya considered returning to Salem to visit Squire's grave and to re-live her childhood memories with him. Yet, she trembled to embark on such an adventure alone. But one night, sleeping fitfully in the house where Junaluska and Nicie had filled her days with so much joy in companionship, she once again heard the strong voice of her aduli that had been silent for so long.

"Madaya! Madaya, listen to me," she called to her daughter.

"Aduli! Talk to me, help me," Madaya gasped.

"Salem is calling you; this is a good thing, the right thing for you to do. This is the answer to your prayer for light for your path."

After each pause, Madaya wondered if she was fading from her yet again and called out, "Wait! Don't leave me!"

"The past and the future will meet there," continued Aduli.

"I don't understand. What does that mean, Aduli?" The fact that she could "hear" her mother from another dimension, although not other sounds always confounded her. *Am I in another dimension, too, when I hear her?*

Excitement mounting, the next morning Madaya decided to book travel on the great Iron Horse, the Western North Carolina Railroaad [WNC RR] having recently stretched its rails from Junaluska, North Carolina, to

Asheville. Lake Junaluska, named for the mountain that honored the old chief, had recently sprung up as a meeting place for Methodists. Madaya would ride the stagecoach from Cherokee to Waynesville, then on to Lake Junaluska to board the train to Asheville. There she would again board a stagecoach to Salem, the more difficult part of the journey through the Smoky Mountains.

A Yankee had written about the railroad in derision, as being " . . . little more than two streaks of rust and a right-of-way; when the wind is just right, the fastest train on the line, the *Asheville Cannon Ball* can make 10 miles an hour!" he joked.

"Well, let them laugh," Madaya told friends who were concerned for her safety, her traveling alone, especially as a female, her venturing that great distance by rail and by coach, neither one safe from robbers and accidents and inclement weather. Aside from those possibilities, a sudden flashback landed her at the slave auction in Charleston where she was considered an imbecile because she could neither understand the strange languages of the Africans, nor the words spoken by the grinning auctioneer who spoke English with what was called a "southern drawl."

Aware that neither her clothes nor her luggage were comparable to those of more wealthy travelers—mostly men—she packed prudently, filling her soft leather travel bag, tanned by Junaluska himself. At last, proudly confident with Aduli's affirmation and the extraordinary opportunity to return to Salem once again, Madaya struggled to contain her growing excitement.

Madaya hid her satchel in the folds of her long muslin dress that she wore for travel. The deep pocket would easily hide her treasures. Her bulging journal could not hold another story, another word, so she tucked it under her bedroll. Leaving behind her moccasins, she wore sturdy lace-up shoes from the Trading Post that she bought for the trip, a bonnet that Will Thomas assured her would help her "fit in," thereby adding to her safety. Will knew that attracting the least possible attention might spare her from too many questions and curious stares, provoking trouble for one who could not hear when spoken to.

Feeling self-conscious in her unfamiliar travel-garb a week later, wearing her aduli's beads, Madaya frequently pressed her fingers against the satchel hidden deep in her pocket, while her other hand clutched the worn handle of her soft leather travel bag. A hand-woven basket held her shawl and some dried fruit and nuts and smoked venison, to be a gift for someone, although most of the food she would eat on the way. She doubted she would still recognize anyone in Salem, as she had been but a child when she left. Then the stagecoach arrived.

Late that day, waiting to board the train at Lake Junaluska that would carry her farther into the beloved Smoky Mountains, she *heard*—or at least watched—a Methodist preach in an outdoor meeting near the railroad station. While other passengers wandered about, Madaya found a seat on a back bench under a tent where the man preached.

While the Moravians, with whom she had become accustomed in childhood, exhibited little drama in their worship rituals, singing the Charles Wesley hymn at the campmeeting—that same hymn that Moravians also sang—she suddenly felt like dancing: *Why, this is as buoyant as our Cherokee dances!* She mouthed the meaningful words and hummed along the still-familiar tune. The lyrics birthed hope in her longing, though she was not sure for what she hoped. At the same time, mourning her loss of hearing in a peculiarly new way, she prayed a question: *Will I ever hear again?* Gathering courage and watching others to get the tempo, she sang with gusto this final stanza of the hymn, a call to wholeness:

> *Hear him, ye deaf/his praise, ye dumb, your loosened tongues employ/ye blind, behold your Savior come/and leap, ye lame, for joy!*

Although deaf, Madaya felt like she *heard* the singing and preaching, stirring the depths of her being. While she struggled to fully embrace the white man's religion, she prayed God would continue to cleanse her memories of injustice with forgiveness and compassion and healing.

With other passengers who listened for the train's whistle announcing its arrival, Madaya waited for the rumble beneath her feet that would signal the train's approach to Lake Junaluska. Often glancing down the tracks, she picked up a discarded newspaper and read about a tragedy that had occurred while railroad workers were building the 863-foot Cowee Tunnel near Dillsboro. With shovels, pick-axes and dynamite, they had tunneled a hole through the mountains through which that set of iron tracks could be laid.

The article included a photograph of nineteen prisoners who were assigned to work on the railroad. Chained together, all of them drowned when their boat capsized while crossing the Tucksegee River, "bound in death as in life," wrote the reporter.

Madaya cringed. *No wonder Junaluska had fought so hard to maintain the Cherokee way of life. Though ancient, it was modern enough for us, and here I am*, she thought, *caught between my simple comfort in Cherokee, teaching the syllabary, telling my story, helping the deaf, privileged in more ways than I deserve, but yet eager to submit to the selfish desire to experience new ways of living, and especially to be in my Moravian community again. Strangely, many voices call me. I am Moravian. I am Cherokee. I am American. I am a doubter. I am Christian.*

Madaya had often pondered the story of Margaret Vann, the first documented Cherokee convert to the Moravian faith in Salem. She wondered about that woman's strength and all she experienced in order to be baptized and accepted into membership in the church. After repeated attempts to find God's will, church leaders cast lots that indicated a negative response to Margaret's request.

When she at last received approbation, she served faithfully, welcomed into fellowship with those who recognized the trauma of her marriage to James Vann. He had fathered her son and children with another wife who had also left him. After his death the complicated estate included disputed business affairs, including a tavern and a ferry service, plus contested slaves that some relatives claimed were theirs, not his. With debts and loans and gossip shadowing all anyone knew about him, poor Margaret managed to escape his clutches, but in the end, she was the only one with her son who had inherited his house and assets, infuriating everyone else associated with Vann. Some praised him, confusing Madaya who wondered about those whose two sides were so pronounced. In the midst of her reverie, thankful she was not a judge, she saw other passengers, having heard the train's whistle, gather their belongings.

She welcomed the vibration of the platform beneath her, announcing its arrival. Clutching her meager possessions, she hesitated only a moment before allowing the conductor to take her elbow to assist her climb up the steps. Finding a seat, Madaya gazed in awe as the landscape outside her window appeared to move slowly away. She settled back into the calming, rocking rhythm, feeling the clickety-clack of iron on steel. *Oh, the wonder of it all!*

Boarding the stagecoach again in Asheville, she completed the rest of her journey to Salem, taking nearly two more days. Arriving at the Salem Tavern and Inn on Main Street, she stepped from the coach into fresh hay spread on the barnyard. The coach driver led the weary horses to the watering trough and grain crib. Retrieving her travel bag and basket, Madaya crossed Main Street and trudged the last few steps of her journey, across the green square to the Single Sisters House on Church Street. Hoping to find a room, at least for the night, Madaya waited in vain for someone to answer her knock at the locked door. She'd forgotten how well the sisters were protected as night gathered.

Exhausted but content to be back in Salem, she wandered down the street to St. Philips and sat on the steps near Squire's grave. Resting her chin between cupped hands, she watched brilliant crimson, yellow, orange and violet bleed from the western skies into the black canopy draped over the little village. Turning to face the gravestone, she said, "You gave me all you had, dear Squire. I didn't have enough time to show you my gratitude and my love, but I think you know! You gave me more than you ever imagined!"

She was right, but neither could she fathom in that moment the gift that Squire had left her that was yet to be discovered.

Nearly too tired to move, and dusty from the long days of travel, she longed for privacy to wash and sleep away her exhaustion. Crossing back to the Tavern Inn, she was given a bed with only one other woman in it. In fact, she was already asleep as Madaya climbed in stealthily, clinging to the edge of the bedstead, so as not to disturb her. At least there were not three strangers to a bed on this night.

Breathless with excitement, Madaya awoke at dawn on Sunday morning and slipped out to the pump on the square to draw water for a bath. Her unknown roommate had already departed. Later arriving at St. Philips, she felt at home in the old church where she and Papa had worshiped. Having been baptized and accepted into membership, she sang the hymns, read the Scriptures and drank in the familiarity, feeling as though she had never left. A young man sat with other men across the aisle from her, and a mother with four young girls sat primly beside her, all likely families of slaves. Disappointed, she realized no one looked familiar.

With a pang of regret, Madaya thought about her forbidden friend Katarina. She would be grown up now, her own age, likely married, possibly moved away. She wondered whether Freihofers would recognize her, or if she would recognize them after twenty years. Of course, the white Moravians attended the larger church on the hill to the north of St. Philips, so they would not likely connect on this day.

Wandering through the village, Madaya absorbed changes in the years since she left Salem as a child, galloping away, clinging to Junaluska on his horse after her dramatic rescue at the slave market. Even where new houses were being built, a garden site stretched behind each lot, confirming the Moravians' mantra: *at every house a garden grows*. In one of those exquisite gardens Madaya noticed a woman picking early greens and stopped to chat.

"I'm admiring your lovely garden," Madaya said in English that sounded rusty to her after so many years away. The woman greeted her in German, "Sei gegrüßt!" Then in English she said, "My name is Katarina." *Katarina? Surely, I did not understand*, Madaya thought, but gasped, "I am Madaya, daughter of Squire!" Watching her closely, she hoped she had understood the way the woman's mouth moved. Then both cry out, as if in a dream, sobbing and hugging and clinging to each other and to their past connection. Twice widowed, Katarina invited Madaya to stay with her in her little house while visiting Salem, for soon she would move into the Single Sisters House yet again.

Talking and listening to each other into the night, Madaya reached into her pocket to retrieve her *satchel* to share with Katarina, so many stories to tell. Holding up the hawk's feather that Katarina had handed to her when they parted as children, overwhelming gratitude and wonder washed over them like a giant wave. They fell into each other's arms again, weeping.

Following a delicious night of sleep, the women spilled out more memories and dreams over a breakfast of hot chocolate and toasted bread with apple butter, both of which Katarina had made.

"Ahhh, my dear, Katarina, I see that your linen bonnet is tied with white ribbon. I weep for you, dear friend." Madaya remembered that the marital status of a female Moravian was identified by the color of the ribbon that ties her cap. Empathy welled up within her awareness that she, too, had lost the love of her life when Astooga Stoga was killed in battle.

Katarina told Madaya about her first husband, the doctor, the man without whom she felt she could never live. "We met because he was the doctor who was called to treat my father when he became too ill to work. He would ask me to help him when treating my father, and I thrilled to his touch! My heart fell hard for the handsome young doctor who cared for him. My stepmother—you remember her, of course— warned me to be careful. When she married my father, I felt I was always a disappointment to her.

"But I knew very quickly that I would marry him. Soon, he was no longer 'Doctor' but quickly became 'Frederick.' But as you know about the Moravians, it was some time before the elders got the same message from the Lord that we already had! When they cast lots to determine whether we were meant for each other, the lot finally fell in our favor— as well as the Lord's.

"But, speaking of losses, dear Madaya, when a fever struck our community, although he was a doctor who brought healing to so many, he could not save himself. I lost my dearest one in the world, my Frederick, but there is more to my story.

"Sister Deborah approached me many months later about three single sisters and three single brethren whose marriages had been approved. They were to meet at their home to get better acquainted, she said, so I thought she was going to ask me to help prepare food for them after their group-wedding the next week. Oh no! Sister Deborah had something else in mind. She told me that she carried a proposal of marriage—my marriage!—to Brother Wolfgang Reich. All I knew was that I had loved my Frederick, and would always love him. So, how could I marry someone else?

"But that night, I had a dream in which Frederick appeared and said to me, 'Dear little one, rest content. Take the hand of this good man and journey on with him. It is ordained that in the world one should marry and be given in marriage.'

"This brought me great relief, Madaya, and on the day of the Lovefeast and marriage, my new husband-to-be, a shoemaker from Wachovia, recently moved from Bethlehem, and so different in appearance from my Frederick, joined with me in the vows. Following the ritual, Sister Deborah replaced the widow's white ribbon on my linen cap with a fresh ribbon of blue. When I turned to face my new husband, so shy, so reticent, Wolfgang whispered, beaming so proudly, as though he were introducing me to the President of the United States: 'My wife!' he said.

"Wolfgang told me about his dream that contributed to his decision to marry me, fears or no fears. One phobia—you know I hate to say this, my dear Madaya—was an unreasonable terror about Indians. His many fears convinced him that he could not leave Bethlehem to fulfill the call for him to go to Wachovia. But in his dream, after confessing his many fears, the Lord told him, 'Surely I will go with you. You need not fear.' All of that led to my marriage to that fine man.

"But now, here I am widowed again; that is why I shall soon move back into the Single Sister's house." She did not explain further. A startling thought penetrated Madaya's whole being: *I, too, am Moravian! God can provide me with a husband! If it is God's will,* she added, thus calming her insight with practical Moravian theology.

"Tell me, Madaya, what else is in your *satchel?* Tell me more stories! How much has happened during our many years of separation!" As they walked together on many paths through Salem, sometimes stopping at landmarks, or pausing for the view, or sharing deeply, they forgot they were simply two women telling their stories. Madaya sometimes pulled from her satchel some treasures, those physical vestiges that primed the deep well of memory about Squire and Aduli, about Junaluska and Nicie, about Sequoyah and her beloved John Astooga Stoga, until they both ended up in the graveyard of loss.

"Loss begins for all of us when we are born." Katarina, always philosophical, was the girl who figured out answers for questions, while Madaya's thoughts tumbled wildly, hoping someone else could figure out the answer.

"Our first loss is the watery protection of our mother's womb and our nourishment through our mother's placenta," Katarina spoke her thoughts. "Birth changes everything, forever!"

"We've both lost our beloved ones. When we lose a parent or child or friend, through death or betrayal , or when we lose our health, or our home . . ." Madaya shuddered, remembering the Removal and her aduli's suffering on the *nu na da ul tsu n yi.*

"But also," Katarina continued, "When we lose respect for any of God's creatures, our natural world, or when we lose our compassion, our dignity, or our innocence, our freedom . . ." The women paused often to connect each generality with real-life incidents.

Back in the little house, Madaya confided in Katarina, "At times I feel I'm destined to lose all I love; sometimes it has been my fault," she said, thinking about her lover's death. "Do you ever feel that way?"

"Listen to us, Madaya!" Both women laughed, old sages that they were, still in their youth, they saw the irony of it all. "Suffering? Yes! But privileged, blessed, thankful, too." cried Katarina. "We are alive! And, we have found each other—a miracle!"

Katarina jumped up, announcing that she had to go to work at the Salem Book Store just across the road from her house. That evening Katarina gave Madaya a gift that she purchased there. "It is my prayer that this journal can help you embrace your many losses. I've discovered that," she told Madaya, "what is found is not always identical to what has been lost." Madaya stroked the soft leather journal with its empty pages and considered those words. Her old journal back home bulged with no room left to record.

"You are wise, Katarina, you are wise. Perhaps I *can* write—in Cherokee," Madaya told her friend. "Perhaps the time has come for me to tell my story for the *Cherokee Phoenix,* before it is too late. Madaya recalled how often Junaluska expressed that possibility. She clung to a new understanding: it is the *story* itself that is sacred. The *story,* when fertilized and tended, sprouts new growth. Its seeds, carried by the winds of everyday living, spread to other fields when shared. Picking up the journal at her side, she began to write.

Sequoyah had urged her to tell her story. It was he who had brought not only condolences to Madaya when he heard about John Astooga Stoga's death those many years earlier, but who also brought the hand-written translation of the book of St. Matthew by her lover.

"If I do not return from battle," John Astooga Stoga had told Sequoyah, "please give this copy to Madaya. She knows of my obsession with this work of translating the Gospel into Cherokee. When I return, my only obsession will be to translate my intense love for Madaya," he smiled. "Also, if I do not return, please ask Madaya to write her story. The world must learn of her remarkable life, young as she is."

"Let us not talk of your not returning," Sequoyah suggested.

"But promise me, Sequoyah," he said. The two embraced before Junaluska's grandson slipped out the door, on his way to prepare for battle.

So, although she had begun to write about her life, she admitted to herself that doing so was a chore, hardly a source of energy. Too great were her sadness and losses.

That evening Madaya told Katarina, "I've resolved an ongoing struggle. I shall tell the whole story—what I lost, yes, but also what I've found." Then Madaya told Katarina about John Astooga Stoga, their love tryst, their plan to marry, her longing to be pregnant with his child, and his death for which she still blamed herself.

"Ma-dá-yaaa!" Katarina called out her musical name as though trying to awaken her from a deep sleep. "Listen! My sorrow is different from yours. Each sorrow differs from another's. Each person's grief is unique. It's all part of our human condition to grieve our losses and even to blame ourselves when what's done is done. The past takes on a life of its own, and when guilt takes the reins, crashing into first one wall, and then another, it can kill us!"

Their heads nodded and their eyes drooped as the moon set in the west. The old friends embraced again before retiring. Not even in her dreams could Madaya imagine what awaited her.

Chapter Fifteen: Tsunami

*Love is when he gives you a piece of your soul, that
you never knew was missing.*

~ Torquato Tasso

A rising early the next morning, Madaya carried the empty journal to the back steps overlooking the garden, already bursting with new life. She set Katarina's clay inkpot beside her on the stone steps and wrote in Cherokee on the first page: *Lost and Found*. As she meditated, both thinking, yet not thinking, she opened herself to feeling the morning sun scattering random gold patches in the garden, on the grape vines, filtering through the pure white dogwood blooms. Drinking in the aroma of peonies, Cherokee roses and rosemary, she breathed deeply the sweet liquor of gratitude and awe spilling over any walled-up divides in her heart.

Writing in her musical Cherokee language, in honor of Sequoyah and all he had taught her, in honor of Astooga Stoga who determined that her story must be told, Madaya began in earnest her gift to honor them, as well as Nicie and Junaluska. She recognized the power of the written word and the extraordinary gift of Sequoyah to their people. At last Madaya began to lay out the planks of a bridge she would build from past history to a new future, for herself and for her people. Words and thoughts coalesced onto empty pages. She wrote of everyday mystery and miracle, of the lost and the found. She drew a tiny flower before each entry:

>❖*Yes, I still mourn the cruel loss of my twin brothers and my edodah, and my dear aduli on the Trail, but I have an ongoing relationship with her 'spirit-presence' through my dreams. ❖After losing Junaluska, I found in Nicie the woman who has helped me tell my story, as well as Junaluska's, now to be saved for all time through the syllabary. ❖After losing my beloved Papa Squire, I got to tell him while kneeling at his grave, how much I love him still. ❖After losing my hearing, I found a new way to communicate through writing and reading lips, and teaching others who are deaf. ❖After losing my childhood friend Katarina, I found her here in Salem. ❖After losing my faith in the Great Spirit, God found me through the kindness and love of so many persons; sometimes what's lost seeks us!*

Turning the page, she continued to write:

>*I looked on the inhumanity shown to my family and nearly became like some white people who cannot understand that the Great Spirit is even bigger than their understanding of God. Their God is too small! The Great Spirit, the Creator, the Golanlati is*

beyond understanding, beyond description, far bigger than the evil around us.

Our earth and its creatures serve us human creatures—not because of their imposing size like the black bear—but because they have been created to accompany us in our earthly journey, like that lowly caterpillar who intentionally spins the cocoon to be born again, reminding me that God creates exquisite beauty out of darkness.

O God, our God, maker of heaven and earth, how great is your name, your creation, your love for your creatures!

Madaya treasured her ability to read and speak not only English and German, but also the Cherokee language of the *Ani Yun wiya*. Having learned to live with her hearing loss, she accepted the power of her words and experiences, a treasure that no one could take from her.

Through the day while her friend worked at the bookstore, Madaya wrote until her fingers cramped, allowing the relics in her *satchel* to prime the well of treasure.

Monday, 10 April 1865. Filled with anticipation, Madaya continued to write in her new journal, describing Easter week with its daily services filled with scripture and hymns to prepare both mind and heart for Easter morning.

Most unexpectedly, Katarina burst through the door where Madaya sipped sassafras tea before going out to walk and further explore Salem. "Madaya!" she gasped. "Hundreds of Union soldiers are marching into Salem! Maybe thousands! Some of them came into the store...they seem nice enough, but you must not go out alone!"

Stunned into silence, Madaya offered Katarina a cup of tea, urging her to sit down. "No, I must return to the store. The Moravian men monitor the streets, encouraging everyone to go about our work calmly. We must act naturally. Someone reported that General Stoneman is leading Federal troops to camp on the high ground above our creek, maybe three thousand men! I've heard that they've borrowed some of our horses! Borrowed? Will they return them?"

"Why here? Why now?" asked Madaya. This is Easter week!" She'd heard plenty about the war raging between the north and the south. But her Cherokee people usually travelled to Tennessee or to Georgia; some even traveled far to the north to fight. She shivered as she thought about Junaluska's war stories, and her beloved Astooga Stoga. "Wars! Will they never cease?" she cried out.

"It's reported that some soldiers caused destruction at the railroad." continued Katarina, inhaling deeply and talking rapidly. "I don't know what happened. But one of the Moravians who keeps watch on our streets saw some soldiers returning to their camp after they caused a ruckus at the railroad, and wandered back to camp through God's Acre."

"God's Acre!" gasped Madaya. "Those burial grounds are sacred to Moravians, and to any human with decency!" she spat out, surprised at her venom.

"But listen to this," explained Katarina, "several of the thirty or so Moravian home guards watched them race into the cemetery on horseback. Then one of the soldiers dismounted and took off his hat when he realized where they were. Most of the others followed his example, removing their hats and walking their horses solemnly through the cemetery."

"Oh." said Madaya. Nothing made sense. Bad in the good, good in the bad. Fleeting memories blended into a confusing collage. She was surprised to learn that Katarina already knew the story she was about to tell her. The tale that Junaluska had told about two wolves had universal meaning: "Which wolf will win, Katarina?" she asked. "The one you feed," Katarina responded as they pondered how to do that on this day.

After Katarina left the house for the bookstore again, Madaya decided to take a chance. *Maybe these soldiers aren't so bad,* she thought as she, too, cautiously stepped out the door.

As casually as possible Madaya sauntered toward Salem Female Academy where girls and young women, as well as slaves, had learned for more than a hundred years, having opened in 1772. Everything was quiet. Obviously, the students had been instructed to stay indoors. She found the path on which she had walked with Katarina and Squire to a classroom twenty years earlier; that had been her last full week with her friend until this week.

Madaya inhaled the beauty of the dell with its honeysuckle, mountain laurel and dogwood shading the bridge. Although she couldn't hear the noisy spring peepers calling from the damp azaleas sprawling near the creek that meandered behind the classrooms and dormitories, the soothing sight restored her calm. It was there that she and Katarina had wandered and splashed, and where Madaya taught her friend to catch spotted salamanders and tiny crawfish with her hands, this Cherokee child with her white friend.

Chuckling to herself, she remembered that Sister Freihofer didn't know half the mischief and escapades in which these two motherless daughters managed to indulge. Recalling those experiences had brought her pleasure during those years of enforced separation from Katarina. She told Madaya that her parents had moved to Bethabara when Sister Friehofer could no longer manage the house and her father became unable to work the farm, even with the help of slaves.

Back at Katarina's house, Madaya picked up her pen again. Now that she'd started her journal, she couldn't stop writing. Considering the losses of her own Cherokee people in the last hundred years humbled her. Wars, culture, politics had changed everyone, everything. That she knew. For the Cherokee, the change was hardly subtle. She began to write in her journal again:

No longer do Cherokee women tend the children, the farming, the cooking, the pottery-making, creating clothes from animal skins, caring for the poor and sick among us—and—taking care of the prisoners of war brought to our village by the warriors. Instead, the women now weave cloth, their looms a gift from the white man who wants them to make "real" clothes, not coverings with deerskins and bearskins for winter warmth. The white settlers sometimes even provide looms and spinning wheels for a village— usually only one at a central location shared by the women, because the equipment would dominate our small houses with only one or two rooms that house whole families. That accomplished, the women are expected to purchase wool and cotton from their European settler-neighbors who gladly teach the Cherokee how to spin on their spinning wheels and weave on their looms.

Of course, the exquisite art of basket-making with dyes made with roots and barks, leaves and twigs, is becoming a money-making commodity, often at the trading posts to which we have become increasingly dependent. Our baskets are becoming an artistic enticement to white settlers, some of whom pay dearly for their find, while the Cherokee creators are replacing many baskets for everyday use with metal containers that they, too, purchase at the Trading Post.

Madaya stopped writing to gaze at the woven river reed basket that held dried flowers and herbs that she had brought as a gift—for someone—never dreaming that *someone* would be her childhood friend. She thought about the women in her village who had learned from their mothers and aunts how to find and strip river cane; how to mix dyes from black walnuts to stain a dark brown color; boiled onion skins to produce a lighter brown; elderberries to dye strips a deep rose-red; the bark of bloodroot twigs to produce shades of yellow, while its root produced a reddish-brown color; and black from butternut. The intensity of color chosen depended upon the length of time the basket reed was submersed in stained water.

Nicie had taught Madaya basketry. Creating a basket pattern evolves slowly from memory and imagination, not from patterns or drawings. Women wove together those images that fed her spirit, arising from living with mountains and streams, with flowers and herbs, with woodlands and gardens.

Oh yes, much has been lost by our people. Madaya frowned and flipped to the flyleaf of her journal where she read again Katarina's words: *Sometimes what is found is not identical to what has been lost.* Then Madaya added these words of her own: *And some lost things are never found, like the loss of my first love, John Astooga Stoga.* She enjoyed writing his name with an artistic swirl, just as the basket-maker creates beauty out of something perceived as ordinary.

For some reason, the day's activities had sapped her energy and deposited the silt of discouragement. Then, she pulled from her satchel Astooga Stoga's handwritten Cherokee translation of the Gospel of St. Matthew, sensing comfort flow from its pages, from her lover, from her God.

The week proceeded without serious incident, although each day the residents of Salem strained to hear any suggestion of change, of trouble. Many Moravians stayed close to home, but Madaya did not want to miss Holy Week services, so poorly attended because of the soldiers' presence. So, on this day she walked to the church and welcomed the joyful Moravian Lovefeast tradition.

Watching the women in white with crisp white aprons and simple coverings on their heads serve the lovefeast buns and coffee during the service, neither she nor anyone present had any inkling that *this* day held extraordinary meaning for two of the young worshipers.

Sipping the steaming hot coffee as the choir sang, " . . . may we all so love each other," Madaya sneaked a look at the soldiers scattered across the aisle from the women, and noticed they sang lustily the same words as she did.

Following the service at St. Philips, Madaya hesitated on the steps before continuing toward Squire's grave, because she noticed the young black man who had sat across from her pew on the previous Sunday. Madaya watched him place a bouquet of apple blossoms tied with a white ribbon on Squire's grave. Puzzled, she proceeded to the grave where the two passed pleasantries and learned that both had spent their early years here. She surmised him to be about her age. Born and taught in Salem, he had lived with his mother, a free woman who worked for the doctor, he told Madaya.

"She died when I was six years-old," he said. She watched him carefully as he spoke, straining to understand his words, spoken in English. "By the way, my name is *Salem*."

Nodding toward Squire's tombstone, he said, "A great man!"

"A great man? Squire?" asked Madaya. She scrutinized his mouth as he spoke, trying to understand. "You knew Squire?" she felt her heart quicken.

"Yes, he worked for Brother Friehofer. Squire was my father," Salem told Madaya matter-of-factly. "You knew him, too?"

Speechless, Madaya gasped, still wondering whether she had understood his spoken words and their meaning.

"Are you all right?" Salem asked, concerned with Madaya's quizzical expression and the sudden silence between them. He realized that she appeared to be deaf, as she stared at him intently, her mouth open. A flashback for Madaya vividly revealed a young black boy about her age, standing alone, with tears flooding his cheeks at Squire's funeral. Surmising that he was the son of a slave, his presence at the service was hardly surprising, because many slaves were acquainted with Squire who treated everyone kindly. She had thought no more of it. Her thoughts a jumble, still unable to articulate her questions, she dropped to her knees at Squire's grave and looked up at the young man bending over her.

"In order to protect him," further explained the young stranger, squatting down beside Madaya, looking her in the face and articulating carefully, "my mother had never told Squire because both Squire and my mother would have suffered had it been known, uh, had it been known." He watched her closely, to determine whether she had understood anything he had told her.

"Known? Known what?" Madaya questioned breathlessly, still unsure she had understood his earlier comment.

"Well, a few months before my mother died, while Squire was on the Trail of Tears, she told me that Squire is my father, and to tell him about his paternity, if he ever returned to work for Brother Freihofer. When he returned, my mother had already died, and I waited for the right time to tell him. Squire was always friendly to me, but he was nice to everyone. If only I had known! If only *he* had known!

"I was nearing eight years-old when Squire died suddenly. My heart broke in pieces. I'd been waiting for the right time to reveal my mother's secret. My mother had never married because she confided in me when she knew she was dying, that she only loved Squire, but they thought it best not to marry until he was free. I dreamed of the day we would live together as family, but first my mother died, and then Squire died in that accident at the well he was digging.

"So, I attended his funeral, without either parent, although I was cared for by the wonderful doctor and his family. But, but how do you know him?" Salem and Madaya faced each other where they knelt at Squire's grave. Attempting to stand up, Madaya's legs wobbled, and Salem reached to take her by the arm, still unaware of the impact of his news on the young woman before him.

Astounded as their stories continued to unfold, yet gently as the opening of a Cherokee rose, the orphaned young adults both laid claim to *Papa Squire,* as the Cherokee woman and African man embraced as brother and sister. The young man's devout mother had named him *Salem,* a familiar word for peace-loving Moravians. She desired peace above all else, causing no trouble for her secret lover Squire, or for her dear son whose name derived from the Hebrew word שלום: Shalom, meaning restoration, wholeness, completeness, and indeed, peace.

The couple agreed to meet again for the Maundy Thursday service. Once again they sat across the aisle from each other, this time sneaking smiles and glances throughout the service. Hours later, after long conversations in which Salem gazed at his newly discovered sister in awe, they planned to meet again on Good Friday, as well as on Holy Saturday morning to continue catching up in the years since Madaya had first noticed him at Squire's funeral.

In that momentous week, Good Friday was on April 14. Brother George Frederic Bahnson—who was both bishop and pastor of Home Moravian Church—preached, but wisely omitted that part of the ritual that referred to the government because of the presence of Federal soldiers. Very few ventured out on that rainy Good Friday, with palpable anxiety still infecting the people like a plague. The bishop wrote in his journal this prayer: "May the Lord soon bring a desired end [to] this horrible war." But Madaya and Salem could not keep a lid on their joy at finding in each other a sister and a brother.

That night Madaya's aduli came to her again in a dream, but all she remembered were these strange words: *Today you will weave a new strand into your story, far too big to fit into your satchel.* Madaya jumped out of bed and questioned, *Do you not know, Aduli, that I have already found a brother?* She shook her head vigorously, trying to loosen any cobwebs, trying to re-capture only the joy in her new discovery of a brother—full of wonder—in spite of questions.

Katarina was at work in the bookstore, so Madaya informed the quiet house: "Well, at least I found Katarina again! And, a new brother!" She hugged herself, as no one else was available. She considered the safety factor in the village, but decided the presence of the soldiers should make it even safer to wander about. Madaya embraced the sunshine and warm springtime breeze. Walking up Main Street, she lowered her eyes and nodded whenever she approached a soldier. They seemed quiet and respectful enough.

After stopping at Winkler's Bakery for sugar cake, she returned to St. Philips to talk to Squire yet again. "What do you know? Why do I hear only from my aduli, but not from you, dear Squire?"

Madaya and Salem could not ignore the tsunami of emotion from which they did not want to retreat, indeed could not. The reality of what was happening consumed them. By evening, their familial affection had exploded into a love far deeper than the well that Squire had dug, that surged as deep as yet unexplored oceans of the earth, teeming with life, and color, and mystery. Aduli had been right again; this day birthed a new kind of love.

"I have something for you, Madaya. You so fully embody all that holds importance to me." She watched his lips, his expression, questioning: *How can this be happening? How could he love me? How could I love him as I do?*

"I have a gift for you, Madaya," Salem laughed and pulled a small package from his pocket to give to her with another long, slender gift, both wrapped and tied together with a small white ribbon. "Of course, Katarina helped me with this," he confessed. "Knowing how greatly you value your satchel and your journal, I made this at the pottery...not knowing then to whom I might give it. Only God knew! From this pottery inkwell you will write words, your story for your people, and perhaps for your son some day."

Unwrapping the duo, she marveled at the two tiny love-birds in a nest etched into the exquisite clay ink pot. The quill was fashioned from the red feather of a cardinal that he had caught fluttering from a nest as he walked by. "You see, Madaya? The whole universe smiles on us!"

They clung to each other as dusk and flowering shrubs protected a long, deep kiss, allowing the gift of human love to penetrate every cell of their being.

Chapter Sixteen: Freedom

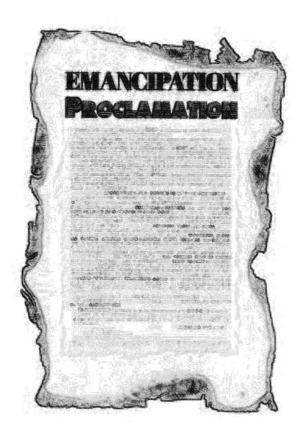

A great human sob shrieked in the wind, and tossed
its tears upon the sea—free, free, free.

~ W.E.B. DuBois

Katarina and Madaya joined Salem in the pre-dawn stillness as they gathered in front of Home Moravian Church on Easter Sunday morning before dawn. The village square filled with hundreds of worshipers, enslaved and free persons alike, waiting for the moment when Brother Bahnson stepped out of the church to signal the news that had stunned early Christ-followers two millennia earlier.

As the silent throng of worshipers marched up the road toward God's Acre, they heard the antiphonal brass choirs converging at the cemetery, answering each other in a holy conversation about resurrection, new life. The band grew and grew, two hundred-strong by the time they converged in God's Acre. Madaya whispered to Salem to tell her if they played Charles Wesley's hymn that she remembered singing on the trip to Salem. Stunned, having heard from her about that experience, he shook his head in a vigorous *yes*, and pointed to his ears and mouthed one word: "Now!" Like a vision for the blind, these lyrics running through Madaya's mind broke through her deafness to further encourage her: *hear him, ye deaf!* She did hear him.

They stood on tip-toe, watching the black eastern sky lighten. Fresh flowers from village gardens adorned each grave. It looked like spring had burst through earth to create a Garden of Eden in the night. As the sun peaked over the rim of the eastern hill, the pastor shouted to the gathered thousands: "Christ is risen!" to which they responded, "He is risen indeed!"

Easter evening brought with it two cardinals building a nest in the corner of a culvert below the young couple who watched from the bridge. With bits of string and twigs and grasses, they shaped a home for their life as a new family. Beside Madaya walked Salem, their arms linked, their hearts too full to speak, overflowing almost violently, like a great cataract after a storm, capturing and sweeping away all the debris. Everything they saw as they meandered behind Salem College was a call to rejoice, to weep, to laugh, to sing, to worship. Looking fully into each other's eyes, Madaya took her cue from Salem. Their voices spontaneously blended in exquisite harmony, drifting from the bridge over the stone culvert, along the clear stream bubbling through the dell. Even flora and fauna appeared to pause and absorb the transcendent moment. Together they sang: *Praise God from whom all blessings flow.*

They paused to sit on a stone bench by the spring. Salem placed a hand on each cheek and lifted Madaya's radiant face closer to his face until their lips touched in exquisite oneness. Their spiritual and sensual connection was too deep, too miraculous, too mysterious for explanation. Absurd as it was, they already spoke of spending the rest of their lives together, but as more than siblings, although they had just met. As night followed day, their awareness of a connection beyond their understanding emerged. Every embrace caused goldfinches to sing, children to laugh, butterflies to flutter, dogwoods to burst into bloom. Surely, the whole world smiled on them.

Down at the springhouse in the dell behind Salem College, they sat on a rock together, touching, their arms entwined as though afraid to release each other. Salem pulled Madaya to her feet and walked to the gurgling creek. Stooping, he loosened a small chunk of clay, moist and gray, and began to fashion two hearts. He pressed the edges of the two together, leaving a concave opening between the layers, then handed it to Madaya to hold while he rinsed his hands in the clear water.

"This," he explained while looking into her eyes, "represents our two hearts, fashioned into one. Our love will forever spring from this open space." He stopped, overcome with emotion. Madaya laid her hand over his, shaking her head in affirmation. Their love bubbled from the deepest recesses of their hearts as eternal as the spring beside them.

Her thoughts tumbled as wildly as her pulses. She reached up with both hands to touch his face, his eyes, his ears, his lips. They fell into each other's arms again, laughing, weeping. To be brother and sister, on their way to becoming husband and wife, was more than they could cognitively absorb in a lifetime, and certainly not in a few days. Salem walked with Madaya to Katarina's house. They agreed before parting that they would speak with the pastor to present to the elders their desire to be married. They would follow protocol. Soon, the wedding that would include three other couples recently approved for marriage was planned for a Sunday afternoon in four weeks.

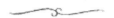

On their wedding day, Sunday, 21 May 1865, they left for St. Philip's Church, hand-in-hand. Katarina walked with them. This was the last day she could share Madaya, as she and Salem would leave for Cherokee on the Monday morning stagecoach. The couple, reluctant to part into separate pews, lingered as long as possible in the foyer before seating themselves in the respective divisions for men and women. During the service Madaya and Salem shot glances like love-arrows at each other across the aisle that separated them. Katarina reached for Madaya's hand, remembering another day they had sat together at St. Philips with Sister Freihofer who had pulled their hands apart during Squire's funeral.

Surprised worshipers cautiously watched a Union Army chaplain in full uniform stand before them. He exhorted the congregation, mostly enslaved Africans, from the text in I Corinthians 7:21 that addressed "servant, ye are bought with a price; be not ye the servants of men." A momentary shiver gripped the congregation, most of whom had suffered numerous insults and orders from white people, both their owners and the United States government, as well as during the kidnapping from their homes in Africa. Anyone in uniform was suspect.

Madaya's left-hand fingers clutched the bench that Squire had helped to build, while her right hand sweated into Katarina's hand, just as it had done years earlier. She glanced at Salem across the aisle who sat ramrod straight with his friend Eneas. One thing was certain: Salem would fight to the death anyone who hurt his beloved. *Damned be that person!* Amazing himself at the animosity he harbored, Salem shuddered, hoping no one could read his thoughts. After all, he was a free man, unlike most others in the church. He winced at the disturbing memories of the tragic torture that his friend Eneas had endured. The two men had met at St. Philips and become close friends. Sitting together, the two men glanced at each other, barely withholding judgment. *What is this all about?* they questioned, scarcely breathing as the Union Army chaplain began to preach.

Eneas had been brought from Ghana. He had arrived in Salem to work for Brother Steiner after being rescued—bought for a good price by the Moravian Church through the efforts of this good Moravian man—from the cruel master of a Raleigh plantation. He subsequently moved into the *Negro Quarter*, a neighborhood separate from Salem. While one was free, and one enslaved, the men found comfort and support in their friendship when both found lodging there.

While the Moravian community conceded that "the help of Negros in many cases is indispensable," and that [while] "it is practically impossible to ban everyone with a black skin from our Community, the board reaffirmed its prohibition on teaching trades to any blacks, slave or free."

Reluctantly, over time Eneas began telling his new friend about his treatment in Raleigh after Salem noticed the raised scars on his back that resembled a rusty washboard. He told Salem that when his pregnant wife, Mbyo, was caught with a book from their master's library, he begged his owner to spare his wife and to give him the punishment, for it was he who had stolen—or borrowed—the book, one and the same to the owner; it was he who had encouraged his wife to read aloud to him. Someone had overheard their murmuring voices and reported them to the master.

The slave owner seldom did his own dirty work, such as emptying his shit-pot or beating his slaves. At the command of the slave-owner, the accused or even the friends or family of the slave, performed his dirty work. At times an enslaved person was made to beat her own child for perceived wrong, such as the mother who was forced to beat her recalcitrant young boy who had taken an extra dipper of water in the fields where children worked alongside their parents from dawn to dusk.

So it was that without warning, one morning Eneas and his pregnant wife were led into the yard by another slave. Eneas was forced to dig a concave indentation to support his wife's eight-month pregnancy, but he assumed the hole was for his own head to rest during the beating, although it hardly conformed to his anatomy. Then the slave owner called Eneas's pregnant wife forward. She was forced to lie face down with her protruding abdomen resting in the hole, so that the baby was "protected," thanks to the master's thoughtfulness, while he commanded her husband Eneas to give her ten lashes with a leather thong laced with bits of spent bullets.

Attempting to be as gentle and merciful as possible, Eneas cried for forgiveness each time he swung the leather thong onto his wife's back as she whimpered. He was willing to "beat" her himself because he would do the dastardly deed with as little force as possible. Obviously guilty of two crimes, of stealing from the master's library and teaching his wife to read, Eneas knew he "deserved" much worse, but was outraged at the master's cruelty to his wife. Both were literate from their years together in the mission boarding school in Ghana, but the slave owner assumed that Eneas had taught his wife to read—against the law, of course.

As she was led away, stumbling and bleeding, Eneas was called to stand facing the cottonwood tree with his arms wrapped around the trunk. Another slave tied a sisal rope firmly around his waist before completing the task for the master: twenty-five lashes for *his* crime, lacerating his back with the same bloody whip with which Eneas had beaten his wife. The lashes on his back shredded the brown skin, stripping it to tear into the musculature beneath it.

Thankful they had survived, Eneas and Mbyo comforted each other as their "protected" first baby was born dead later that night. Two years later, having been brought to Salem by the Moravians who had rescued the couple, Eneas had leaned heavily on his new friends, especially Salem. That's when the next tragedy hit him: his wife died in childbirth along with their second son, a stillborn infant.

So, on this day, Salem and Eneas gazed sternly at the Union Army Chaplain, the Rev. Clark, who sounded official and congenial enough, but was white as cotton in the fields. Oh yes, they had witnessed such calm on other occasions, but the whole congregation listened, stunned, to the announcement that followed the Army chaplain's sermon:

The Emancipation Proclamation, the officer intoned,
By the President of the United States of America:

A Proclamation.

Whereas, on the twenty-second day of September, in the year of our Lord one thousand eight hundred and sixty-two, a proclamation was issued by the President of the United States, containing, among other things, the following, to wit:

"That on the first day of January, in the year of our Lord one thousand eight hundred and sixty-three, all persons held as slaves within any State or designated part of a State, the people whereof shall then be in rebellion against the United States, shall be then, thenceforward, and forever free; and the Executive Government of the United States, including the military and naval authority thereof, will recognize and maintain the freedom of such persons, and will do no act or acts to repress such persons, or any of them, in any efforts they may make for their actual freedom.

While gasps and sounds of weeping and exclaiming reverberated through the congregation at St. Philips, with brief calculations, some wondered why the official announcement had not reached them two and a half years earlier. Moments later, everyone mingled, no longer talking in whispers, but breathlessly questioning, exclaiming, with an occasional *Amen!* Or, *Praise the Lord!* Or, *Did he say 1863? This is 1865! Is this one more empty promise? What will this mean for us now? Nothing has changed for us in those years since the President proclaimed freedom for enslaved persons, years ago!* On and on their exclamations and questions clouded what might have been pure celebration.

Reaching toward Salem, Madaya called to him, seemingly stunned by the news. The aisles overflowed and they could not reach each other. Katarina realized that perhaps Madaya had not fully grasped what the officer had announced. She turned Madaya to face her and cupped her chin in her hands and said with tears running down her cheeks: "The slaves are free, Madaya! Squire is free!"

One of few white persons present, Katarina pushed Madaya forward into the aisle toward Salem. He wrapped one arm around Madaya and held her shoulders as he explained excitedly, pausing frequently to add: *Do you hear me?* as she watched his mouth and expression intently. Once assured that she understood, Salem pulled Madaya through the aisle toward the site of Squire's grave in the churchyard to tell him the astounding news; the official word had been spoken. Squire was free.

Falling on her knees beside Squire's gravestone, in an emotional rendezvous with the spirit of Squire, Madaya blurted out the news: "You are free, *Papa Squire*! You are free!"

They ran toward Katarina's little house hand-in-hand, breathless with joy and excitement. Their wedding was scheduled for three o'clock, but Katarina announced, "First, this day calls for dinner at the Tavern! President George Washington ate here," she laughed, "but our celebration *today* hallows this place much more significantly!"

This day called for a celebration! Katrina led her friends to the Tavern for lunch before the scheduled wedding later that afternoon. While waiting to be seated, a white man—an owner of slaves?—expounded rather noisily about the inconvenience perpetrated by the announcement in the church. He had attended because the Union chaplain, apparently a friend, had urged him to be present. Suddenly angry, the man pulled from his pocket a copy of the proclamation that had been read in the service that morning. With some vehemence, he tossed it into the fire where it landed toward the outer edge. Salem who stood closest, thrust his arm into the flames and snatched up the copy, its edges already charred, and pressed it to his breast. Other guests silently looked away without comment. Salem held it up triumphantly and announced to any who would listen: "Justice eclipses convenience," and handed the singed document to Madaya.

Still waiting to be seated at the Tavern, the young people gathered with others around the fireplace to chat about the momentous morning. Earlier, a downpour had drenched everyone with much-needed rain during a serious drought. One pastor suggested they had experienced "a drought of justice and emancipation." A drought indeed! Of course, some felt "inconvenienced," he said, not only by the rainstorm, but more especially by the sudden release of enslaved persons, leaving some owners mightily bothered. Certainly, even some "good Moravians" felt "inconvenienced" on that day.

When seated, Eneas—himself free at last—offered a prayer of Thanksgiving for the happy couple and for the pronouncement in church, intensely aware of the extraordinary day these friends witnessed together.

The couples could not ignore the imminent wedding, but the enormity of the President's proclamation led ultimately to conversation about his recent murder. Although all four had witnessed much pain, suffering and tragedy in their young lives, they cringed with the knowledge that Abraham Lincoln had suffered the indignity, the tragedy of assassination by one of the country's white citizens, in a theatre, on Good Friday, no less!

"Well," remarked Eneas, "at least, it was not one of us. It was not an African or an Indian, it was . . ." Salem held up a hand. "Ahh, actually, my friend, he was 'one of us,' a citizen of this country—of his country—of our country, one of the human race. Yes, friend, it *was* the action of one of us," he said, his voice quavering. "We are in this together." Later, in the quiet of the evening, several Moravians wrote about the momentous day.

Eneas recorded in his *Lebenslauf,* his memoir, additional history that he wanted to preserve for all time. Often completed or even written in its entirety after the death of a Moravian, the memoir was usually prepared by the pastor, and generally dealt with the spiritual condition of the deceased person. But Eneas, both educated and baptized, knew that his story could describe details and bring clarity to the history of some enslaved Africans that needed to be passed on. The announcement made on this day would become part of an emotional transcription of the President's proclamation. Eneas could do no less than pay tribute to his deceased wife Mbyo and his two sons who now would also experience freedom, had they survived.

In his own handwriting, the enslaved African Maximilian E. Grunert wrote in his diary about that day: "The church was crowded with colored people, and a few whites. Rev Clark [the chaplain] encouraged [the slaves] to industry, honesty and pie. Br. Brahnson closed with remarks and the Lord's Prayer and singing." Interestingly, he did not mention the Emancipation Proclamation read by the chaplain. Perhaps it was because the enslaved persons *did* know, had known earlier. News travels, but the looming question was: *Why now? Why not a long time ago? Why does Justice travel so slowly?*

Not only the Moravians, but also the *white pastor* of the African Methodist Episcopal [A.M.E.] church in Wilmington, North Carolina, was "mightily put upon" as another chaplain in the Union Army, William H. Hunter, took charge of that pulpit, announcing that: "a black man as ever you saw preached to the Congress of the United States. Another colored man was admitted to the Supreme Court as a lawyer. One week ago you were all slaves; now you are free. Rebels have been driven back in confusion and scattered like chaff before the wind."

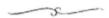

Following the simple marriage ritual late that afternoon for four Moravian couples, Salem and Madaya finally returned to Katarina's home to prepare for their trip and to spend the night together before leaving for Cherokee together. *Together!* Each of them mouthed the miraculous word: *together*.

Katarina had retired early, but had written in a note to the couple of her joy in their union, a vivid reminder that not too long ago she and her late husband had lain together in that room next to hers. She had her own losses to think about. Reading these words of comfort in her Bible, although not written for her, she clung eagerly to God's message to the Babylonian exiles through their prophet Jeremiah: "For I know the plans I have for you. They are plans for good and not for disaster, to give you a future and a hope." Embracing that promise, she was content.

The newly married couple read her note to them together—at last, *together!* Eagerly retiring to their little nest, they became one with each other in superlative joy and passion.

The next morning Madaya set out for Cherokee, not only with her brother-husband Salem, but also with more than a satchel, overflowing with love and discovery: Madaya's new journal, written in Cherokee, about *Lost and Found*. She would freely admit to all who would hear her story, she had *not* lost everything! *One doesn't, you know,* she wrote. *There is always more, the grace of abundance, of gratitude, of self-discovery, of miracle.* This Madaya believed.

Chapter Seventeen: Miracle

Miracles are a retelling in small letters...the very same story which is written across the whole world in letters too large for some of us to see.

~ C. S. Lewis

Salem yearned to learn Cherokee ways. A free black American, he absorbed like a sponge the mores of his wife's people. Human dignity for both had been attacked and lacerated, but now restored, they were one, united yet separate, equal yet unique. Salem looked at his new wife as they jostled along in the stagecoach to a new identity together in Cherokee. He tilted Madaya's face to his own so she could watch his lips move with this message:

"My dear love, like my name *Salem*, we both are restored to wholeness, to peace. I had never expected to find release from my failure to tell Squire that he was my father. All these years I had lived without hope. This embarrasses me, because you found ways to forgive others and yourself."

"Yes, but I need to tell you something, dear husband," Madaya began, moving even closer as they bumped along. "You, Salem, you have already brought me a measure of peace that I thought never to attain again. Even with my deafness, you grasp what not many others can do. Yes, Nicie and Nanyehi understood me, but your understanding reaches even more deeply.

"Let me explain. When a person is blind, like Bent Twig in our village, everyone admires her courage, her abilities, her presence, anything she accomplishes. Tell me, who admires the courage of a deaf person? Bent Twig easily joins every conversation. And, when she is old, people will— whether they know her or not—will continue to invite her into their conversations.

"Deaf persons are usually known for their oddity, not their kindness, not their courage, not their wisdom. As a deaf child, I was considered an imbecile. Do you understand what I'm telling you?" Madaya was hopeful, although they were barely beginning to grow their understanding and acceptance of each other. So much they had not had time to explore.

"Maybe I do, maybe I do not." Salem studied her closely, astounded by her beauty and love for him. "But, what does that mean for you?" he asked her.

"Usually, when someone is deaf, the person who is talking easily becomes annoyed. When I ask people to repeat what they just finished telling me, some say: 'Oh, it's not important.' But to me, it *is* important. Then, it's easy for me to blame the hearing person for not speaking clearly, or not looking at me so I can read her lips, or mumbling rather than articulating clearly, or talking quietly, or running their words together in the way our thoughts tend to do. So, while the problem is *mine*, I secretly blame the one who is speaking. And, that person blames *me* for not understanding. Does this make any sense, Salem?" Tearful, Madaya looked at Salem, tugging at Salem's tender heart, trying to make her dearest one understand.

Salem pulled Madaya even closer and started to respond, but Madaya laid a finger on his lips and continued. "But you, Salem . . ." Tears trickled down her cheeks as Salem blotted them with his finger-tips.

Madaya continued in a rush of words and love, "You understand me, and hear me, and love me, even when I don't understand. You are patient; you are kind; you . . ."

Laughing, Salem kissed her and showed a dismissive gesture to stop her. Grasping her shoulders, as he faced her he said, "*You* are the patient one; *you* are kind; *you* are forgiving, and I AM PROUD OF YOU, AND PROUD TO BE YOUR HUSBAND!" he almost shouted. They had been talking quietly, but others in the coach smiled at his outburst, having been introduced earlier to the couple. In spite of the outburst, they surely were not quarreling.

Ignoring the other passengers, Salem kissed her as passionately as he dared with others watching them. Their connection was far deeper than any stranger could fathom. "Thank you, dearest one. It's no wonder that I *hear* you better than anyone I know," she whispered into his ear, dissolving into his embrace.

Although already married as Moravians in Salem, both Madaya and Salem began to prepare for their Cherokee wedding. Typically, the suitor offered a gift of prime venison to the parents of the beloved with his offer to marry their daughter. But without parents, without Junaluska and Nicie as stand-ins, this gesture was impossible to fulfill. Besides, Salem would not know how to hunt. *Have I already failed test number one?* he asked himself. But the village medicine man performed rituals that confirmed their acceptability for marriage.

One night, local male friends of the newcomer carried Salem with much hilarity to the council house, away from the women. The council house is no miserly structure. Built on top of a mound with open sides, it is a seven-sided, open building where all seven clans sit with their own clan members during meetings. The roof peaks, with a hole in the center of the thatch to allow the smoke from the fire—burning continuously—to ascend. The young married men joked and issued ribald warnings about their union as man and wife. Amused, Salem had already passed that initial stage in his marriage. Even the marriage of a Cherokee to an

African was not unknown in the village. Salem embraced their acceptance of him into Cherokee life, feeling content and at home.

Meanwhile, the women feted Madaya with a feast of favorite foods, and waited on her with tenderness and adoration. She and Nicie, whose presence Madaya sorely missed, had taught many of these women to read and write using the new syllabary. When Bent Twig knelt before her to offer best wishes, Madaya remembered her conversation with Salem in the stagecoach. Tears like gentle rain washed over both of them as they embraced in mutual understanding of and appreciation for each other.

Suddenly aware of her sisters' admiration and respect for her and the husband she had chosen, Madaya basked in the accolades poured out from her own people. With laughter and singing and dancing, the women crowned her with their blessings and prayers—and good advice from those acquainted with marriage, that, of course, is neither understood nor accepted by young lovers.

The sun-splashed day arrived at last. As men gathered in the council house, women entered to stand on the opposite side. Salem stood, surrounded by new friends, gazing across the room to Madaya whose joy bubbled like the river-rapids, filling every cell of her being. Although Salem had yet to kill a deer or any other animal, he carried a venison roast to offer his bride, one that he had lovingly prepared with assistance from the amused women. It symbolized his promise to provide meat. Madaya carried a fresh ear of corn, assuring all that she was prepared to plant and harvest to provide bread for their sustenance.

Each also carried a blanket. Madaya cradled Nicie's quilt, feeling the presence of both her and Junaluska. As the two walked slowly toward each other, they met with their blankets open. Madaya folded them together—her quilt and his blanket—symbolizing their unity in sharing the same bed, the same future. The announcement followed in Cherokee: *The blankets are joined!*

Weeks later, the news bolted like a flash of lightning to light up the whole village: Madaya is with child! The women gathered in the Oconaluftee River to pray, as was their custom. They invoked the Great Spirit for a successful pregnancy, an uncomplicated delivery and a long, happy life for the Cherokee-African offspring. Madaya, having experienced much trauma in her lifetime, longed for even more than most young mothers would think to express. With the changes among her people and the young nation to which she belonged, she prayed, like Solomon in the Hebrew tradition, for wisdom, for courage to teach and nurture her child in this strange new world in which he or she would live.

Madaya felt the spirit-presence of Junaluska and the strong women in her lifetime, not only her aduli and Nicie, but also Nanyehi and Katarina who rejoiced with her. Both she and Salem sensed the blessing of their beloved Squire and Precious.

When the time came, Madaya felt her responsive body answer the call of birth pangs experienced by mothers everywhere, from the beginning of time. *We are one, we mothers give everything we have, our determination, our strength, our courage to this moment. We welcome this day, this child.* Madaya understood.

Clinging to her aduli's assurance in a dream during the previous night, Madaya embraced the process of birthing: *Believe, my dear child, believe in the miracle.* That was the short message, nothing more. Belief in the miracle and mystery of childbirth gave her strength to breathe deeply. Push and breathe. Push and breathe. Squatting, with Salem bracing her back as she pushed, Madaya watched the infant's dark crown slide onto the soft skins laid out beneath her.

"It's a bow, not a sifter," someone announced. A boy–child sucked in the air, blinking and kicking in his new world. He welcomed his own arrival with a mighty howl that reverberated throughout the small room and into the village. Madaya gasped, acknowledging the miracle of her son's birth and the sound that shook her to the core of her being.

Weeping, she tried to communicate to any who would listen in the excitement:

"I *hear* him...I *hearrrr* him..." she cried out, panting with exertion.

"Madaya! What? You *hear* him?" Disregarding protocol dictating his position behind her, Salem fell forward to kneel at Madaya's side, to smother her with kisses.

"I *hearrr* himmm!" Madaya's cry co-mingled with the cries of the infant, a celebration cradled in blood and tears, the messy stuff of life, yet saturated with joy and awe. As though waking from a deep sleep, her body opened initially to a cacophony of sounds, until baby-cries and laughter coalesced into a finely tuned symphony to fill her ears, her whole body and spirit.

Like wildfire the news raced through the village: Madaya can *hear*! *Atsutsa sdiga Chunaluska* has arrived! Unlike most newborn Cherokee babies, her baby is already named. The son of a Cherokee mother, the boy-child began his life not only as Cherokee, but also as the namesake of the beloved Junaluska and heir of African grandparents that included his parents' own courageous Papa Squire. Madaya treasured the ongoing spirit-presence of her aduli, and believed that she with her edoda rejoiced in this miracle of which they, too, were a part.

Choosing a different spelling than Junaluska's for her son's name, Madaya recognized that names evolve through a lifetime of experiences. But the legacy was his. The profound connections between his parents and grandparents made believers in Aduli's prophecies, as well as Madaya's firm faith in the God of miracles she honored.

Later that night, listening, oh the bliss of that word, that experience, Madaya watched Salem leave to carry the placenta up the mountain. Madaya laughed aloud, loving the sound of her own voice. Dancing upward, climbing ever higher, jumping over rocks and skirting trees, bearing the pottery bowl with the placenta that had nourished their baby, the new father—the edoda—stepped lightly in his moccasins and deerskin pants. "Look, Squire!" he lifted the bowl heavenward with both hands and laughed aloud.

Ten days later, Madaya tenderly lifted from her baby's naval that last shriveled vestige of his physical connection to her before birth. Placing the tiny brown, dry stem into a small rabbit-skin pouch, she knotted the tie and slid it into her story-satchel.

Chapter Eighteen: Story

How much more like a [satchel] were our stories? They held our fear and hurt and resentment and anger, a place to order our disorder, a direction for our directionlessness.

~ Maritole's father: *Pushing the Bear*

Part One: 1891

Little persuasion was necessary. Chunaluska, now 24 years-old, handed the acceptance letter to his mother Madaya. In it, he was offered work at the Gottfried Aust Pottery in Salem that had become renowned for its fine artistic creations. His father Salem had already worked with the potter as an apprentice for several years prior to finding—and marrying—his mother Madaya. His grandfather Squire had aspired to do likewise following his indenture with Brother Freihofer, so when his life was cut short—young as Salem was when he heard about the plan after his father's death—he determined to do that himself one day, to apprentice himself to a master potter at Gottfried Aust Pottery. And now, Chunaluska would live that dream.

Although Aust was no longer living, it was he who had found the red clay in Bethabara, built a kiln, hung a sign announcing his business within the year after moving to Salem, and even fired a "set of mugs of uniform size" for the Moravian Lovefeast within short order. Aust also trained apprentices for thirty-three years in the art of pottery. His successor began the trend of producing animal bottles, from turtles to foxes, to respond to the market for "fancy" decorative arts in the nineteenth century. And, as Moravians, the potters also continued to create pieces representing Christian iconography.

Chunaluska recognized his good fortune to work with potters who would carry on their tradition of excellence for one hundred and fifty years in Salem. While they had changed methods and even moved toward less practical but more artistic objects to accommodate the growing market, they continued to showcase their superb work. The earthenware of Daniel Krause enticed visiting potters, both to learn from and to praise his creative excellence, as Chunaluska learned and watched.

Overjoyed, Madaya and Chunaluska prepared to spend at least the year of 1891 in Salem. Finding it difficult to maintain calm with their emotions bubbling, their excitement mounted even as their friends and neighbors in Cherokee had wept to see their preparations for leaving.

"Just for a year," they promised, for this is what the officials at the pottery had offered. Chunaluska's pottery provided a livelihood for him and Madaya following the death of her beloved Salem, the father of Chunaluska. At first, the whispers about his work did not please the Cherokee men who wanted Madaya's son and namesake of Junaluska to learn the fine points of warring as it became necessary. Pottery was women's work.

Having emerged from the Civil War, the Cherokee already feared rumblings of more battles among tribes as well as national leanings toward war, even overseas, some suggested. Madaya recalled Nanyehi's commitment to peaceful solutions; she had learned the hard way with the loss of her husband Kingfisher. But war appeared to be the way of the world, if not its eventual demise as brothers killed off one another in escalating numbers.

As mother of Chunaluska, Madaya boasted of his fine taste and extraordinary artistic ability. It was a display of his pottery that had appealed to a group of potters from Salem who visited Cherokee earlier that spring. His detail and craftsmanship astonished them. They would pay him for his work, they said, but he would need to live in Salem and work six days a week at the Gottfried Aust Pottery.

Edward Belo, known for his generosity, had built an extraordinarily massive Greek-revival house on Main Street in Salem for his family that included seven children. His three sons served in the Confederate Army during the Civil War. One son offered Madaya and Chunaluska two rooms for a small rental fee. Madaya would tutor several children in Salem in arithmetic and writing while her son worked in the pottery next door. Nearing sixty years of age, Madaya relished her new opportunity.

Perhaps she and Katarina might connect again! They had exchanged a few letters, but Madaya's sudden plans for departure gave her no time to post her old friend who now lived in Bethlehem, back in Pennsylvania. Within two weeks both mother and son were ready. With the loss of her dear husband and the father of her son a year earlier, Madaya had plunged perhaps too quickly into writing for the The Cherokee Phoenix newspaper, telling her stories and encouraging other women to do the same.

The women did not want her to leave, so Madaya met with the women yet again, telling them she planned to return. "With or without a story-satchel, or a journal, your story deserves to be heard," Madaya reminded the Cherokee women who admired her, as well as her stories. "You do have a voice," she said. "For some of you, telling your story may follow other pathways." Madaya glanced at Marigold who spent her days designing quilts to tell her story. Another drew pictures of their village, their mountains, and even her family who honored her work. Even Madaya's own son Chunaluska told his story through his exquisite clay creations.

The women had accustomed themselves to gathering in the evenings, "just the way our ancestors did hundreds—no thousands—of years ago," someone explained their practice. Wanting a name for their activity, most unexpectedly, Chunaluska suggested the one they liked best: *ada ni di ut sa ti na*, translated in English: *the Giveaway*. This would be something one treasured so greatly that she wanted to keep it, but, too precious to keep only for herself, she would give it away, making it a true gift for the receiver. Especially delightful were the gifts passed on to grandchildren who treasured this connection to their enisi.

"All of it, any of it, we can pass on," Madaya reminded the women. And who better than she could facilitate this life-giving, life-preserving activity? Of course, as the women talked, or read aloud what they all now could write in Cherokee, some memories, some experiences harbored deep pain, intense regret, unbearable guilt. But invariably, such tales also unlocked secrets, enabling them not only to empathize, but also to share their own anguish with one another. "The *story*, when fertilized and tended, when remembered and shared, sprouts new growth as it spreads," Madaya reminded them.

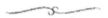

Finally back in Salem again with her son, Chunaluska, Madaya picked up her journal often. She embraced the possibility that others might even read her story one day, providing one more link between past and future, in honor of Astooga Stoga, no, in honor of Salem, or Junaluska, or Sequoyah, no, in honor of *Story*.

Occasionally Madaya carried her journal, not her heavy satchel, so she could make notes through the day. Realizing one evening that the journal was missing, she panicked. Rushing into the streets from their comfortable little rooms at the Belo House, she searched everywhere she had been that day, from the gardens behind the Single Brothers House to the pottery where she had watched Salem work. She also worried that she may be going the way of the forgetful old *enisi. But*, she asked herself, *what might I still learn from this loss?* Experienced in this task, she had learned the ritual repeatedly throughout her life until it had become habitual to ask the question, even if not discovering an answer.

Later that evening, weary with the day's activities that included tutoring several Moravian children, she considered her most recent loss. As she could not write in her journal, instead she sat in her bed doing something she had not done for a long while. Pouring out the contents of her satchel, one by one she picked through the treasures. From the little brown pebble that reminded her of another life-changing day in Salem when she was five years-old, to the pitifully ragged puppet Junaluska had brought her from Washington, from Thistle's horse-hair braid to the hawk's feather from Katarina, she laughed at some memories and cried over others, cleansing her mind and spirit.

Finally, even as she noted the empty spot on the little round table by the bed where her inkwell and quill sat alone without the journal, she welcomed a conversation with Chunaluska. As usual, when ready to sleep—especially since losing Salem—she held her satchel close to her bosom, shifting the bulky items several times to allow a more comfortable repose. Moments later, she slept, comforted somehow in spite of the missing journal and the objects pressed against her heart—some of them inside, some of them in the satchel.

During the night, a voice called her, a voice she had not heard for a long while:

"Madaya!"

"Aduli!" she answered.

"You are troubled with yet another loss, dear child. But hear this: you will not find your journal; look for it no longer; you will not see it again. Although you still have your satchel, remember that Nicie asked you to bury her satchel with her. That was a wise thing, for it is the *story* that is sacred, that is valuable, not the little earthy relics to which you attach importance. Remember, dear Madaya, it is the *story,* not the satchel, not the *stuff* that must last. While your satchel will disintegrate with time, one day, someone will find your lost journal. She will continue your story, continuing to build that bridge between the past and the future. Until then, you can begin telling your story in new ways."

Madaya sat straight up in bed. "I know that, Aduli, but I still want my, my *stuff.*" Madaya repeated the new word that was already familiar to her aduli. Madaya had recently heard the word elsewhere, referring to any collection, generally unimportant and without value to most other persons, the woman had explained to her. But to Madaya, these items in her satchel were invaluable treasures, no matter what others thought about them. *New ways? Someone will find the journal? She will continue my story? Who is* she? *What does this mean?*

Moonlight shone from the western sky through the high window. All was quiet, serene, filled with light. Wide-awake now, she felt for her satchel and smiled when she felt its tangible presence. But, its importance, her aduli had said, was in the *story,* the story that never ends as it connects with others since the beginning of time, to the end of time, link after link after link, never ending.

The next morning Madaya, sans journal, hurried to Salem Book Store to purchase another, then continued to Salem College. Opened in 1772 with three students, it had never closed its doors to any girl or woman, not even during the Civil War. Remembering the day about three thousand Union soldiers had marched into Salem reminded her that she had seen more in her lifetime than most other women she knew. But now, here she was with her precious son, Chunaluska, the grandson of Squire. They had visited his grave even before going to the Belo house. He and Salem would be so proud of them both.

Bounding into the office of the single sister's house that morning, Madaya made her request. "I am doing some research," she told a young student at the desk. "Can you tell me how to find out whether any Cherokee girls have attended the Academy or the College?"

Within minutes she was seated before a large catalog that held the names and other pertinent—though not personal—information about its students. "You see, I am Cherokee," she told the young assistant. "Having lived in Salem for several years as a child, I attended the Salem Female Academy. But I did not know other Cherokee students here. Their stories interest me."

She had to smile at this admission. Of course, *story* would always entice her; she had already bought a new journal to replace the lost one. Then she stared wide-eyed at the information she retrieved.

Remarkably, even while Madaya walked "the trail that made us cry," Jane Ross, the daughter of a Cherokee chief, had been enrolled at Salem Academy, but had left school in order to walk with her family on the westward journey. Of course, the two had not met, as Madaya was only four years-old. Then she learned that Sally Ridge, the daughter of another chief was the first Native American to graduate from the school. Breathless with excitement, Madaya continued to read and take notes in her new journal. *Was this what Aduli meant?* she wondered, *telling the story in new ways, like researching, so she might learn the stories and pass them on?*

Part 2: 1915

Eighty years-old now, back in Cherokee alone again, Madaya sat with her satchel in her lap, sifting through its contents. Although the story-satchel was heavy, she still liked feeling the weight of it, linking her to the past. *I lived a glorious past; I am at home with it*, she mused.

She rummaged through her memories that she'd kept vital with the acquisition of these relics that lay scattered across her bed. They had become the catalyst for her stories, whether spoken or written or even acted out in her dreams or imagination. *Human beings can do that,* she mused, *but can animals, especially wolves and dogs? They have memory.*

Madaya recalled the story about one dog—whether legend or not she did not know—who had found his way back to Cherokee after having been taken from his owner, an old man who had chosen citizenship in North Carolina rather than walk the Trail. But a soldier snatched up the dog for his own and forced him to walk with him, a distance of twelve hundred miles.

Within days after arrival in Oklahoma, the dog disappeared. Although the owner back in Cherokee had died, nine months later his family recognized the skinny, pitiful dog that showed up one day, cocking his head just the way Moonlight used to do to ask a question. *Of course, dogs can remember and feel connections,* Madaya concluded.

These many years later Madaya, sitting with her satchel emptied into her lap, picked up a string of beads. Colorful, they were a happy reminder of her dead aduli who had become a heroine to her daughter. Often appearing to her in dreams, Aduli imparted wisdom and empathy, courage and strength, even at that late stage of Madaya's long life. She fingered each bead that seemed to represent prayers, like a rosary prayed by the devout. Madaya recalled the moment Junaluska had given the beads to her. It was he with Squire who had buried her aduli along the Trail, and who kindly thought to remove the necklace to give to her little daughter.

Madaya had heard rumors in the village about some of her people wanting to create a drama about the Cherokee story to be acted on stage so that visitors could learn about their rich—if tragic—history. Of course, Madaya had learned to observe such spectacles as she re-lived those experiences of her lifetime.

Aduli had been right again. Madaya never found that journal that bulged with her written memories, but often she wondered who might find it, and wished she could be present to walk through it with her. But that was not to be.

Part Three: 2015

A hundred years later in Salem—now known as Old Salem in North Carolina—an extraordinarily loud pounding at the front door sent me scurrying to answer. Three men from Duke Power asked me to move the car parked in front of the Stockton Missionary House next door. Not knowing the owner, I called several persons to expedite its removal so workers could cut off the gas lines in the old house. Obviously, at last the decrepit old house with its dangling shingles and sagging porch would come down.

From archeologists to historical preservationists, the arguments between Winston-Salem and Old Salem, between the historical purists and the modern progressives grew, then withered, then sprouted again, then seemingly died an unworthy death. Given a year to find a buyer, who actually would not have to purchase the house, but only move it elsewhere, the community—especially neighbors—watched and waited. Of course, a house can be moved. Some examined the possibility, even imagining a handsome, grand abode with its wide front porch that would be reached by a winding, tree-lined lane, but moving it was completely impractical for any who were interested. The slow demise of the Stockton House escalated when its tenants found other housing.

Giant boxwoods and flowering trees and shrubs around the property had already been cut down a year earlier. When asked whether they would cut down the crape myrtle if I tied myself to it, they said not as long as I was in it, but they would surely return later to do the job. It would come down.

One morning, if not a historic dinosaur, what looked like a Disney-set monster with giant steel jaws arrived to accomplish its work in a day. Great clouds of dust were somewhat quelled by the man who pointed a powerful stream of water onto the crashing debris. Within two days, nothing but the footprint of the Stockton House remained, looking extraordinarily small. Its paved, though crumbling driveway was yet untouched. The lure of a kiln buried several feet below it was reported to hold nineteenth century pottery from the Gottlieb Aust era. Questioning how anyone could lay a driveway over such a historic treasure, I then remembered the site was not considered historic at the time. How frequently does every generation run rough-shod over what often is a treasure, or, if not, at least harbors a ghost of the past? For a long time the remnant of the Stockton Missionary house waited, while visitors to Old Salem often passed by without a glance.

The sunken, pock-marked and cracked cement slab of the house-basement was now all that remained, along with a set of five concrete steps leading down into the pit from the southeast corner. It looked small, barely reflecting what had once stood there, even as a museum's ancient shrunken head is a poor intimation of the human being to whom the skull had once belonged before the misfortune of beheading by a cannibalistic tribe.

When the big day finally arrived, archeologists and their assistants began to mark off sections that would engorge its buried treasure. Fascinated, I watched, and even begged to help, but—reasonably so— my offer was disregarded as one might dismiss a kindergarten child observing the action, offering to help dig in a giant sandbox. But night after night, at least when moonlight waned, I stood there, shivering with the immensity of it all. Immense because families had lived there, because the Moravian "missionary house," as it was called, had gathered beneath its protective walls, children, pastors, bishops, maybe kings...of course, I let my imagination run wildly, rough-shod over the *real* history to create my own story. (That's what writers do.)

One night after a heavy rain, I donned boots and told my husband I just wanted to "check on things." He's a generous, understanding man, given to pampering—and protecting—those he loves. Suspicious, he offered to go with me, but I told him I wouldn't be long. I just had to slip into the pit; one never knows what might surface after a rain. With great care I slipped under the police tape guarding the site, feeling a twinge of conscience, and stepped gingerly down those back steps of rock and cement chunks. I felt for my flashlight, and figured my husband would watch from the dining room window that faced the pit. Even if I fell into the muddy darkness, he would rescue me. Feeling safe, I shone the beam into puddles and along roughly hewn walls.

At least no snakes, no monsters down here, I thought. *This is silly of me.* With gloved fingers—of course, I would not use even a garden spade to disturb the sacred place. Clinging to the history of this space, thinking of those potters who had worked and created right here, I shivered in awe.

Choosing one spot, I persevered, feeling for just the right space that was sure to give me, well, squishy mud. Or perhaps a pottery shard! Even the thought quickened my pulse. But even that I would have to put back into the place where I found it, just as a decent fisherman would not keep the fish he had caught when out of season, or when too large, or too small, or one of an endangered species. No, I'd definitely replace it where it belonged.

Running my gloved fingers along the northern wall nearest the driveway, I thought if I found any pottery, it would likely be here. Not that my reasoning was accurate, but, I did envision such a find. That's when my foot felt something not so soggy as most of the ground surrounding me. Steadying myself by leaning against the wall of the foundation, I wiggled the toe of my boot deeper into the space around whatever was buried there. Stooping to grasp one corner, I nearly fell backwards, because I'd expected the object to be heavy, like a rock or a brick, but there it was, a nearly weightless, oblong piece of debris with nothing to announce its importance or identity.

Simply staring at it, I wondered if it would disintegrate in my hands before I could examine it more closely. But it stayed there, so I squeezed the object lightly. It did not disappear, nor did it feel, well, squishy like everything else I touched. Definitely solid. I shone the light on it, but no new information popped into my reasoning. I could not remove it, but neither could I place it back into the mud at my feet. But yes, I would have to leave it there, hoping for no more rain, and talk to the workers in the morning, although, because of heavy downpours, they would not likely return for a few days. What to do?

Obviously, as four more inches of rain were predicted throughout the weekend, I needed to take the object into my house—to protect it, I reasoned. Neither heavy enough for a brick, nor light enough for a— nothing came to me. Yes, I would carry it into the house, and put it back later, or, simply report what I had done, feeling like a five year-old with her hand caught in the cookie jar—or worse, maybe like a criminal. (Perhaps it was only a workman's leftover lunch in a sack. I hadn't meant for this to happen, but didn't know how to escape my dilemma. I felt like I was being chased through a maze in a nightmare.)

Stealthily I continued, although no one—not even my husband I later discovered—was watching me. Slipping and sliding back to the steps leading out of what felt like primordial ooze, I held my find with one hand while clutching the crumbling brick walls with the other. Safely inside my back door, I called Ray to help me.

"Please hurry! Cover the table with newspaper! Put some on the floor so I can walk to the table!" He looked at me, struck dumb as Zachariah. "Ohhh, sorry," I apologized. "This is important, Ray. I need your help." He reached for the muddy object in my hand. "No!" My rebuke was sharp. "What in samhill have you done?" he stammered, reaching for another stack of old newspapers. Even in that extraordinary moment, I questioned the etymology of that word: *samhill.*

Laying the treasure—I was sure of that much—gently on the table, I stood back, wondering if it would take on a life of its own, like some sleeping creature that had only to be wakened, but again, nothing happened. Removing boots and gloves, I stepped closer to the table to run a bare finger over the muddy find. Ray stooped closer, wide-eyed. With a few more gentle swipes I had uncovered what looked like a book, brown with mud; could it be a brown leather book?

Positioning it by moving the paper on which it rested, I looked at it from all sides. Hesitantly I lifted a corner to take a peak, and saw there, smudged and nearly indecipherable, handwritten words that I recognized. Cherokee! In a 19th century Moravian pottery.

A brilliant *aha* moment split my understanding like a lightning strike. This lost artifact would add significantly to Madaya's last journal written in old age with a shaking hand in which she had described relics in her story-satchel, and what each represented. Although her satchel itself was lost in time, just as Aduli had predicted, her *story* would bridge the chasm between them and us, right where they had once walked, and where I now live, *on common ground.*

At last, the Cherokee lioness tells her story, hidden secrets, forbidden sex, forgotten slaves, a deserving chief . . . Madaya tells all.

Epilogue: The Rest of the Story

The past isn't dead. It isn't even past.

~ William Faulkner

Salem <oldsalem.org/250/2>

To commemorate the arrival of ten Moravian brethren who arrived in a wagon from nearby Bethabara in North Carolina in 1766, a reenactment of the original trek will end at the archeological site of the Builder's House in Old Salem. There began the building of the first structure erected in Salem, located at the corner of Brookstown and Old Salem roads, across the street from the Children's Museum of Winston-Salem. Nightly illumination of a unique student art exhibition, created by Norman Coates and Jack Miller of the University of North Carolina School of the Arts School of Design and Production can be viewed nightly through 2016.

Throughout the year, numerous programs, lectures, displays and events are available for the enjoyment and education of both adults and children in this "living museum" of Old Salem, as well as elsewhere in the city. Details, listed on the website listed above, include such events as a visit with George Washington, the Moravian Speaker Series, the 250th Anniversary Community Day, and the annual naturalization ceremony on the Salem town square on Independence Day. It was here that the first recorded, annual) celebration occurred on 4 July 1783 with a concert titled, *Psalm of Joy* by Johann Friedrich Peter.

St. Philips Moravian Church

<oldsalem.org/building/st-philips-african-moravian-church>

It is on this site on Church Street in Old Salem where the enslaved African Squire was buried in the churchyard. Unlike most other grave markers on this site, his grave is in its original location in the "strangers" graveyard where non-Moravians were buried. You can find his gravestone by walking south on Church Street, up the steps toward St. Philips, the first grave on the left.

The log church now houses the museum of St. Philips with interactive audio-visuals, including a video with a docent available for interpretation. After visiting the log church/museum, you can visit the brick church next door with the interpreter who describes the significance of their vibrant history. It was here where the Emancipation Proclamation was read to the stunned congregation on Sunday, 21 May 1865.

The Moravian Church [Unitas Fratrum: Unity of the Brethren] <Moravian.org>

Moravian congregations that survived persecution, including martyrdom of John Hus in the fifteenth century, arrived in the new world in 1735. With it they brought the Bible in their own language, a passion for mission and music, with extraordinary dedication to record-keeping.

Lasting customs, such as the lovefeast, or *agape* meal, usually include a bun and cup of steaming coffee, served with dignity during the service of hymns and scripture. Likewise, the candle tea attracts hundreds nightly during Advent with no regard for sometimes cold and snow as folks line up at the Single Brothers House for their turn to enter and experience the spirit of Christmas. They walk on ancient cobbled floors through semi-dark, candle-lit rooms with rough-hewn stone walls to watch costumed women dip beeswax candles. Sitting on handmade wooden benches, guests are warmed by fire in the ancient fireplace, and served the lovefeast bun and coffee before continuing to view the miniature display of a wintry street scene of Salem about 1900, built to scale, culminating at the crèche (nativity) in a cave-like opening in the wall.

Moravian Archives, Winston-Salem <moravianarchives.org>

A visit to the vaulted, two-story Archie K. Davis Center allows both the casual visitor and the serious researcher to absorb the beauty and the wonder of Moravian history, Southern Province.

Meticulous records with stories/letters/diaries/genealogies/minutes and other resources cover the ongoing history of the Moravian Church in North Carolina from 1753. In the research room one can access Memorabilia and other significant historical records that describe life from early days to the present, including family histories of church members.

The climate-controlled manuscript vault holds more than eight thousand acid-free boxes with records that pre-date the American Revolution. The book vault protects rare volumes of the Music Foundation as well as Moravian Archives.

Museum of Southern Decorative Arts <mesda.org>

Frank L. Horton and his mother Theodosia "Theo" L. Taliaferro, may have been originally dismissed by other professionals in the world of antiques, but today their legacy lives on as the Museum of Southern Decorative Arts. Renowned internationally for its collection of southern arts and material culture in the American South, it is one of the "must-see" museums in Old Salem.

Salem College and Girls' School <salem.edu>

Begun in 1772 by Elizabeth Oesterlein, the school is the oldest continuing educational institution for women in the U.S. Four single sisters and twelve girls, ages 13-17, walked from Bethlehem, Pennsylvania, to Salem in 1766. Oesterlein opened the school, inspired by Bishop John Amos Comenius (1592-1670) who wrote: "No reason can be shown why the female sex should be kept from a knowledge of languages and wisdom."

True to its earliest philosophy, the first black student was admitted in 1785. Whether free or enslaved, Cherokee or African or Caucasian, young or mature, Moravians believed that all deserve an education. While it continues as both a liberal arts college and boarding school for girls, it now offers graduate degrees and a Continuing Studies program that welcomes male day students. "Our fathers were men of wide vision," wrote Emma Lehman, teacher at S.C. for 51 years. "They planted a small seed which has grown and developed into what we are today."

Lake Junaluska, North Carolina < lakejunaluska.com/about_us/>

Lake Junaluska Assembly became an integral part of Methodists in the Southeast Jurisdiction on 25 June 1913 when they convened for the first time with four thousand participants in the George R. Stuart Auditorium. Participants initially arrived from Waynesville, as no overnight accommodations were then available, but once the lake was filled and an inn was built, folks arrived by train with trunks and boxes and crossed the lake by boat, often to spend the summer. Many persons not Methodist, such as Eleanor Roosevelt, have visited the site with its stunning views year round.

Although this venue for numerous events, from Bible studies to country music festivals, carries the name Junaluska, it was not until 1988 that sculptor Paul Van Zandt was commissioned to create a statue of Cherokee Chief Junaluska. A service of dedication included the great, great, great grandson of the chief with his son Carl, Jr. Standing in front of the historic auditorium, the memorial bronze bust inspires thousands of visitors to embody inclusiveness, acceptance and generosity to all persons.

Museum of the Cherokee Indian <cherokeemuseum.org>

Time-travel *is* possible. Just visit this museum to experience 13 thousand years of Cherokee history. Van Romans, of Disney Imagineering, called it "a model for museums." Three life-size figures of Cherokee men who visited King George III to explore a path to peace were developed from descriptions in Henry Timberlake's *Memoirs*. In addition to photographs, such as David Fitzgerald's "Trail of Tears Photographs" and another collection of 40 black and white photos of the Eastern Band of Cherokee Indians by Shan Goshorn, you will see reproductions (such as the Cherokee petition against Removal), and a "250th Anniversary Exhibition" creation of the "Emissaries of Peace" as part of a travelling exhibit. From artifacts like beads, stamped pottery and baskets typically found in Cherokee, you will also note added trade items (like scissors and guns) that became available through the incursion of European settlers.

You can visit the official Cherokee Qualla Arts and Crafts across from the museum, before a stroll through Oconaluftee Village, depicting village life, customary clothing and crafts practiced as long ago as ten thousand years. An evening in the outdoor amphitheater showing "Unto These Hills" may raise more questions than it answers, and may even encourage you to sign up for classes, hike the Great Smoky Mountains National Park where you can fish for trout, swim, canoe, climb and even bicycle (where the Tour de France cyclists have trained).

Sequoyah Birthplace Museum <sequoyahmuseum.org>

The genius of an illiterate man, born lame in Tennessee about 1778, is best known for his invention of a way for the Cherokee to write and read. But this is only half the story. He was also a silversmith, an artist and a blacksmith who started a salt works and later built his own cabin in Oklahoma.

He worked for years to create a way for the Cherokee to communicate as the white people did with their "talking leaves." He finally invented a symbol for every sound in the language, of which there are 85 in the "syllabary." Experimenting first with his young daughter, his extraordinary accomplishment provided literacy for his people, for which the Cherokee National Council awarded Sequoyah a medal for his ingenuity.

Indeed, *the past is not dead; it is not even past* . . .

AFTERWORD: Tracks

We will be known forever by the tracks we leave.

~ Dakota

FULL CIRCLE

There is a mysterious cycle in human events . . .

~ Franklin D. Roosevelt (1882-1945)

Born in Allentown, Pennsylvania, to a clergy-father and both parents teacher, I lived on a college campus, knowing I was loved, unconditionally. Growing up on a college campus, I inhaled learning, loving it. My faith-community included my home-life where my parents nurtured us to love God and humankind. Two thick, worn books—the Bible and Webster's Dictionary—rested on the edge of our kitchen table where six to nine of us crowded around it for meals and celebrations. As an adult student, I graduated from United Wesleyan College, Sacred Heart Hospital School of Nursing and George Mason University, and was awarded a Doctor of Humanities degree from Methodist University of Liberia.

Married to my college sweetheart in Bethlehem, Pennsylvania, from earliest childhood I experienced a magical immersion every Advent season as my parents took my three brothers and me to see the crèche created there by the Moravians. Initially settling in Bethlehem, they named adjacent towns with other biblical names before moving south to North Carolina where they settled Bethabara, meaning *house of passage*, and Salem, meaning *peace*.

Today living again among the Moravian people, this time in Old Salem, I welcomed close proximity to the Cherokee, providing renewed inspiration to write historical fiction about what happened here in the nineteenth century. With abundant and available research material for my next book on Chief Junaluska, a new trajectory emerged as I learned about enslaved Africans who lived in Salem. I welcomed the gift of having come to this time and place.

As a United Methodist who frequently visited Lake Junaluska, North Carolina, named for the mountain that overlooks the lake, so named to honor the chief, I became enamored with the chief whose statue resides prominently in front of the tabernacle by the lakeside. Eager to learn more, I participated in a "Cherokee Immersion" not far from Lake Junaluska.

Although our three children, their spouses and our six grandchildren live in five different states at some distance from us, our foster daughter and her family, one brother and other relatives live nearby. Living in a historic house built in 1831 in Old Salem, my husband and I embrace the beauty and meaningful setting in this Moravian community, now known as Old Salem. The 250th anniversary of the founding of Salem celebrates those who earlier walked this land, and where I, too, now embrace the privilege of living on this *common ground,* having come full circle, indeed.

TELLING YOUR STORY

Rather than homo sapiens, *human beings should be known as* homo narrans, *for we are the only species that can tell its stories.*

~Richard Leakey, anthropologist

How often through the years I have dreamed of finding a journal or a letter to her two young children written by my biological mother when she knew she would not live to see them grown. Although I continue to search in my dreams, apparently it was not meant to be. When my dad married another winsome bride, she became—even to two more brothers she birthed—the *mother* that all four of us children called through early childhood, "our second mommy."

Shortly before my second mother died, I gave her a silk-covered journal for her to record some of her stories about growing up as one of eleven children on a farm in the Shenandoah Valley. Finding the journal in her bedside table after her death, I sat on the edge of her bed, my hands shaking with excitement and gratitude as I opened it. But, its pages were blank, still empty. Astonished, although I should not have been because she had always insisted modestly, "Oh, I don't have anything to tell." Having heard some of those stories, I knew better. Fortunately, my parents' love letters to each other survived, now treasured by our family today, as well as some of my dad's sermons and theological discourses.

So, it is hardly surprising that for years I've encouraged and facilitated telling one's story, benefitting the teller as well as those who hear others' stories. These precious vessels connect us to one another as well as to our past, riding the waves of time to reach even those who are yet to be born. Even now I have access to "My Story" file on my computer desktop. It begins before I was born, for our lives do not begin with our birth. As long as I am able, new tales will appear on its pages, stories of living with my clergy-husband, our children, our work in many states and countries where friendships abound. My life as a daughter, mother, grandmother, wife, sister, student, a patient and a nurse, a missionary and teacher, pastor's wife and bishop's wife, youth counselor, a clown, facilitator, friend, a mourner and survivor, a believer, a struggler, a winner and a loser, a behind-the-scenes actor and activist, a leader and a follower. It's all there, for my children and grandchildren, nephews and nieces, but if not for them, for the writer herself who needs to tell her stories.

If you don't tell your story, who will?

COMMENTS

Disclaimer: It has been suggested that stories in the oral tradition are like trees, *real*, while written stories are but a *reflection* of what is real, like a shadow. Or, can it be said that what is *real* is any given event or experience, and that *any* interpretation or re-counting is a *reflection*?

With each repeated telling, our stories undulate, change and ripple like a pond in the breeze. All representations (oral or written or any method used to tell a story, like live theatre, mime, opera, film, etc.) are just that: representations/symbols, imagination mixed with memory.

Historical fiction collects imagined details, growing like kudzu, but not as *real*, until both writer and reader are sucked into the story, reminding me of the *Alllegory of the Cave* (Socrates). So, without apology, but aware of my ignorance, I attempt to "tell the story again," by engaging *imaginative speculation* to remind us of our history and the life-supporting practice of telling and hearing personal and collective stories. Before adding these few comments, I again leave you with this reminder and disclaimer:

All eighteen chapters are a work of fiction, drawing on historical background, including the nineteenth to the twenty-first centuries in North Carolina. It is neither my intention to misrepresent historical facts nor to represent a chronological reconstruction of the era. Yes, I employed *speculative imagination* to birth this story. The following comments include few references, as this is not a scholarly or academic dissertation, but they may entice you to explore more fully this century in our history. Read on!

Information about Cherokee words from resource person of Cherokee (Tslagi) descent, Darlene Ousley. Many tribes in North America have adopted some nomenclature of the *real* people, the *first* people, the *principal* people. The Cherokee people still refer to their tribal chief as Principal Chief.

Nu na da ul tsu n yi means: "trail where they cried," usually referred to as "the trail of tears."

Tsalagi represents what the Cherokee people call themselves. The word *Cherokee* is not a Cherokee word.

Ani Yun Wiya means: The Principal People, the Original People, or the Real People. Unlike Tsalagi, Ani means "people of" so this phrase means "all of us" or the group of us. A *Tsalagi* person belongs to the *Ani Yun Wiya*.

Chapter 1: *The Removal,* was ordered by President Andrew Jackson and carried out by General Winfield Scott. Sixteen thousand Cherokee were forced to walk in 1838-39 to Indian Territory (now Oklahoma.) Some left willingly at an earlier time. *Historical records* indicate the occurrence of a *meteor shower,* just prior to their expulsion from their homes, as well as the burning of villages, gardens, crops, animals. *Cherokee horses* descended from the introduction of Spanish horses mid-seventeenth century; less than three hundred survive now in Oklahoma.

Chapter 2: The *Rhodesias* (now Zambia and Zimbabwe) were "discovered" by the son of a British clergyman. *Cecil Rhodes,* who became known for exploiting the Africans in central and southern Africa, was the antithesis of *Dr. David Livingstone,* the first white man to transverse the African continent (from the Atlantic to the Indian Oceans), discovered the upper Zambezi and Victoria Falls, purposed to interrupt and destroy the evils of slave trade, preached to "tens of thousands," was generally accepted and revered throughout his travels, died on his knees and was buried at Westminster Canterbury in 1874, honored by Africans and British alike. All that to say, missions in Africa expanded as a result of his influence and love for the people.

Diseases like small pox, tuberculosis, measles, STDs, typhus, diphtheria, pertussis and others, killed 25-50 percent of the natives who had no immunity to these diseases. The white man (beginning with the invasion of the Spanish in seventeenth century), introduced *Intentional infection* ("germ warfare"), practiced during the French and Indian War. One official, *Jeffery Amerst* was quoted: "You will do well to try to inoculate the Indians, by means of blankets, as well as to try every other method that can serve to extirpate this execrable race." Another, *William Trent* wrote: "Out of our regard [to] them we gave them two Blankets and an Handkerchief out of the Small Pox Hospital. I hope it will have the desired effect."

The negro quarter is likely where *Squire* lived in Salem when it was home to slaves on a farm owned by Moravians in the nineteenth century; many of the lots were later sold to the Afro-Americans there. It was later (1874) re-named *Happy Hill*, where today a plaque marks the location.

Chapter 3: *General Andrew Jackson's life* is reported as being spared by Junaluska, who suffered a lifetime of regret for having done so. Some reports of the Battle at Horseshoe Bend do not mention Junaluska, although he is revered for having served in that battle, as well as others.

Accounts (during the Removal) of drowning, epidemics, frostbite, freezing to death and starvation are not exaggerated; an estimated *four thousand* (twenty-five percent) Cherokee died on the journey over land and water; during that winter walk, many boarded boats, ferries or rafts to cross larger rivers like the Ohio, Tennessee, Mississippi and Arkansas.

William Holland Thomas was a cousin to Confederate President Jefferson Davis, and was the adopted son of Yonaguska, a chief of the Eastern band of Cherokee. Thomas was the only white man to serve as a Cherokee chief, as well as serving as a colonel in North Carolina's sole Cherokee legion in the Civil War, known as the *Thomas Legion*. Accolades abound for his relationship with the Cherokee, because without his assistance, they may not have survived in North Carolina. He became a wealthy landowner, and some believe his wealth exceeded that of the Vanderbilt family. He was also a primary source (along with Swimmer) for James Mooney's remarkable research for his book: *History, Myths, and Sacred Formulas of the Cherokees*. Again, "facts" vary, but it is generally agreed, at least among the Cherokee, that *Tsali,* his *brother and two of his sons,* were shot by Cherokee prisoners of war who were coerced into killing their brothers, all as a result of a scalping that had occurred in an earlier provocation. Also, *Elias Boudinot* who published the *Cherokee Phoenix,* along with two of the *Ridge family* were murdered. The assassins were never apprehended. *The walk home:* Some reports indicate that Junaluska walked back to North Carolina from Indian Territory about five years later; others suggest he did an about-face while his people were still walking the Trail. Also, there is no indication that anyone accompanied him on his walk home.

Chapter 4: *Sequoyah/Language* The story of Sequoyah's life and work are generally verifiable.

Barbara Duncan, director of the Museum of the Cherokee Indian in North Carolina, suggests that because the speaker of the Cherokee language needs to identify the physical state of an object, such as liquid, or flexible, or moving, and so on, it provides "a whole way of looking at the world and classifying the world that is unique." Today, children are not generally exposed to spoken Cherokee, other than through classes now offered in some public schools in the Cherokee Nation, both in Oklahoma and North Carolina. Of two currently spoken dialects, the *Kituwha* is spoken by the Eastern Band in the Qualla Boundary in North Carolina, and the *Overhill* or Western dialect is the most commonly known/spoken Cherokee with the most speakers in western Oklahoma and Snowbird in North Carolina. One linguist suggested that Cherokee and Greek are the most "perfect" languages.

Chapter 5: *Kidnapping:* Squire told Junaluska he was from Mukoni, about 10 km. from present-day Livingstone (founded in 1905). British rule did not end until 1964. The story of kidnapping by an African raiding party was customary, in which all—except the enslaved—benefitted, from the African kidnappers, to the white persons involved in transporting them to the new world, as well as those who conducted the slave markets at the end of the transaction. *A slave owner,* Andrew Jackson not only owned 161 slaves at the time of his death, but was also a slave trader. To see a shocking pictorial reminder about U.S. history, do a Yahoo search for: *mulatresses,* women slaves sold in New Orleans. *Records of the War of 1812* do not always mention Junaluska's role, but examining the *Battle of Horseshoe Bend* shows him to have played a significant part in Jackson's success, in addition to saving his life. Part of the War of 1812 involved major battles from New York to Baltimore to New Orleans and Florida. *Tecumseh* did eventually develop the *Confederacy* of northern Indian tribes, but finally died in a battle in Ontario, after which the Confederacy dissolved.

Chapter 6: *Enslaved persons* were conscripted to walk the Trail, to help move the Cherokee to Indian Territory.

Chapter 7: *Baptism* was likely for *Squire,* who (according to his gravestone) was a Baptist, although he is buried in the "strangers' graveyard," so designated for those not Moravian, as well as working as an enslaved person for a Moravian. The practice of *Brand and Baptize* added to the head-count for "converts" who were enslaved Africans. In Maputo, Mozambique, I stood in the "holding room" and listened to stories of kidnapped Africans who had walked from that spot to be branded and baptized before boarding a ship for the New World, where they would be sold (again).

Squire's death did occur while digging a well for Brother Fries (according to his gravestone). As nothing further is known about his history, his story is conjecture.

Chapter 8: *Enslaved persons*, considered property, were considered merchandise and were sold at markets; one of the largest on the coast was in Charleston, South Carolina. But the historic town of Charlotte was one of many "good places" for slave markets.

Chapter 9: *BIA Schools* were first established by Christian missionaries with the purpose clear: "to civilize and Christianize native children." While most schools were established in the late nineteenth century, earlier missions dot the landscape; the descriptions of treatment and purpose are well-documented. The boys at the Carlisle School (established in 1879, ran a print shop that produced thousands of forms for the Washington, D.C. government offices). *Jim Thorpe* (at Carlisle) shocked white boys in particular with his athletic prowess in track and field; he won two gold medals at the Olympics in 1912; he also played football successfully and was praised by Dwight D. Eisenhower, a cadet at West Point. Many graduates of the BIA schools excelled: *Susan Fleisher,* the first Native American woman doctor who returned to work with her people; "Even Indian women can learn," was the shocking news whispered—though not broadcasted—to the world. *Charles Eastman* became a physician and Indian rights activist; others include actors, authors, professionals in every field, all of whom became political activists.

To quote *Thomas Jefferson to the Choctaw:* "A little land cultivated, and a little labor, will procure more provisions than the most successful hunt; and a woman will clothe more by spinning and weaving, than a man by hunting." In 1813 the North Carolina General Assembly passed a law forbidding anyone to teach African Americans to read and write. Not until 1924 did the Indian Citizenship Act make Native Americans legal citizens of the land that the white man stole from them. Finally, in 1946 they achieved the right to register and vote.

Chapter 10: *John Burnette* wrote a much longer treatise about the Removal and his discouragement that he'd lived with all those years (not much more than a boy when he walked the Trail with the Cherokee). The full text of his lengthy birthday letter to his children written when he was eighty years-old, is available at <*learnnc.org*>. In it he wrote: "Murder is murder whether committed by the villain skulking in the dark or by uniformed men stepping to the strains of martial music." *John Astooga Stoga,* the grandson of Junaluska, died in battle as described. In addition to his military service, he persuaded the American Bible Society to translate the Bible from English into Cherokee, published in 1857.

Chapter 11: *Beloved Woman* with her swan's feather cloak of peace would always be known as one of the War Women, but she could not, would not participate in the torture rituals that women were expected to perform on their prisoners of war. Instead, *Nanyehi* chose peaceful rituals. She had followed her warrior husband *Kingfisher* and watched him die in battle and that changed everything. *Balance:* Historian James Adair writes that the spirits of those killed by the enemy could not go to the *Darkening Land* until their deaths had been avenged. "To exact retribution is the primary reason for declaring war." This notion of *balance* reflects similarity to an ancient European cosmology in which balance is key to survival. "An eye for an eye" was not only an ancient Judeo-injunction, or a pseudo-Christian imperative, but also the linchpin of Cherokee belief.

Chapters 12/13: *Legends of the Sacred Pipe* and the *Great Yona* and *Yuktena* and *Arrow Woman,* as well as the stories of *Kan'ati and Selu,* and *creation,* and the story of *Good Wolf, Bad Wolf* are among well-known legends of the Cherokee people. The uncle did indeed contribute to the child's upbringing.

Chapter 14: *Nicie, Junaluska's third wife,* is buried beside him in Robbinsville, North Carolina. *Burial practices* changed through the centuries, but always reflected a thoughtful, spiritual understanding of the body and spirit. The body was prepared by the women and wrapped before placing in a *casket* of cane or woven rush. *Mourners* for a period of seven days were not to show great emotion such as joy or anger, after which they participated in "going to the water" for cleansing rituals. The family gathered before burial to hear the shaman relate tales of life of the deceased, the contributions and exploits, and references to the void that remains with the loss of a loved one. In centuries past, bodies were buried in the great *earthen mounds,* some of which were built about 1000 CE. Citizens deposited stones around the periphery; a fire was kept burning in the center. The *Kituwah mound* is still visible today.

Chapter 15: The arrival of *Union soldiers* (3 thousand troops) in Salem on Monday, 10 April 1865, followed by other stories about Holy Week, are all well-documented in Moravian Archives.

Chapter 16: *Reading the Emancipation Proclamation on Sunday, 21 May, 1865* at St.Philips in Salem is well-documented. Description of events experienced by enslaved Africans (such as *Eneas and his wife)* is a composite of practices documented during this time, with the reality much more harsh than the related story. *The Rev. Russell May,* a Moravian pastor in Winston-Salem, made these remarks at a re-enactment of that day in 1865, at St. Philips, about the "drought of justice and emancipation" and the "inconvenience" experienced that day. *Maximilian E. Grunert* did write in his diary about that day. More than one couple was typically married in the same Moravian service.

Chapter 17: *Wedding customs* of the Tsalagi in this description are documented as practiced, as well as *birthing customs* and the ritual of carrying the placenta to bury on a ridge, believing that the number of ridges climbed would be the same number of years to pass before another child would be born. *Childbirth:* In the event that a child is born weak or malformed, the mother can decide to abandon the infant in the forest, the only form of birth control considered acceptable. Use of the contraceptive *cicta maculate* (spotted cow-bane), is frowned upon, and infanticide by anyone other than the mother is considered murder.

Chapter 18: *Gottfried Aust Pottery* was the actual site that now awaits excavation and exploration, next door to the author's home in Old Salem, next to the *Belo House*, still standing, owned by the Moravian Church. The *daughters of two Cherokee chiefs* did attend the Salem Female Academy, one of whom graduated and the other having left to walk the Trail of Tears with her family.

RECIPES

AFRICAN

Two dishes I prepared while living in Zambia, Africa, are *ensima*, similar to Cherokee cornmeal mush, and cabbage relish, served hot as an accompaniment to the cornmeal recipe. These are the same as the dishes Squire and Eneas would have prepared, both in Africa and the United States.

ENSIMA (ZAMBIA)

See Momfeather Erickson's recipe for Cornmeal Mush. Although a Cherokee recipe, ingredients and preparation are the same for this dish familiar to many cooks worldwide. Zambians, and I, would serve this mixture thick, breaking off small chunks of ensima from one bowl in center, with everyone dipping it into the cabbage dish (or other "relish," such as chicken with broth). In the villages, many eat it with fingers, even as the Cherokee would have done and as we do when serving this meal at home. Salt is always added to taste. As a gift to the hundreds of worshipers, many of whom walked miles to the mission on Christmas Day, we gave a treasured bag of salt to each person.

CABBAGE RELISH (ZAMBIA)

Wash a cabbage and slice into thin strips. Heat several tablespoons of oil and add cabbage. Rather than adding more oil, I sprinkle with water if it starts to stick to pan, but most add generous amounts of oil. Stir and cook until soft and translucent. Add salt and pepper if desired. (Most villagers would have few condiments; simple and plain is preferred.)

CHEROKEE   [from   Nanataka   American   Indians   Council: <nanataka.org> Momfeather Errickson's Recipes [translation from Tsalagi (Cherokee)]

CORNMEAL MUSH (SELU'DA ANISTA)

Corn meal 1 part corn meal to 4 parts boiling water) and salt

Put water in saucepan. Cover and let it become boiling hot over the fire; then add a tablespoon of salt. Take off the light scum from the top. Take a handful of the cornmeal with the left hand and a pudding stick [or wood spoon] in the right [or vise versa if you're a southpaw]; then with the stick, stir the water around and by degrees let fall the meal. When one handful is exhausted, refill it; continue to stir and add meal until it is as thick as you can stir easily, or until the stick will stand in it. Stir it awhile longer. Let the fire be gentle.

When it is sufficiently cooked which will be in half an hour, it will bubble or buff up. Turn it into a deep basin. Good eaten cold or hot, with milk or butter and syrup or sugar, or with meat and gravy, or it may be sliced when cold and fried. (Or, eat hot as African ensima with cabbage relish.)

THREE SISTERS

Depending on ingredients available, this dish can vary greatly. To be authentic, it has to contain corn, beans and squash. This is my (modern) version of the dish described in chapter eleven, and is tasty served as a side dish, or with rice, or with mush, or as soup. Nutritious.

Corn (canned/frozen or freshly cut off cob; Cherokee cooks would have used stored, dried corn)

Red kidney beans (including juice if canned)

Squash (any variety) If using crookneck squash, simply cut into small chunks, skin and all. If tougher-skinned squashes, you may cut into large pieces to microwave to simplify peeling before cutting in small pieces. Could also substitute pumpkin for squash.

Onions chopped finely, sautéed in oil

Rosemary, chopped and added to onions

Salt and pepper to taste; other herbs and spices, such as curry, increase the appeal for some

Vegetable or chicken broth (or water); adding half of cooked mixture to a blender thickens it nicely. This is a good crockpot recipe, or just cook until desired consistency.

SASSAFRAS TEA (GA NA S DA TSI)

Red Sassafras roots and water
Boil a few pieces of the root in water until it is the desired strength.
Sweeten with honey if desired. Serve hot or cold. Note translation about
how to collect roots: *Gather and wash the roots of red sassafras. Do this
in the spring before the sap begins to rise. Store for future use.*
(Or, buy store-bought, dried sassafras.)

SALEM RECEIPTS [SIC; 19TH CENTURY SPELLING FOR RECIPE]

The Winkler Bakery in Old Salem, North Carolina, was built by
Moravians in 1800, and named for the first owner Christian Winkler.
The bee-hive brick oven still operates on south Main Street as the
oldest, still operating, wood-burning oven in the United States. Here are
three favorite receipts [sic] with a modern twist that you can use in the
21st century. Authentic, freshly baked Moravian sugar cake can be
purchased at Winkler's today, as well as recipes for some dishes. Or,
specialties like Tomato Pie and muffins can be enjoyed at the Tavern on
Main Street, prepared by the Rick and Lori Keiper family, owners. [It was
here that President George Washington ate and stayed overnight.]

WINKLER'S MORAVIAN SUGAR CAKE
[modern, from recipe card available at Winkler's]

Into ½ cup warm water (110°), add ½ teaspoon sugar
Sprinkle with 2 packages active dry yeast. Set aside until yeast
bubbles.
Into measuring cup mix together ¾ cup brown sugar plus 1 teaspoon
cinnamon; set aside.
In large mixing bowl:
¾ cup warm water (110°)
½ cup sugar
2 tablespoons dry milk powder
¼ cup dry instant mashed potato flakes (modern!) or ¼ cup mashed
potatoes

½ teaspoon salt
½ cup melted and cooled butter
2 eggs
1 cup flour and the yeast mixture
Mix 2 minutes on medium speed or mix with wooden spoon.
Add an additional ¾ cup flour and mix until well blended.
Place dough in greased bowl, grease top of dough, cover and let rise until double, about 1 hour.
Punch dough down and place in greased, shallow pan (17" x 12" x 1" deep).
Let rise 30 minutes. Spread dough evenly in pan, butter top of dough with melted butter.
Make shallow indentations with fingers; dribble 1 stick melted butter over top.
Sprinkle evenly with brown sugar and cinnamon mixture.
Let rise 30 minutes and bake until golden brown (12-15 minutes) in a 375° oven.
[No, you don't want to know the calorie count.]

TOMATO PIE

[Not necessarily Moravian; recipe adapted by Ray Chamberlain]

Pre-heat oven to 350°
1 pre-baked 9-inch pie crust (You don't want a soggy crust.) Cool.
6 finely chopped green onions, including the stalks
10 fresh basil leaves, finely chopped
8 Roma tomatoes, or other types, but sliced thinly and drained thoroughly in colander; blot with paper towel if still juicy.
1½ tablespoons balsamic vinegar, divided in half
salt and pepper (salt helps to absorb juice)
1 cup mayonnaise
1 cup grated cheddar
1 cup grated Mozzarella
Lightly combine the cheeses and mayonnaise; divide in half.
Layer ingredients in cooled crust in this manner:
Layer drained tomatoes on crust. Sprinkle with salt and pepper and half of balsamic vinegar.

Add half of each, green onions and chopped basil.

Add half of mixture of cheeses with mayonnaise.

Start second layer with remaining tomatoes and repeat process above, ending with cheese mixture on top. (Add more cheese if desired.)

Bake at 350° on bottom rack of oven, about 30 minutes until lightly browned.

If necessary, cover crust edges with a cuff of aluminum foil. Let it set before cutting. (Guard it from those who, like our nephew John, would eat the whole pie at one sitting.)

OLD SALEM PUMPKIN MUFFINS
<myrecipes.com>

1/3 cup golden raisins
1 tablespoon all-purpose flour
1/3 cup butter or margarine, softened
3/4 cup firmly packed brown sugar
1 cup canned pumpkin
1/2 cup milk
1/4 cup molasses
2 eggs, beaten
2 cups sifted all-purpose flour
2 teaspoons baking powder
1/2 teaspoon salt
1/2 teaspoon ground ginger
1/2 teaspoon ground nutmeg
1/8 teaspoon ground cloves

Combine raisins and 1 tablespoon flour; stir well, and set aside.

Cream butter; gradually add sugar, beating well. Add pumpkin, milk, molasses, and eggs, beating well.

Sift together flour, baking powder, salt, and spices; add to creamed mixture, stirring just until dry ingredients are moistened. Stir in raisins.

Spoon batter into greased muffin pans, filling full. Bake at 375° for 20 minutes. (Or, cook in miniature pans for 10-12 minutes). Serve with cinnamon butter (combine spice and softened butter).

REFERENCES

Rather than a bibliography, seldom included in fiction, this lists some of sources that informed my writing. Without them, this book could not have become what it is.

Avery, Laurence G. Ed. *A Paul Green Reader*, 1998.

Bender, Margaret. *Signs of Cherokee Culture: Sequoyah's Syllabary in Eastern Cherokee Life,* 2003.

Bower, Jennifer Bean. *Moravians in North Carolina*, 2006.

Bricker, Michael. *Winston-Salem Through Time*, 2014.

Bunn, Mike and Clay Williams. *Battle of the Southern Frontier: The Creek War and the War of 1812.* (2008).

Carolina Avenue Press. *Preserving the Past: Salem Moravians' Receipts [sic] & Rituals,* 2006.

Conley, Robert J. *The Long Way Home, 1994.* (F); *Dark Land, 1995. (F)*

Cooper, Michael. *Indian School: Teaching the White Man's Way*, 1999.

Crow, Jeffrey. *A History of African Americans in North Carolina*, 1992.

Crum, Mason. *The Story of Lake Junaluska,* 1950.

Dubois, W.E.B. *Darkwater Voices from within the Vale,*1999.

Duncan, Barbara R. & Brett H. Riggs. *Cherokee Heritage Trails Guidebook,* 2003.

Duncan, Barbara, Ed. *Living Stories of the Cherokees*, 1998.

Ehle, John. *Trail of Tears: The Rise and Fall of the Cherokee Nation*, 1989.

Ellington, Charlotte. *Beloved Mother: The Story of Nancy Ward*, 1994.

Finger, John R. *The Eastern Band of Cherokees, 1819-1900*, 1984.

Flint, Eric. *Trail of Glory.* 2006. (F)

Frazier, Charles. *Cold Mountain*, 1997.

Fries, Adelaide L. *Road to Salem,* 1993.

Foster, Sharon Ewell. *Abraham's Well,* 2006. (F)

Glancy, Diane. *Pushing the Bear*, 1998. (F)

Hifler, Joyce Sequichie. *A Cherokee Feast of Days*, 1992.

Hildebrand, Reginald F. *The Times Were Strange and Stirring: Methodist Preachers and the Crisis of Emancipation,* 1995.

Hudson, Marjorie. *Searching for Virginia Dare*, 2002.

Jacobs, Harriet. *Incidents in the Life of a Slave Girl*, 2001.

Johnston, Carolyn Ross. *Voices of Cherokee Women*, 2013.

Jones, Randell. *Before There Were Heroes*, 2011.

Judd, Cameron. *Daniel Boone: A Novel of an American Legend*, 2005.

King, Duane, Ed. *The Cheroke Indian Nation: A Troubled History*, 2000.

King, Martin Luther. Why We Can't Wait, 1964.

Lovett, Charles. *The Bookman's Tale,* 2014. (F)

Lawson, John. *A New Voyage to Carolina,*1709.

McBride, James. *Good Lord Bird*, 2013.

McCullough, David. *Brave Companions: Portraits in History, 1992.*

Miles, Tiya. *Cherokee Rose*, 2005. (F)

Miller, Adrian. *Soul Food with Recipes*, 2005.

Minges, Patrick, Ed., *Black Indian Slave Narratives*, 2004.

Mooney, James [1861-19121]. *History, Myths, and Sacred Formulas of the Cherokee*, 1992.

Moravian: *Records of the Moravians among the Cherokees*, (Vol. 1 & 2), 2010.

Morgan, Robert, *Gap Creek, 2012. (F)*

Morial, Sybil Haydel. *Witness to Change*, 2015.

Morrison, Tony. *Song of Solomon, 1987.* (F)

Moulton, Candy. *Everyday Life Among the American Indians, 1800-1900,* 2001.

Nathans, Sydney, *To Free a Family: The Journey of Mary Walker,* 2012.

Peacock, Nancy, *The Life and Times of Persimmon Wilson,* 2013. (F)

Perdue, Theda, *Cherokee Women,* 1999; *The Cherokee,* 1989.

Phillips, John Franklin. *Chief Junaluska of the Cherokee Nation,* 1988.

Rozema, Vicki, *Cherokee Voices, 2006; Voices from the Trail of Tears,* 2007.

Moravian Church in America. *Moravian Book of Worship,* 1995.

Sensbach, Jon F. *A Separate Canaan: The Making of an Afro-Moravian World in North Carolina, 1763-1840,* 1998.

Skeate Stewart, *A Nature Guide to Northwest North Carolina*, 2005.

Sink, Alice. *Wicked Winston-Salem*. (2001).

Walker, Corey D.B., *A Noble Fight, 2015.*

Williams, Heather Andrea. *Help Me To Find My People: The African American Search for Family Lost in Slavery*, 2012.

ARTICLES and other sources

Annotations from Moravian Archives, Winston-Salem, N.C., Vol.3, No. 3 "A 250th for Winston-Salem."

Basket, Nancy. "Native American Storyteller and Fiber Artist." Brochure. <nancybasket.com>

Bartlett, Donald L. and James B. Steele. "Wheel of Fortune." *Time.* (December 16, 2002).

Cecelski, David S. "The Shores of Freedom: The Maritime Underground Railroad in North Carolina, 1800-1861." *The North Carolina Historical Review, (Vol. LXXI, Number 2,* 1994).

Freeman, G. Ross, "Lake Junaluska." *The Heritage Center, Southeastern Jurisdictional Commission on Archives and History.* Brochure.

Frizzell, George E., "The Quallatown Cherokees in the 1840s: Accounts of Their Condition and Lives." *The Journal of Cherokee Studies (Vol. XXIII,* 2002).

Fawcett, Thom White Wolf. "Doctrine of Discovery Legislation Proposed by NAIC." *Love Your Neighbor News. (* April 27,2012).

Georgia Tribe of Eastern Cherokee. "Junaluska." *Web Archive: Historical Places. Historical People.* (4 November 2014).

Godbold, E. Stanley, Jr. and Mattie U. Russell. *Confederate Colonel and Cherokee Chief: The Life of William Holland Thomas.* (1990).

Harbold, Laura. "Cherokee Work To Save Their Language." (*National Archeological Archives).*

Hildebrand, Reginald. *Speech at the Juneteenth Luncheon: A Celebration of the 150th Anniversary of Freedom in Salem.* James A. Gray Auditorium, Old Salem Visitor Center, Winston-Salem, N.C. (4 June, 2015)

Honeycut, James M. "A History of the Friedberg Moravian Church Land." (1979). Brochure.

Horowitz, Tony. "The Horrific Sand Creek Massacre Will Be Forgotten No More." *Smithsonian Magazine.* (December 2014)

Jones, Landon Y. "Tribal Fever." "Mortal Sickness Among the Indians." *Smithsonian.* (May 2005).

Kimzey, Bob. "The Life of Will Thomas: a Review and Critique." Junaluska Book Club. (2007).

Kernell, Chebon. "Commemorate in a Way That Really Matters." *The New World Outlook.* (January/February, 2014).

Lowry, Bill. "Lake Junaluska Assembly: A Brief History." *The Heritage Center, Southeastern Jurisdictional Commission on Archives and History.* Brochure.

Mangino, Stephanie. "Narratives of Freedom...Stories of slavery," *Shenandoah.* Vol. 5, No. 1. (2015).

May, Russell. *"Remarks at the Reenactment of the Announcement of Freedom in the African Church [St. Phillips]."* Old Salem, North Carolina. (16 May 2015).

McLachlan, Carrie A. "The Dog in Cherokee Thought." *The Journal of Cherokee Studies (Vol. XXIII).* (2002).

Thomas, David Hurst and Jay Miller and Richard White and Peter Nabokov and Philip J. Deloria with Introduction by Alvin M. Josephy. *The Native Americans: An Illustrated Histor.* (2001)

Thomason, Phil. "Hill Road: A Visible Legacy of the Trail of Tears in Tennessee." *Bulletin of the Sequoyah Birthplace Museum, University of Tennessee, Department of Anthropology and Frank H. McClung Museum.* (December 2006, No. 3).

Toner, Mike. "Where the Trail of Tears Began." *Bulletin of the Sequoyah Birthplace Museum, University of Tennessee, Department of Anthropology and Frank H. McClung Museum.* (December 2006, No. 3).

National Museum of African American History and Culture, *"Changing America."* Washington, D.C. (2013). Brochure.

National Museum of African American History and Culture [NMAAH].*"The Emancipation Proclamation, 1863 [and] The March on Washington, 1963, Vol. I. Issue II.* (Fall 2012). <AfricanAmerican.si.edu>

North Carolina Department of Cultural Resources. *Official Archives and History.* (2011).

Perdue, Theda, "The Trail of Tears as Seen Through the Eyes of a White Man." *The Cherokee.* (1989).

Sensbach, Jon F. "Culture and Conflict in the Early Black Church: A Moravian Mission Congregation in Antebelum North Carolina." *The North Carolina Historical Review, (Vol. LXXI, Number 4).* (1994).

Southern, Ed, "North Carolina Literary Hall of Fame, 2013 Inductees . . . John Lawson" *Weymouth Center for the Arts.* (2012).Program.

Steinman, Edna. "Native Americans Suffer 'Historical Trauma.'" *United Methodist News Service: Faith Focus.*

Swanson, James L. "The Blood Relics." *Smithsonian Magazine.* (March 2015)

Takei, George. "An American Family." *Human Rights Campaign, Equality.* (2015).

Tobiassen, Virginia, "Let the Record Show," Sermon, *Home Moravian,* (31 May 2015). *"For the Common Good,"* Sermon, *Home Moravian,* (24 January 2016).

Toomlin-Sutker, Sandi, "Marie Junaluska: Reviving the Mother Language." <WNCWoman.com>

TO LEARN MORE ABOUT THE AUTHOR AND THIS BOOK,
PLEASE VISIT

WWW.CHAMBERLAINBOOKS.COM

Made in the USA
Charleston, SC
16 March 2016